The Olympian

A TALE OF ANCIENT HELLAS

By
E. S. Kraay

ISBN: 1-4392-0167-6
ISBN-13: 9781439201671

Visit www.booksurge.com to order additional copies.

DEDICATION

To My Babcia
Marcianna G. Orzolek, 1895 - 1975

The strongest person I ever knew…

The Olympian: A Tale of Ancient Hellas

CHAPTER ONE

The Pythia Speaks

I was 12-years-old when my father took me to my first Olympic Games. That was a long time ago, but I remember how, even then, he concluded that his only son would not be an athlete. Other boys' fathers would have been disappointed at such a thought; my father was not. Born on the Island of Ceos surrounded by the clear waters of the Aegean, I was raised by my elders to achieve a balanced state of sound mind, body and spirit. It is not that I lacked the physical tools or prowess to achieve success in the gymnasium—though my girth today might influence you to think it—I was simply meant to take a different path. While Ares and Apollo whispered in the ears of many of my classmates, more often I heard the soft sounds of the Muses and received special blessings from Euterpe. Language became my friend. My father knew it and took no shame, rather pride that I could wield the reed with the same dexterity that the athlete tosses the discus or throws the javelin.

My father and I attended the games at Olympia through three Olympiads before illness prevented him from travel. He taught me to love the games, and I am grateful to him for it.

My words have made me a wealthy man. Without woman or wife and with a full purse, I am free to do what the gods bid me do and I am free to come and go at my own leisure. My benefactors have been fair and good men, but I owe no debt to them; what they have given to me has been just compensation for what I have given to them. Satisfaction is mutual. My responsibility is to the gods and to myself. I honor them in accordance with custom and our ancient ways; they reward me with health in my old age. I've been tempted to lose count of the years as each comes and goes, but I remember. Remembering is important. Unlike the wheat and barley that find birth, life and death through the seasons, I have only found life. But no man can stop the cycles of the moon and other heavenly bodies that mark the passage of years; my hair is thin, and I know with certainty that my time on earth grows shorter each time Helios drives his flaming chariot into the sea. No man lives forever, though what he leaves behind can endure so other men might benefit from each man's knowledge.

I move through life with purpose and am always alert to the signs that the Pantheon places before me. The gods lead all men. Happy men see the signs and abide by them; they follow the gods of their own accord. Not sparing the whip, the gods pull other men like beasts of burden. Alas, they are sad and lonely men and their lives are often filled with tragedy. They need only to open their eyes and their minds. The signs are always there and the guidance true if only we are prepared to follow it.

The worth of a man's life is made more complete by the depth of his knowledge and his willingness to share it with others. If a man continues to learn, he continues to enrich his life and the lives of those around him. And so it is with this old man. I continue to learn, every day, and I am compelled to pass on what I have learned to all those who will listen. My voice is my song, and I sing for all men to hear.

I have seen that of all men, those who attain the highest esteem and regard in the eyes of their fellows are the athletes, the men of beautiful body whose brawn often times exceeds the power of their brains. They spend their days in endless pursuit of physical perfection manifest in one, flawless burst of energy that lifts them above all other men and earns them a place in history to be revered eternally. We overlook the faults of the men who win the crowns of the wild olive and laurel. Above all other rewards a man can earn for himself, the crown never passes unnoticed and the man who wins it endures unending fame and renown. The athletes' popularity is abetted by poets like me who compose the victory odes and play them throughout the land, and by other artists as well who sculpt their images in wood and stone to challenge the test of time. Even today, I can stroll through Olympia and gaze upon the statues of men who won the crowns in games long past, even before the time of my father's father, and his father, too. We are compelled to praise the athlete and are helpless to ignore his achievements.

In some ways, I regret my part in diverting the minds of common men to these heroes of extraordinary athletic feats for I have come to question the value of athletic accomplishment and its subsequent adoration. I do not doubt that these men have earned their victories. But, the true value of a man's life is not to be measured, as we are so apt to do, on the friendly fields of contention, but on other fields and other days, when the scales are not tipped by the mere veneration of fellow men.

What a man does in the gymnasium, he does for himself. His accomplishment has not improved the quality of the lives of those who praise him. For what can a man say who has won the crown? That I am faster or stronger than you are? Does it really matter if he is?

These things I learned not so long ago in the company of a young man, dead now, who came to know that the true champion is made of firmer stuff than just the meat that clings to his bones. The true champion competes for more than personal glory and for stakes much higher than a crown of leaves that will wither and fall from the vine. We call the purity of a man *kalos kagathos*, and it is not found only in a man's muscles. It pervades his brain, his heart, and the depths of his being.

I call all of Hellas my home. Even though my whiskers are white, my calves remain hard and my heart is strong for I make journey often, certainly more than most men whose vision of the world is limited to their own city and the fields and forests that surround their homes. I have many acquaintances, but few friends. I have yet to decide if that is a good or bad thing. I may rest my head in a single place for one night, for one month, maybe even a year, and then I move on to share my time and learn from others. Knowledge is not to be gained from a single source.

I attend many games. I do admire the athletes, though in recent years my admiration lacks much of the enthusiasm of my youth. Every four years, as I learned from my father, I heed the call of the Elean runners and find my way to the stadium at Olympia; it is a grand and festive sight. More frequently, I travel to the holy grove at Delphi to take the Pythia's counsel. As the gods weave the pattern of my life, I am enlightened and seek the words the priestess imparts to me and to others as well.

I sit now alone this night on an open beach that bleeds sand to the Aegean from the Island of Thasos, many days north from my boyhood home. The waves lap the land with a soft and comforting sound. The breeze is warm like puppy's breath. The stars are brilliant, and I can see the Bear that points our way north to the land of the Hyperboreans that some say is forever covered with ice and snow, where Apollo dwells with the people of his mother. I contemplate the life of a man born here on this island and known to all men of Hellas as a great Olympic champion.

For the glory he bestowed on this island, his countrymen honored him with a bronze statue that was displayed in the heart of their *agora*. His name was Theagenes, Theagenes of Thasos, though his friends, thinking that 'Thea' passed the lips with a feminine inflection that did no justice to the mighty, if not heroic image that he presented to friend and foe alike, called him Theo. Theo won the *athlon*, the sacred olive crown, twice at Olympia. I knew him as a boxer when he won his first crown, but he returned again to win the *pankration*. Our paths never crossed at those second games he competed in, the 76th, though I hoped they would.

Theagenes is dead now for five years though to me it seems much longer. They called him the bull of Thasos because of his powerful stature and his unbending will to stand and fight any opponent. But in my time with him, I have seen the bull weep; I believe no other man has. It pained me to learn of his demise. He had seen only 25 years when, as I've been told, he simply slipped and fell to his death at the quarries in Aliki, not far from where I now sit. There have been times when I wonder if he slipped or if he fell of his own accord. I dispel the thought for it disturbs me and leaves me empty. I traveled with him once. It was a journey that began at Olympia and ended at the Hot Gates at Thermopylae, a journey inspired by his misguided anger and personal vengeance and by my greed to capitalize upon it. It ended in revelation for both of us.

This is my second trip to Thasos; my first was but one year ago. I return to give tribute to Theagenes, and I plan to return every year as long as the gods favor me with life. Theo has earned that much from me, and I regret that I did not make that promise to myself sooner.

Theo returned to his homeland following his second Olympic victory. He was a brooding and introverted man who kept to himself. He lived alone in the hills and went to the quarry every day to cut stone. He exchanged few words with anyone and no man could call him friend. Here was a champion whose athletic achievements had earned him a lifetime of money, but in a few short years he gave it all away. Unlike other athletes, he did not squander it on foolish diversions like women and wine, or even a fine house. He just gave it away. All cities offer their champions a free meal in the *agora* every day so that young and old alike can gather to meet the man who brought fame to his homeland. The citizens of Thasos came to the marketplace and waited, but Theagenes never appeared. He spent his days in the quarry and rarely frequented the village; he bothered no one and no one bothered him... until after his death.

I truly wanted to attend the ceremony when his statue was raised on Thasos. I considered making my way to his island at that time but was waylaid at the bidding of the Spartan *gerousia*, the old men who, not for the first time, sought words from me for the tomb of a departed comrade. I respect them, the Spartans, for their way of life, for their commitment to something much larger than themselves, but it is not a life I would be pleased to follow. I am not made of such hard stuff.

Not attending the dedication, I thought to pay my respect to it the following year. But the shallow and uninspired men of Thasos played a cruel trick on their departed Olympian. Incredibly, not long after the statue was erected, the Thasians threw it into the sea!

Disgusted, I somehow managed to laugh at the ignorance of the Thasians. I deduced that the gods were not so humored when I heard of the fate cast upon the island. In his wrath, Poseidon commanded his sister Demeter to turn her back on Thasos. The land became barren and refused to bring forth food or fruit or flowers of any kind.

In its odd way, it was the famine that brought me here to the island of Thasos the first time, one year ago, and through no coincidence...

In the month of **Maimakterion**, when people pray to
Zeus the Storm Bringer to be kind to their crops and houses
as the cold, northern winds approach, I made my journey
to Delphi from Syracuse. I had been visiting a friend and
stayed longer than I had planned. I normally travel to Delphi when the weather is warmer, but I would not deny myself the Pythia's counsel. It was unusually mild for this
time of the year, and the auguries favored continued good
weather. The voyage across the Ionian Sea was calm, and I
was well rested when I began my long climb up the twist-
ing path from the water's edge to the **Altis**, the holy grove
which sits high on the rugged hillside looking back on the
gulf far below. Hours later as I approached the site, I could
hear the cheerful voices of young men toning their bodies in
the nearby gymnasium; their laughter filled me with a sense
of embarrassment at my own bulk though I carried it well
on strong legs. Oh, to be a young man again, the thought
fluttered through my mind and disappeared as quickly as a
butterfly that you catch in the corner of your eye as it darts
into the forest. As custom would dictate, I cleansed myself
in the chilly water that fed the Kastalian fountains. I felt
alert but still had to stop and sit to catch my breath before
it fled me forever, though I did not fear it; there were far
worse places to meet the gods than at Delphi.

As I rested on the side of the path, I could not help
but overhear a group of men who sat opposite. It was the
same men who had lodged with me the night before in
Itea's small inn, a common gathering place for visitors to
the Oracle. Though I was on the road much earlier than

they were, my age had allowed them to nearly overtake me as we climbed toward the temple.

"What more can the priestess tell us?" one asked his companions. "Our people have done her bidding and still we hunger."

Whoever these men were, I thought, they would have to consider what the Pythia had told them more deeply if their response to her previous guidance had not produced the expected results. The Pythia's words are rarely straight-forward and are more frequently as mystical as the source of her power and sight. One must consider them long and hard, and often an initial interpretation may not be accurate. Such is the way of Apollo and the priestess through whom he speaks.

I took a deep breath and assumed my proper place in the line of supplicants that continued to grow and move forward slowly; patience is a requirement for those who seek the Pythia's counsel. The blue sky provided vivid contrast to the ancient, gray cliffs of Mt. Parnassus that rose steeply in the distance behind the sanctuary. As I waited in line, I watched the shadows shorten, and I pondered the move-ment of objects in the heavens. Within two moon cycles, the day would display its greatest imbalance between light and dark; when the winter winds turned the land cold, He-lios would give his steeds more rest.

I will not repeat, as others do what message and in-struction I received that day, only that the priestess told me my path would cross again, and soon, with Theagenes. I took her at her word.

Certain that I could clarify her message, I left the temple grounds and retraced my steps back toward the gymnasium where I stopped to purchase a small loaf of bread and cheese. A grove of trees shivered in the breeze and invited me to enjoy its shade while I took my lunch before I began the long trek down the mountainside to Itea and its harbor. As I ate, I pondered the Pythia's conundrum. If I would cross paths again with Theo, and Theo was dead, did her message portend my own death? How else would I encounter a dead man? Would Theo greet me at the Styx with Charon? If that would be the case, I concluded it should be of no concern to me. I have lived a full life and so I do not fear death (but as a younger man I would not have said the same). If the gods were calling me home, then I would obey, willingly. Still, when a man accepts his death as imminent, he is inclined to cling more tightly to his life. I fought the urge to do that, and attempted to resolve myself to the destiny that Apollo had decreed. I prayed that it would be painless. I have seen death in its most gruesome form and I have no desire to be counted in that lot of men whose final moment is embroiled in agony.

I was lost in contemplation and prayer but remained attentive, though undisturbed, to the sounds that surrounded me. Birds sang sweetly from the olive trees under which I sat; they lifted my spirits and implored me not to dwell on dire thoughts. Cheers erupted sporadically from the nearby gymnasium. Men passing by on the path whispered nervously amongst themselves, some chanted and even sang. Quiet laughter mingled with louder tears. Some men were happy, others sad, but all puppets on the strings that descended like an invisible web from Olympus. Why bother to weep, for no man can change what has been ordained in heaven.

I shook my head to clear it and breathed deeply, steadfast to accept the direction I would be led. With my resolution came satisfaction and I smiled. Death is merely a part of life, though it is, indeed, the final part.

Unexpectedly, like a clap of thunder on a clear day, I heard the name of Theagenes' homeland spoken, "Thasos." It was but a single word of one man's conversation to which I had not been privy nor had I any reason to believe I would or could be part of. Nonetheless, the spoken name of his island caused me to turn quickly to identify its source.

The same group of men, those I had seen in Itea and the same I had sat near earlier in the day, had taken seats on the grass not far from me. Although I stared, no one seemed to notice; they were rapt in an intense discussion. I strained to hear their words and, assuming that their conversation was none of my business felt guilty, like a thief with a conscience.

They numbered four and they sat in a tight circle. The elder, though not nearly as old as I, rested against the base of a crooked tree. A troubled look etched wrinkles in his brow. The others leaned forward and waited impatiently to hear his words. After gazing back up the hill at the temple from where they had come, he spoke in a tired voice. "I am as befuddled as each of you," he began. "Let us consider our actions. The Pythia told us months ago to welcome back all exiles. Does any man here deny that we have complied with her instructions? Has any exile been forgotten or overlooked in our haste to satisfy Apollo's wishes?"

The four exchanged a glance of resignation. I recalled the earlier statement on the path to the temple and quickly deduced that these were men of Thasos and they had returned to the Oracle for more guidance. The famine retained its hold on their island, and whatever they had done to appease the gods had failed to loosen its bony grip. After a moment, one said, "We can think of no one, Parmenides."

Parmenides nodded gravely and folded his hands in his lap. "And that is the source of our confusion." I listened closely as he continued. "We must carefully meditate upon what we have been told. The priestess directed us to call back all men who were banished from the island. There have been few during my lifetime. I can count their number on my hands. We followed her instruction, though in some cases it pained us to welcome back men of poor character who can only make our island weaker. Empedocles and Archytas refused our invitation, but they have been gone so long from Thasos that it comes as no surprise; they have made comfortable lives for themselves in other lands. But the remaining men returned and were greeted cordially, even those who have led contemptible and despicable lives. Our response was true to Apollo's wishes: we welcomed them back, all of them."

As Parmenides ran the palm of his hand over his bald head, his gaze turned toward me. Our eyes locked. He caught me staring at him and his fellows. Embarrassed, I averted my look to the ground and feigned disinterest by gathering my things. I glanced up to find his eyes had never left me. "Friend," he called, "I see by the few remaining gray hairs on your head that you are old. Old men can be wise and we have need of wisdom. What is your name?"

I called back, "Simonides," and added, "of Ceos."

Despite the gravity of his situation, his face beamed, if only for a second, "The poet?" he asked.

I answered with a smile.

"Then we are in luck! You are known as a truly wise man, Simonides of Ceos, and we would welcome any advice you might offer us." He beckoned me to join them. I approached slowly and lowered myself to the ground while bracing myself on the same tree against which Parmenides sat. One of the younger men offered to assist me, but I respectfully refused his arm.

"I am Parmenides," he introduced himself. "My friends and I have traveled here from Thasos. One season ago, our island, a place of beauty as all Hellenes will attest, was struck by famine. No crops would grow. Our fruit trees were barren. We struggled to understand why our island alone, and not the mainland, not Thracia to the north or Chalcidice or Macedon to the west, or even Troa or Mysia to the east felt Aethon's flaming hooves.

"We sacrificed to the gods as custom and logic would prescribe, but to no avail. Our island turned to dust; it resembled more a lump of dried clay than the jewel all know it as.

"We turned to Apollo and made our journey to Delphi and presented our case to the Pythia. Her message was clear and not veiled in mystery: 'Welcome back all exiles,' she said." I raised my eyebrows reflexively as few of the Oracle's messages are 'clear.' Parmenides continued, "We returned to Thasos and did her bidding. It has been six months now, and the crisis has only worsened: our children cry and our treasury is empty as we trade what little we have left with the mainlanders to keep food on our tables." Drawing strength from one another not to weep in my presence, the Thasians joined hands in their small circle. I watched uncomfortably as they fought back the tears that welled in their tired eyes.

"Today, we met again with the priestess and implored her to unveil the secret that the gods heartlessly hide from us." He paused while looking at his fellows, and raised his arms in abdication.

"And what secret, may I ask, did the Pythia reveal?"

"In her trance she smiled and laughed. In that high-pitched and cracked voice she whispered, 'You have forgotten none but the greatest.' That is all she spoke. She turned her back and retreated to her lair. We could see her slender shoulders quiver and she cackled undecipherable words as she disappeared into the fog. I fear she taunted us.

"So we sit here and rest and search our memories for whom we might have forgotten. The greatest of our exiles? Certainly we Thasians consider no man who has been exiled as great, rather the opposite. Those who have been banished in the past were sent away with good reason. Still, we have welcomed all back though not all have returned." Parmenides reached to his side and offered me a draught of warm wine. "So tell us, wise poet, what do you think? What can be done to appease the gods that we have not already tried? What hidden meaning lies in the Pythia's message?"

I wiped the wine from my lips with the back of my wrinkled and spotted hand while I considered what he had told me. The Pythia's instructions did seem as simple as they seemed clear. But the Thasians' response to her first directive had not produced the intended result. If there was not a deeper meaning to her words, there may have been a more obvious interpretation.

"I sympathize with the plight of all Thasos, and trust that I will offer my own prayers to the gods on behalf of you and your countrymen," I answered. "However the gods are unlikely to listen to this aged frog's prayers if indeed you have not satisfied Apollo's bidding." A bright beam of sunlight found its way through the leaves above me and struck my face, momentarily blinding me. I raised my hand to shield my eyes and asked innocently, "Whom do you consider the greatest of all Thasians?"

One of the younger men raised his voice while the others shrugged their shoulders. "We are not from Athens or Sparta," he said. "You, Simonides, are well-known amongst all Hellenes, and you have traveled our country far and wide. The greatest men in Hellas are not from Thasos. We have no Pindar or Heraclitus to call our own. The great warriors who repelled the Medes are not from our island. Whom do we consider the greatest man from Thasos?" He mimicked his comrades and shrugged his shoulders. "There is no living man from Thasos whom we would consider great for no man from our island is known through all of Hellas. We four serve our state as best we can, but none of us, not even

Parmenides with all due respect, considers himself 'great.' We are simple men. Certainly none of the few whom have been exiled from Thasos was a great man in our esteem nor in the mind of anyone else."

I raised my hand to calm him and offered, "You say there is no living man from Thasos whom you would consider great. I ask you to reconsider the Pythia's statement from a different perspective. Whom do you call the greatest Thasian, be he living or be he dead?"

All but one smiled broadly and Parmenides answered with confidence, "Surely you and all men of Hellas would answer: none other than the great Olympian, Theagenes. Of all Thasians, his name is known best in Hellas and even beyond."

"No man would disagree with you on that point. Therefore I say to you Thasians: Theagenes is the answer. It is Theagenes to whom the Pythia refers. You have forgotten Theagenes." I rested my case and reached again for the wine.

They looked from one to the other in disbelief, and each shook his head 'no.' "Surely you can't mean that, Simonides," my new friend stated without reservation. "Theagenes is dead. He is no exile from Thasos. His broken bones lay buried near the quarry into which he fell several years ago. I mean no disrespect, sir, but Theagenes is no exile and cannot be the one Apollo orders us to welcome back."

"Think deeper, Parmenides, and free your mind from conditioned thought. It is true: all Hellenes, if not men of the entire world, revere Theagenes for his accomplishments at Olympia and the other games. None, however, admire him more than you Thasians do. Yet in your ignorance, you have exiled him from Thasos." Distrust appeared on their faces like a dark and threatening shadow, and they mumbled among themselves that I may not be as wise as they might have hoped or expected.

"Please hear my thoughts, friends," I implored, "—all of my thoughts—before you judge the merit of my words. You may find that what sounds false may well be true, and if it is so, you may discover your answer and thereby dispel the famine that threatens to destroy you and your island."

"We have a long journey before us, and we need to be on our way," Parmenides said on behalf of his fellows, "but in respect to you and your work, we will hear you out. How can you say we exiled Theagenes? Quite the contrary is true. We honored him with a statue in our *agora*."

"And where is that statue now?" I asked.

"I'll speak for the fate of that statue," one said.

"Calm yourself, Xeno," Parmenides interceded. "What's done is done."

"True, Parmenides, and it should not be undone." Xeno stood and began to pace behind his countrymen. I could see the young man's frustration as he raised his hand above his head and roughly raked a cluster of green leaves from their branch and threw them into the air. They floated to the ground in a haphazard way. Xeno pointed at me with anger in his eyes. "You know as well as all of Hellas what happened to that statue. It rests at the bottom of the Aegean where it justly belongs."

"I want no conflict Xeno, if that is your name. I ask a simple question because you men, in service to Thasos, want answers." My voice remained steady but before I could continue, Xeno interrupted.

"You'll get no conflict from me, only the truth. My brother was murdered by that statue." His companions closed their eyes; they had no doubt heard the story before and did not need or want to hear it again. "My brother was destined to be the greatest athlete from Thasos, maybe in all of Hellas. Theagenes' death in the quarry robbed him of that chance. Some say that Theagenes even took his own life, miserable wretch that he was. As if that was not bad enough, the statue toppled from its place in the *agora* and fell on my brother and killed him." He turned violently and glared at Parmenides and the others. "You know it's true. That statue killed him and for its crime, it was rightly dragged through the streets and dumped into the sea where it will rot forever."

Parmenides' face reddened and the others looked away. Apparently the fate of the statue was not something all Thasians took pride in.

I had come to know Theagenes in a special way, and I was prepared to make a stand in his behalf against this whiskerless youth that refused to face the reality of what had actually happened. I knew I could emerge the victor in any battle of words with this inexperienced young hothead. I have been known to use my tongue with the efficiency of a trained *hoplite* wielding his sword. "As I've heard it, Xeno, your brother was an arrogant fool and in his drunkenness he would sneak to the *agora* at night and strike the statue with his fists. Who is to be surprised that it fell upon him? As I've heard it, your brother got what he deserved." I continued undauntedly before Xeno could interrupt again. "You are correct, young man: all Hellenes know the story. Only the wealth of your family allowed this silly trial to transpire, and only the wealth of your family convicted the statue—if convicting a statue is possible—and sent it to its current resting-place in the harbor. Thasos would have never tasted famine had your father's coins not found their way to the pockets of those responsible for justice. You are fortunate that all of Hellas does not judge Thasos by this silly incident alone. If it did, your island would have more worries than just a famine." I panted now, nearly out of breath from the force of my tirade. I had no overt intent to offend this young man, though I cared little if I did, but I could not restrain myself from telling him exactly what I thought in defense of my one-time friend.

Xeno moved threateningly toward me, but Parmenides and his comrades stepped in quickly to restrain him. Xeno was slightly built and it was difficult for me to imagine that his brother had been so powerful of stature that it would have been possible or conceivable for him to challenge Theo in the *pyx*. From the looks of Xeno, even at my age, I feared no physical abuse although I was glad that the young man's companions had prevented him from causing a regrettable incident.

"You know nothing, old man. Justice was served," he shouted at me through watering eyes.

You need a healthy dose of good, Spartan discipline, I thought, but I calmly replied, "To which event do you refer,

Xeno: When the statue toppled upon your brother or when it was cast into the sea?" I could not check my final words and added, "Even as the great Hesiod has written: *neither famine nor disaster ever haunts men who do true justice.* You have offended Dike. Your laws are flawed and true justice has not been served despite what you may think!"

"Shut up," he yelled and now began to sob. "This is none of your concern." Parmenides placed a comforting arm around the young man. It was clear to me that although Parmenides and the others recognized the stupidity of the Thasian court, they were not prepared to abandon their companion.

"I think it is time for us to leave," Parmenides said.

"Do you return to Thasos directly?" I asked feeling some remorse that I had upset the lad to satisfy my own vanity. Parmenides nodded 'yes' as the four men gathered their few belongings.

"If you could abide my presence, I would like to accompany you upon your journey."

"And for what reason does the great Simonides wish to return to Thasos amid its famine and pestilence?" Parmenides asked as he pulled his satchel high on his shoulder. His demeanor turned cold and suggested that I was not welcome.

"For the simple reason that I consider myself a friend of Theagenes of Thasos." The four stopped in mid-action and stared at me, even Xeno whose eyes were moist and red.

"It is true," I continued. "I witnessed his victories at Olympia. More importantly, I journeyed long with him in a time of peril that changed my life and his as well. There may be more to tell of Theo that will help convince you that he is the one Apollo seeks redemption for. Theo is the exile that can end your famine." I looked directly at Xeno. "I am sorry to have offended you, young man. I will agree with you on one point: Theo was as arrogant as he was skillful with the *himantes*. Like you, young Xeno, he was impetuous." Then I turned my gaze to the others, "But you know Theo's greatness only from his exploits in the games. His true triumph as a man occurred far from the games at Olympia. In your own words, you recognize him as the greatest Thasian. When you have heard my story, you will know him as you have never known him before. Greatness can be measured in many ways and by far more significant parameters than a man's proficiency with his fists. You need to know what I know. When you do, you will have no doubt that Theo is with the gods and they tell you now to return him to the status that he deserves."

The stunned look on their faces told me I had captured their interest. I could see it in the eyes of each man, even through the tears of Xeno. I waited for an answer hoping that Parmenides would offer me the invitation I sought. A gust of wind tickled the trees, and a single, unusually large, ripe olive fell from its branch and landed squarely between the Thasians and me. I bent to pick it up and studied its perfection; it was marked with no blemish, just soft, moist fruit dropped from the heavens by the gods. I saw it as an unmistakable sign from Demeter that my deduction was true: Theagenes was the exile that needed to return to Thasos to bring an end to the famine. Although I could see that the Thasians failed to understand the significance of the fallen fruit, that it was a good omen from the gods, I thought it best not to interpret the event for fear of offending them further than I might already have. And so, I extended the olive to Xeno. "Peace to you, young friend," I said.

He stared at the offering in my open palm without moving. Slowly, he reached for it. In a soft, hurt voice he whispered, "He can come." I joined the group and we headed down the path that would lead us to Itea.

CHAPTER TWO

In the Path of Agamemnon

I consider myself strong for my age, and my gait was equal to that of Parmenides and the three younger Thasians whose names I learned, in addition to Xeno, were Episcles and Cimon. Every so often, I think to test my fitness, one would increase his pace and the others would follow. They soon learned that I was equal to the task; I stayed with them like their shadows.

Xeno's stature and the impertinence he displayed in our previous conversation were physically and mentally characteristic of a boy even though I put him at twenty years, an age when young Hellenes have completed their *ephebike* and are ready for citizenship. Most 20-year-old men enter the military reserve; Xeno could not survive the rigors of military life. His attire and his fair skin indicated that he was from a family of some wealth; that much I was sure of when he did not deny my accusation that his family's financial status had influenced the trial of Theo's statue.

As for the other two, they smiled frequently but said little. I guessed that Episcles approached thirty, and Cimon forty. They were tanned and muscled. Wrinkles like thin spider webs ran from the corners of Cimon's eyes. His deep brown skin and slightly bowed legs told me that he spent many hours each day on the sea guiding his boat on the rich waters of the Aegean; he was a fisherman. Episcles' sandals were thin and I felt hard calluses on his hands when we took each other's forearm in greeting. His shoulders were thick and I surmised he spent his days in the quarries breaking rock with heavy tools. The Thasian contingent to Delphi covered a broad spectrum of experience.

The weight of age was not hidden in Parmenides' sixty some years, and it was accentuated by his bald head that glistened now with sweat as we moved carefully down the narrow, rocky path. I always find it harder on my legs in the descent than in the climb. On a long step down, my higher leg shakes in its flex as my lower leg searches for sure footing below. Occasionally, we stepped to the side to allow others to move by us on their climb to the sanctuary.

We talked little and saved our breath as we made our way down the mountainside to the harbor. Darkness had fallen by the time we reached the inn at Itea. Exhausted, we took our meal of bread and fish. Sullenly, Xeno immediately retired. Episcles and Cimon joined three other men who were throwing *knucklebones* in a dimly lit corner. With little interest in games of chance, Parmenides and I walked outside for a last breath of fresh air before we took our places on the hard mats the innkeeper had reserved for us.

"The hunter is on the prowl," I said. Parmenides looked at me quizzically. I pointed into the clear sky. "Orion," I clarified, "The hunter... He searches for game."

Parmenides turned his gaze to the heavens and replied, "And soon the scorpion will follow."

I smiled, pleased to be in the company of a man who understood the movement of the stars in the night sky.

"I have some concern," Parmenides said as he stifled a yawn.

"Have no worries," I replied, "Xeno is a confused young man and his hot blood is fortified by the wealth of his family. His wounds will heal and he will come to know the truth. His travels with you and the other two will serve him well. He may not know it now, but in time he will be thankful for the days he shared with you and your friends."

As we walked toward the dock, Parmenides scanned the shoreline illuminated now by a rising moon as Selene's silver chariot replaced that of Helios. "While I agree with you, Simonides," he answered, "My concern now is not for Xeno, but for our passage home to Thasos." His eyes continued to search the harbor. "Our ship is no where in sight."

A large Athenian trireme sat far out in the deep water. At 120 feet long, it loomed amid a handful of smaller vessels, merchants and fishers, and rocked almost imperceptibly to the rhythm of the small waves as they rolled toward the beach. Further down the wharf we heard loud voices, some female, and laughter, and then music. The windows of a storefront glowed from the hearth inside that was surely preparing the victuals for the officers of the warship. Sparks flickered and flew haphazardly into the night sky from large bonfires set not far from the water's edge where the remainder of the crew, mostly rowers, picked their spots on the beach to rest for the night. Forty sailors and warriors joined them. They would entertain each other with the tales of Artemisium and Salamis, stories they had heard a hundred times before but never tired of. Men of war take great honor in their victories.

"The trireme was not anchored in the harbor when I departed for Delphi early this morning," I observed.

"Nor was it here when we left," Parmenides replied.

"Perhaps the sailors can tell us of your vessel."

Parmenides nodded. "I think we are more likely to get the information we seek from the officers than from the men on the beach."

We continued to stroll down the wharf to the inn. The smell of roasting goat meat, a rare luxury for these men of the sea greeted us at the door as we entered. The four officers sat at a wooden table, their hands and faces bathed in the light, shiny from the greasy meat that they pulled from the bones of the roasted goat and shoved into their mouths. More than enough female company crowded behind the table to keep the men's cups filled with wine and the platters piled high with foodstuff. Above the aroma of the meat, the innkeeper and his brothel smelled money from the officers of the trireme. Military men live a tenuous life never certain when Charon will ferry them across the river Styx, and for that reason, they are free with their coin, unlike the stingy merchants and traders who are inclined to preserve their profits.

As we entered, the *aulos* player hidden in the dark corner ceased his tune and all eyes turned suspiciously toward us with no intent to disguise their annoyance at our intrusion upon their personal revelry. I had been with soldiers before during their warring season. Like them, these men gazed upon us disdainfully for we shared not the bond of brotherhood nor the threat of certain confrontation with violent death that draws men of war closer together be they friend or foe. A soldier was apt to confide in an enemy before he would trust a man who did not bear arms.

The oldest one, an ugly, heavily bearded man with thick, tangled black hair wiped his mouth with the back of his free hand and rudely questioned, "Who goes there and what do you want?"

"Are you the captain of this group of heroes?" I asked boldly.

"Do I look like the captain?" he fired back. Bits of meat flew from his mouth when he talked and grease dribbled down his chin. The others, save one, laughed. Neither Parmenides nor I bothered to answer. "No," he finally said through a mouthful of goat. "I'm the helmsman." He sucked the juice from his fingers and wiped his hands across his dirty garment. "He's the captain." He used a bone not yet cleaned of its stringy meat to point at the youthful man seated at the end of the table.

Without introduction, the young man rose from his seat and spoke most respectfully, "I am the captain of the trireme, sir. How can I be of service to you and your friend?"

I was tempted to begin by suggesting that he school his fellow officer on proper etiquette, but thought better of it believing that such a public reprimand might place the captain in jeopardy with his simple and provincial crew. In all likelihood, this man did not earn his captaincy; his family bought it for him. The heavy scarlet scar that ran down the helmsman's forehead from his scalp to the bridge of his broken nose told me he was no stranger to combat.

His battered face left no doubt in my mind that the *ky-bernetes* had more knowledge of naval warfare in his little finger than the captain had in his entire brain. That would change over time, but for now, there was no need to ruffle the helmsman's feathers.

Parmenides attempted to cool the flames but failed when he innocently said to the captain, "I arrived here yesterday morning on a Macedonian merchant vessel from my home in Thasos."

The ugly one interrupted, "Thasos?" He turned to his fellows and guffawed, "The brave Thasians! As a hoplite aboard a trireme in the Straits of Artemisium, I have recollection of Thasos. When the Medes advanced through the Northern Aegean during the Great War, no man from Thasos took up arms. They turned meekly, like lambs before the sacrificial blade. It was we Athenians who saved all of Hellas no thanks to the timid men of Thasos who offered no resistance and allowed the Persians full access to their island. And now," he concluded, "look at what has happened. The gods justly reward you with famine." He turned his back on us and called for more wine. "Play, musician," he ordered.

The captain presented apology with his eyes and led us out the door. "I'm sorry," he started to say.

I quickly countered, "Don't be. When you find yourself in battle, you will be thankful that you have such a crude and angry man steering your ship. His meanness is more apt to win an engagement on the open waters than his lack of politeness is to win friends."

The captain smiled timidly and said, "Nonetheless, it is foolish to make enemies with our words which I am afraid he has done."

"Rather with words than the point of a sword," Parmenides concluded. "Can you tell us anything about our ship?" he asked.

"Only this," the captain answered, "We entered the harbor mid-morning. There were no fewer than threefold the number of fishers and merchants when we arrived than what you see here now." He pointed toward the four or five small ships moored this side of his trireme. "We are not so welcome here as in our own ports to the east. As we rowed into the harbor most scattered like a school of frightened fish and took to the deep water. I suspect your vessel may have been among them."

Parmenides shook his head. "Never trust a Macedonian trader."

"True," the captain responded. "In my few months at sea, I've learned they make far better pirates than merchants." In the dim light, the captain saw the look of consternation that spread across Parmenides' face. "I might offer you a suggestion if you are willing to accept one."

"Please tell me, young captain, for my comrades and I need to return to our homeland."

"For thirty days, my ship and I have sailed our waters and visited many ports. While the port at Piraeus that serves our city at Athens teems with ships, I make a case also for the port at Aulis that lies on the straits between Boetia and Euboea. Though not as busy as Piraeus, I have noted a considerable number of traders at that port that move both north and south around the large island. I am certain you can find passage to Thasos from Aulis."

"What thoughts, friend?" Parmenides asked me.

"I agree with the captain. By my count, Aulis lays three or four days' march to the east, maybe less. I make it a few days' voyage from there to your island by ship. We should heed his advice and turn our steps toward Aulis when the sun rises."

We thanked the young captain, prayed that the *Moirai* would offer him good luck, and took our leave, determined to be on the road to Aulis early the next morning.

I awoke before the others. Only the first blossom of sunlight tainted the black orchid that lay upon the horizon, slowly transforming it to a deep purple. I made my habit to rise early each day; there was too much of life, even at my age that I had yet to learn and experience. Perhaps foolishly, I feared that something of significance would pass me by unnoticed while I slept. When a man rises early, he hears the quintessence of music as the awakening birds fill the air with their sweet songs. No man and no instrument can feign to accurately capture that magic though many have tried with no success; the earth's song is pure and untainted as life awakens each morning. No matter what follows, my day starts right.

The surface of the sea was like glass and there was no movement from the sleeping crewman of the trireme. That would change in an hour or so when the churlish helmsman stormed to the beach and roused his sailors. Until then, the world was still and peaceful as I made my way through a natural barricade of huge rocks to a secluded pool of seawater where I bathed to replace the salt of my own sweat with that of Poseidon.

By the time I returned to the inn, the few clouds on the eastern horizon blushed red to announce the return of Helios. I never tired at the sight of a blazing sunrise. Parmenides stood in the doorway and stretched his arms wide. He twisted his body at the waist from right to left and back again to relieve the small pains that assault old men when they first rise in the morning. He greeted me cordially as I walked up the steps. "It appears that we will have a fine day to begin our journey."

"The gods have blessed us," I answered, "That is a good sign."

In a short time we were on the path that led us east through the mountains toward the port at Aulis. We left the sounds of Itea behind us but not before we heard the angry call of the *kybernetes* as he raced through the camp on the beach yelling gruffly, "On your feet, you drunken dogs of Sirius." And indeed the sailors howled like angry beasts as he rousted them roughly from their dreams of a better life. I swear I saw the short hairs on the back of Xeno's neck rise when the helmsman issued his commands; I suppressed my laughter.

We made good time through the mountains, and as darkness approached, so, too, did towering, thick clouds. We were well inland at some considerable elevation where the chestnut, elm and beech trees afforded us some protection from the rain that threatened to fall from the flashing and rumbling skies to the west.

"Without fire," Xeno pouted much like a woman, "we are apt to be in for a cold and damp night."

Spoiled child, I thought but said, "The gods may favor us and let this storm pass. In either case, I have fire." Though my memory fails to recall the name of the man from whom I learned it, I have the secret of the stones.

"You have fire?" Episcles asked, not understanding what I meant.

I smiled and nodded. "If you and the others gather a supply of wood—and I see there is much at hand—I can make fire. With it, we can ward off wild animals and dry ourselves if we are unlucky enough to take the brunt of the storm we see brewing in the distance." With no hesitation, Episcles and Cimon scrambled into the foliage to retrieve a supply of wood. For his part, Parmenides foraged for a number of rocks with which he built a small circle to retain any heat I might generate with a fire. Xeno sat on a fallen tree and watched skeptically, unaccustomed as he was to manual labor.

In a short while, Epi (as I came to call Episcles) and Cimon returned with an ample supply of dry twigs, sticks, and even some larger pieces of broken limbs and branches. They watched closely as I made a small, loosely compacted ball of wool that I scraped from my own, worn tunic. I dropped to my knees and placed the ball in the center of the ring of stone that Parmenides had built. It was becoming difficult to see in the darkness and I worked quickly to construct a mound of the smallest twigs around the wool. A night bird made an unusual sound in a nearby tree, and I could sense if not see Xeno's trepidation when he heard the ruffle of dry leaves not far from where we were assembled. With little time before total darkness engulfed us, I reached into my satchel and rummaged at the bottom of the bag; I withdrew a pair of small stones. I prayed silently to Prometheus, and moved my hands as close to the wool ball as possible without disturbing the wood that enveloped it. After three, sharp quick motions as I struck the one rock to the other, a small, hot spark flew from the one and landed squarely in the wool. A thin column of white smoke rose from the center and I leaned closer to breathe softly upon it. Even Xeno had moved near and the four Thasians watched as the glowing redness from the single spark spread through the wool and abruptly burst into a small flame. I was pleased with my success. The five of us huddled around the stone ring, our faces bathed in the orange light of the crackling fire I had created.

"I've seen this done before," Parmenides commented.

"It is less a secret today than it was for our fathers," I replied. "My journeys require that I know this skill to warm myself on the many cold nights I spend in the mountains far from the comfort of a friend's warm home."

"We are grateful that you travel with us," Cimon thanked me.

Each of us carried a small quantity of *maza*, barley bread. Throughout the day, I constantly watched the ground for wild onions and had accumulated enough to share with the Thasians. We supped on the bread and onions as we kept a close watch on the flashes in the night sky. The four winds battled like angry children to set the path of the storm. From what I could tell, Notus was winning on this night.

"The gods are with us," I said to Parmenides. "Zephyrus and his brother take the storm to the north. It will pass us."

"I for one am glad he shows his mercy," Cimon said.

"Me, too," Epi echoed. He rubbed his thighs and added, "I can only imagine how your legs must feel. The path is difficult enough for a young, fit man. Do your legs ache and burn with fire like mine do?"

I looked at Parmenides and grinned. "No," I answered, "All feeling left my legs many hours ago, but the rest tonight will revive me. I will be ready for the road again tomorrow."

"Well then," Epi concluded, "I agree with our silent friend." He nodded toward Xeno who had pulled further away from the fire and into its flickering shadows. Xeno had taken a place on the ground and curled into a sleeping position with his cloak pulled around his body and his satchel positioned beneath his head. "It is time for sleep. Morning will come soon enough."

As Epi and Cimon made their places on the ground, I remained seated on the large log that we had pulled closer to the flames. "Let us sit for a while and talk," Parmenides said to me while the others retired. "The journey has been hard and we've had better things to do with our breath this day than waste it on words." I pulled my cloak higher around my shoulders in the Spartan way. The mountain air was turning cooler even as the storm passed to the north.

"So you believe that Theagenes is the exile to whom the Pythia referred?" My silence was enough to tell him that I did. After a brief moment where we only heard the crackling fire and the wind through the trees he asked, "And you knew him well?"

"Our paths crossed at Olympia," I answered, "when he was a young man, maybe not even quite so old as your friend Xeno, and truly, I spent a mere ten days with him, just he and I. The ten days we shared were hard days, the most difficult in my life, but they changed me deeply and rocked the very foundation of my life right down to the core of my soul. I imagine they changed him as well."

"Strong words," Parmenides said gravely.

"And meant to be," I answered. I gave him a moment to weigh my response. A night bird whistled. "I will share the story with all of you before we reach Thasos, but for now, let your friends rest." I stirred the fire and watched the skittering sparks rise like nervous fireflies. "And you?" I asked. "Did you know him well being countrymen of Thasos?"

"Yes," he sighed, "at least for the time he lived among us. As young men, his grandfather and I were as close as the twins, *Castor and Pollux*." He gazed upward, but the clouds continued to obscure the Gemini and the other denizens of the night sky. "As such, I knew Theo, and I knew Theo's father as well... I watched the young lion cub grow and leave the den. He was a happy and carefree boy and all could see he was destined for deeds and accomplishments beyond what is expected of normal men. But his young life was not easy and when he returned to Thasos an Olympic champion, he was not at all like the free-spirited boy I re-membered."

My silence encouraged him to continue.

Parmenides' shoulders shook as he laughed privately, then settled, as the humorous thought vanished. "Much like Xeno here, Theagenes was a proud and arrogant youth. Un-like Xeno, however, Theagenes had reason to be. His pride and arrogance swelled from his physical stature and talents, not from the wealth of his family. Theagenes left Thasos as a boy. He ran away—I'll wager you didn't know that, but it's true—he ran away to what fate no one knew until word came to us, many years later, that he had matured into a fine athlete who was victorious in the games. His deeds won praise for our island. He himself did not return to Thasos until he was a grown man. When he did return, he was not at all what I would have expected a champion to be; he carried himself with none of the haughtiness of his child-hood. Some say the change was good. I am not so sure, but I do know that with his victories, he gained humility and that cannot be all bad. That was the biggest change I saw in him when he came back. He was quiet and humble, not loud and brash."

Parmenides glanced at the three younger men, who lay motionless on the ground, sleeping deeply now, their exha-lations not natural to these mountains. "I knew Theagenes at the time of his death, a distant man who avoided the company of other men. I remember him, however, as the happy boy he was before he left Thasos and became the Olympic champion he was fated to be."

A full minute passed silently, neither of us offering further comment. At last, Parmenides looked me square in the eye and said, "I am going to share a story with you that I have shared with no one. But as you claim to be Theo's friend, I sense your relationship with him was special. It is not often that an elderly man befriends a young man, and even rarer when a young man takes an old man for his friend. In respect to you, Simonides, and your relationship with Theo, I will tell you a story that no other living man knows."

Before he continued, we gathered more wood and added it to our fire. We watched as the small flames licked the dry wood and rose higher, dancing towards heaven.

CHAPTER THREE

Parmenides Tells of a Divine Birth

If you have never been to our island, you will see that Thasos is a beautiful place even with the scourge that now threatens to destroy us. We are peaceful and care not for war and combat, as do our neighbors on the mainland. We have no army or ships of war. Call us cowards if you must, but we have no taste for combat and are more inclined to search for peaceful solutions to impending conflicts. Our ancestors built a wall around the city, but it serves more as a token of defense than of any strong will to fight. Alas, the helmsman was right last night when he said that Thasos cowered before Xerxes and offered no resistance. I share the shame of our unwillingness to take up arms to protect our own freedom from enslavement. Because of our disposition, it seems unlikely that a young boy from our island would become such a great boxer, a champion in a combative sport, and even more startling, a *pankratiast* for that activity is even more violent than boxing.

No, our men till the soil and fish the fertile waters that surround us. We are blessed with mines and quarries. From Aliki we take the marble and in other places, our island brings forth even gold. If I said Thasos was home to a great sculptor, you might believe me, but a boxer? Doubtful. We trade the stone and metal to Athens and beyond, even to the Medes in the east. We prosper from it, but this famine puts us at the mercy of others to supply us with the staples of life that keep men happy and healthy. For this, my heart is heavy, but your interest lies not in our misfortune, but in young Theo.

His mother's father was my best friend. As young men, we labored in the forests and felled trees from which lumber was made to build our fleet of merchantmen. Theo's grandfather was a good and kind man who worked hard. His wife, a portly girl, died giving birth to his only offspring, a daughter whom he named Selene, after his wife, so that he would always remember the woman he married every time he saw the moon rise and shine on his daughter's face. Young Selene grew into a beautiful girl. She would often follow us into the forests carrying fresh water to quench our thirsts as we labored. Unlike her mother's body, hers was long and lean and muscled, much like her father's. Selene was the envy of all young men on Thasos, and she frequently caught the eye of many a man who visited our harbor. She could have had any, but showed no interest and favored no one special, though several suitors had approached her father with great interest and heavy purses. Her young heart beat solely for her father and no one else. He alone was the object of her affection, but I say with gladness that she treated me with the greatest respect and courtesy.

In Selene's 15th year, a stranger found our shores. His name was Timosthenes. I remember well the first day I ever saw this man who came to us from Thebes. He assembled

our people in the *agora* for council and told us his own
countrymen elected him as a priest of Herakles, born of
the gods in the very land from which Timosthenes came. I
have told you with certainty that Theagenes is the greatest
of all Thasians. If you ask, however, who is the greatest of
all Hellenes, the answer would not come so easily. Many
men, however, would argue, and rightly so, for the mighty
Herakles whose twelve labors are without equal. Here was
this stranger telling us that Zeus himself, the father of Herakles, had ordered him to journey to Thasos that we might
build an altar to the Great Protector's son for no such place
existed on our island.

I know of no man who does not fear his gods. On the
other hand, we are not so intimidated by our priests, particularly strange ones whom we do not call our own. Still, our
elders and our priests concluded that it was wiser for us to
build the altar than to risk the consequence of the wrath of
Zeus if, indeed, he had spoken to this man Timosthenes.

The stranger delivered his message with confidence. I
will admit that he was a handsome man, and our young
women found him so and swooned in his presence. He told
us it was his duty to supervise the construction of the altar
and to take up residence in Thasos so as to lead our worship
to Zeus's son. As Timosthenes spoke, Selene watched him
closely and attentively, wide-eyed, an innocent but beautiful
smile stretched across her face. We stood close to the steps
from which the priest spoke, and for one brief moment his
dark eyes met those of Selene and he smiled. It was clear to
me, if not to her father and other citizens nearby, that the
smile was intended only for this beautiful young woman

who watched him intently from the crowd. That is what I remember that day: Selene's unforgettably beautiful smile as she listened to the Theban priest of Herakles.

I will not bore you with the details of their courtship only to say that Selene and Timo (as he preferred we call him in the privacy of our circle of friends) were wed within six months after the altar was completed and dedicated to the great Herakles. Both the young maidens of Thasos and the young men ached with disappointment, but all agreed that the gods themselves ordained the union of Selene and Timosthenes.

So how does a young boy from our peaceful island become a great boxer and *pankratiast*? You can see the influence of the mighty Herakles, but as I will tell you, the connection may be deeper and even more direct.

I, like you, Simonides, am without wife, but I was married in my youth so long, long ago. My wife was barren. That was unfortunate for I longed for offspring, a son, but I loved my wife no less than if she had given me a tribe of children. A short three years after our wedding, she took ill with the fever and died. I lived alone for 15 years until Selene and Timo were married. At that time, I asked her father, my friend Iphicles, to come share my empty house with me so that his daughter and son-in-law could begin their lives together in the privacy of their own home. I considered an arrangement of that sort would work well in the best interests of all, the newlyweds and the estranged father. For my part, I would welcome the company of my good friend.

Iphicles was reluctant at first to accept my invitation and he stayed with his daughter in his old home. Selene was concerned that if she recommended the move to her father, he might interpret it as her desire for him not to live with her and Timosthenes. This was not the case for like most young women, she loved her father as much as life itself and respected the influence he would always have on her. Iphicles made his decision when, five months after the wedding, Selene's belly began to swell with child.

"If you had a mother," he told her, "I would stay, but I am not qualified to assist you with childbirth nor with the rearing of your baby. It is time for me to go." Iphicles packed his few belongings and joined me in my small lodging in the Dimitriades quarter of the city. I still live in that house, and it is the same one in which I invite you to lodge during your time in Thasos with us.

The compromise was good for me and for Iphicles. Often when good friends share the same dwelling, it tears them apart as each sees the faults and shortcomings of the other on a regular basis. Such was not the case with us. It drew us closer, for our friendship was profound and each recognized the weaknesses and peculiarities of the other with no ill will or disappointment. Our friendship became even stronger. We shared our deepest thoughts with each other and became of one mind.

Not a week had passed since Iphicles had taken residence in my house when one night, shortly after we had both retired to our mats, I heard him whisper, "Parmenides, are you asleep?"

Though my eyelids were beginning to get heavy, I answered, "No, not yet."

"Me neither," he replied. That much was quite apparent to me. I heard the crickets chirp as he rolled on his mat and waited for further response. He prodded me again with the obvious, "I can't sleep."

I moved to my other side and faced the center of the room for we slept at opposite ends. Sleep was now escaping my grasp and my alertness was returning. "And why can't you sleep?"

"I don't know," he answered, but I could tell he wanted to talk.

"Does something trouble you?"

He sat up and leaned his back against the stone wall. "Perhaps, but it may be nothing."

I rose from my mat and moved to the table where he joined me with two cups of watered wine. "If it is nothing," I said, "It wouldn't be keeping you awake. What bothers you?"

Iphicles proceeded to tell me a strange story. I will share it with you in absolute confidence. I have told no one else in respect to my old friend who left this earth not long after his grandson ran away from Thasos. Alas, Iphicles never knew of Theagenes' exploits in the games or of the fame he brought to his homeland. Iphicles would have been so proud!

Two days ago when we met on the road from Delphi, you told me, "When you have heard my story, you will know Theagenes as you have never known him before." What I tell you now, Simonides, no one else knows, but what I tell you will add more depth to your understanding of our Olympic champion. On the other hand, you may think me daft. If you do, I will understand...

"Not long after Timosthenes had taken my daughter as his wife," Iphicles told me that night, "he explained to us that he was required to return to Thebes. He would be away for one week to assist in a ritual that his countrymen performed every year to gain the favor of their Theban son Herakles. Selene and I did not think it unusual and considered it a legitimate part of his duties as a priest.

"The parting of my daughter and her husband brought tears to her eyes, but she knew that he would not be gone for long. As he wrapped her in his arms beneath his dark cloak, his eyes were turned toward the heavens, and there was a hard coldness about them that sharply contrasted the gentleness with which he held his wife. Timo caught me staring and quickly lowered his head to hide amidst Selene's long, blowing hair. I found it strange that as we watched from the pier and waved goodbye, Timo did not return our parting gesture. Rather, he turned his back toward us and moved to the fore of the boat and faced the open water. Selene seemed to notice no peculiarity in his action and made no comment. I remained on the pier with her while she continued to wave until Timo and the boat cleared the point to the west of the harbor and sailed out of sight.

"Three nights later, the most unusual thing happened."

Iphicles moved uncomfortably in his chair. By now, I was wide-awake and listened closely as I refilled our cups with wine. Iphicles continued his story.

"I know the sounds of lovemaking," he said with some embarrassment. "I know from my own experience, and I know as the father of a new bride living in the same house with his daughter and her husband. Forgive me if what I say makes you uncomfortable, friend."

I told him to pay no mind to me, but to continue with the tale.

"More than once since their marriage, I had heard them as Selene and Timo took pleasure in each other and consummated their marriage beneath their blanket in the middle of the night. They made soft, sweet sounds. With my face to the wall, I would smile and think tender thoughts of my own wife now gone so many years." Iphicles blushed and lowered his eyes when he said, "Yes, Parmenides, I will save you from asking for I know what my thoughts would be in your place: I was aroused and I touched myself. But more often, the sounds would lull me to sleep like a mother's song to her child and I would always have sweet dreams. After my initial excitement during that first week, I learned to ignore them." I envied Iphicles the chance to return to the warm, loving days of his early manhood and to relive them so vividly.

"But three nights after Timo had departed from Thasos, I was awakened in the pitch dark of night by ugly, cruel noises of coupling. This was not lovemaking but the wild lust that might be found in the barnyard or the forest. The hard, angry grunts disturbed me, but I was afraid and dared not turn toward the center of the room." Iphicles raised his hands to his head.

"I was ashamed because I knew that the moaning female sounds came from my daughter. I squeezed my eyes shut with the hope that the action would deafen me to the

repulsive uproar that came from the mat in the opposite
corner. My tactic did not work; not even the pounding
blood that rushed through my ears could render me impervious to the sounds I had no desire to hear. I waited through
several painful minutes until the rhythm slowed and the
wet slobbering faded into the walls. The torturous groans
became no more than heavy, deep breaths. Mercifully, Selene's breathing steadied and returned to the restful rhythm
I was so accustomed to. I heard a few, mumbled words that
I could not understand for they were whispered, meant not
for my ears, but for hers alone.

"I dared to roll over, quietly, and as I did, I saw the
form of a large and powerful man rise from the mat. The
moon was full, and when the light from the window caught
his face, he turned toward me. It was Timo. I was shocked
because I did not know he had returned so quickly from
Thebes, and more so because I had never known him to
be such a big and aggressive man. I could only think that
the light was playing tricks on my eyes. He raised his index finger to his lips to quiet me. I remained stunned and
stared silently as he covered his nakedness with a cloak and
walked out the door.

"I had great difficulty returning to sleep. I gathered my
courage and walked outside into the empty street, fearing
all the while that I might encounter my daughter's sated
husband. There was no one in sight so I crept back into the
house. Selene had returned to her slumber. I sat and pondered what I had seen and heard. Nothing made sense. I am
certain I had seen Timo, and I am certain I heard him rav-
aging my daughter, now his lawful wife. Still, his actions

were unlike anything I would have expected from him, and though it was Timo's face, I cannot say that it was his body I saw.

"I dreaded the morning light when I would have to face my daughter and her husband. Would Selene feel the same embarrassment that I did?

"She awoke early that day as she normally did and greeted me with a pleasant and innocent smile that I returned in a fatherly and compassionate way. After preparing our bread and eggs, she sat at the table with me and said, 'Father, I have wonderful news.' 'And what might that wonderful news be?' I responded as I tore a small piece of bread from the loaf and dipped it into the yolk. Selene reached forward and took both of my hands in hers. She looked into my eyes and smiled. 'I am with child,' she said.

"Although I was pleased that I would be a grandfather, my protective nature got the better of me and I responded, 'Then perhaps you and Timo should be more gentle in your lovemaking.' I raised my eyebrows to her. The look on Selene's face told me that she knew I was referring to the previous night. 'Forgive me, father,' she said, 'but the child was conceived last night, and its father is not Timo. I beg you, let it be of no concern to you, rather rejoice in what has happened.'"

I have never seen such a look of bewilderment on a man's face as Iphicles continued to tell me what his daughter claimed had occurred that fateful night.

"I was stunned and confused," Iphicles continued. "What was my daughter telling me? How could Timo not be the father? 'Where is your husband?' I asked her with anger creeping into my voice. 'I think it best that he is here as we discuss your secret indiscretion.' She answered calmly and matter-of-factly, 'Timo is in Thebes, father, and will not return for several days yet, and you know that.' 'What joke do you play on me, daughter?' I responded, 'for surely Timo returned last night. I saw him with my own eyes as he left your bed after your love-making, if what I heard could be called that.'

"She shook her head 'no,' and the smile never left her face. It was then that Selene told me what is so difficult for me to believe and that keeps me awake at night." Iphicles stood from the table and began to pace around our small room like a frightened and confused animal. I told him to calm himself and not to continue if the tale caused him so much pain.

He turned to me with outstretched arms and said, "My daughter claimed that it was not Timo with whom she had lain that night, but with Herakles himself, the last mortal son of Zeus. My face could not hide the disbelief that seized it. 'With Herakles?' I said raising my voice in surprise. 'Yes' she answered calmly, 'With Herakles. He came to my bed last night, and together we conceived a child. I know it is so. He said but few words to me and only after the act had been completed. He said, 'I give you my son.' That was all he said, father, and I believe him.'"

Iphicles returned to his seat at the table and buried his head in his hands. "Have I lost my mind?" he asked me. "Or is it my daughter who is crazy?"

I struggled in vain to find words to console my friend. Iphicles had revealed his secret and had nothing more to say. The candle burned low. We returned to our separate sleeping mats and somehow managed to find a few, fitful hours of rest.

The next morning, Iphicles acted as if no words on the matter had passed between us, and I responded to him likewise. Our lives moved forward, but I watched with great interest the interaction between father and daughter and between daughter and husband when the child was born several months later. No words or actions from Selene or Timo would ever suggest that the conception and birth of their son be due in any way to divine intervention. It is only the deeds and stature of the child that causes me to remember my conversation with Iphicles that one night in Thasos, and to share it with you.

I ask that you keep this tale of heavenly mischief between you and me, Simonides. To my knowledge, my friend Iphicles had related the story to no one but me. We've not spoken of it since that night in my home so many years ago. But I find that my mind has wandered to it now and again through the years. I doubt my reason and even question my faith when I think of it. We have heard such stories about our gods from the priests in the temples. Do we believe them? Do we believe that a god would take human form to conceive a child with a mortal woman? I don't know. Those tales are tales of antiquity, passed down from one man to his son. Yet I find myself struggling to believe that a young girl whom I have known as a child gave birth to a god's son. Tales of such events are ancient and come from a time long past when it is said that the gods did walk the earth and ground that we stand upon. Could Iphicles' story be such a one? Iphicles told me of an event that happened in our own lifetime. It gives me pause for thought, and it truly tests the depth and core of my faith.

CHAPTER FOUR

Helen Plays the *Aulos*

Typical of my time with the Thasians, I woke before the others. My legs still felt the long climb from the previous day, but I was rested and ready to move on. Even at a moderate pace, by late afternoon we could crest the mountains that would lead us to the port near Aulis. The air was calm and still. The strong and angry winds of the night had fled to battle each other somewhere else, maybe in a land far from here that I knew nothing of.

I lay on my back with my hands behind my head and thought about our destination: we were on our way to Aulis, the ancient port from which Agamemnon launched his fleet to lay siege to ancient Ilium. It was at Aulis where the king sacrificed his daughter Iphigenia to Artemis. The thought troubled me, that any man could take the life of his child, his own flesh and blood for any reason, even at the bidding of a priest. But then the first chirps of the waking birds ruffled the serenity of the mountains in their pleasant way and distracted my mind from distasteful thoughts. I recognized the babbling tune of a mountain stream that I guessed correctly was not far from where we camped.

One by one, the Thasians awoke, and like me, remained huddled under their cloaks to fend away the morning chill. We were all aching from the trek into the mountains, but only the youngest, Xeno, voiced any complaint. "My feet are sore." He frowned as he sat upright and strapped on his sandals.

"Then it is you and not the old men who will lag behind us today," Cimon commented cheerfully. "Perhaps when we return to Thasos, you can find a profession that takes you away from your father's house. You sit around all day and count money. It makes you soft."

"Better to send him to the Spartan *agoge*," Epi laughed, "That will toughen him up."

I whispered rhetorically under my breath to Parmenides, "Have you seen the *agoge*?"

"No," he answered, "but I have heard of its horrors."

I shook my head and nodded toward Xeno, "I have glimpsed small parts of it. That one wouldn't last an hour even if they would have him, which they wouldn't. They destroy his kind at birth." It was a cruel statement but true.

Xeno did not take the chiding of Epi and Cimon kindly. "Say what you will, fools," he said pointedly to them, "but when you grow old, you will live like the beasts of burden that you are. I will count more money in one day than either of you will acquire in your lifetimes."

"And will that make you happy, Xeno," Parmenides snapped back, "Or will you still be unable to smile as in your miserable, friendless youth?"

I did not want to waste the day in fruitless argument. We had too much ground to cover. Given his defensive

attitude, I was surprised when Xeno re-directed our attention to the journey before us, and when doing so, he deferred to my experience. "What about it, firemaker?" he
said, but still almost rudely to me. "Are we lost in these
mountains or can you lead us to Aulis? I wish to spend as
little time as I can with you and these commoners who have
no ambition to better their place in life."

I wanted to slap his face in exchange for his impertinence, but I maintained my dignity and withheld any harsh
words or actions. Young Xeno was determined to test my
patience, to break me and thus to reduce me to the old fool
that he himself was destined to become. I knew better and
hoped by my example to demonstrate to the others the path
of honor in the face of impudence.

I turned toward the morning sun and felt its warmth
as I gathered my bearings. "I have been in these mountains
before. My companion then..." I paused and looked each
in his eyes, "Your own Theagenes. It was many years ago,
but Theo and I were headed north. Our path today takes
us east toward the sea. I've heard by its voice a stream not
more than a stone's throw from where we have rested. We
will follow it up through the pass to its source. From there,
we will smell the salt of the Aegean as it sneaks behind the
large island and hugs the mainland. If my calculations are
correct, we make Aulis late in the day tomorrow." I said no
more and walked into the woods where I found the stream
that flowed from the crest of the eastern range. The Thasians followed.

Our pace had slowed, as much by the weariness in our
legs as by the steep goat path that followed the stream to

the top of the rocky range we mounted early in the afternoon. Xeno's constant whining about his sore feet could be considered a welcome distraction from our toil. His overstated misfortune had become our secret pleasure. As darkness approached, we made our way to the home of a widow I knew who lived on the outskirts of Chaironeia.

Her two-room home was perfect for her and even had a small courtyard in the back. She insisted that we use her sleeping room. All but Xeno declined, agreeing that we would place the mats she offered in the courtyard and sleep on the soft grass that she had cultivated there. With barely a word of thanks, Xeno retired quickly to the house after our hostess served us a tasty meal of cheese and bread, which we dipped into a seasoned bowl of olive oil. Like all of us, Xeno was tired, but it was obvious to everyone, even Helen (for that was the name of our hostess) that Xeno had no desire to partake of our company. Sleep provided the better alternative for him than conversation with us. He continued to eye me with suspicion; his glance told me that he believed I had turned his companions against him. It was plain to see that Xeno's own ignorance had alienated him from his fellows, and it was an estrangement that did not occur just in the last few days, rather one that had been brewing for quite some time. Each Thasian's respective profession, his age and family background widened the gulf between him and the merchant's son. My presence only gave the other three somewhere else to turn to express their feelings without the sarcastic rejoinders of their spoiled companion.

After clearing the small table in the courtyard where we dined, Helen returned with an urn of wine. "This," she said proudly, "could be the best wine in all of Hellas! It has been a long time since I have had company in my home. I want to share this with you, Simonides, and with those who travel with you. Only the gods know if and when we shall share one another's company again." She bowed and filled our cups ceremoniously with her deep red ambrosia.

Epi sat on the stone bench by the wall and was the first to respond. "Dionysus himself would be pleased to partake of such a drink," he said after his initial, small sip. He closed his eyes and took another draft. His face expressed his pleasure. "It would not surprise me to learn that it comes from his own *Thyrsos!*" Helen playfully did not deny it and returned Epi's praise with a wink toward the others to suggest that maybe it did!

Helen, now as old as Parmenides, was a professional musician in her youth and I suspected that she still maintained her unmatched proficiency with the *aulos*. Age had not stolen her beauty though her long hair was streaked with gray. She and her husband, a Thespian, had met in the theater. One beautiful evening many years ago, I made their acquaintance in the great amphitheater in Athens as they performed Aeschylus's brilliant new play *Prometheus Bound*. I was captivated by the clarity and purity of the maiden musician's sorrowful instrument, even more so as it mourned the painful words of her husband's Prometheus...

> *"Wretched that I am—such are the arts I devised*
> *for mankind, yet have myself no cunning means*
> *to rid me of my present suffering..."*

I was compelled by their performance to seek them out when the stage emptied at the conclusion of the final scene. I have never been bashful to approach people whom I admire and these greeted me warmly and respectfully. We dined together that evening with the playwright who, at a mere 30-years-old, had demonstrated in that one composition the quality of his work that would endear him to all Hellas. More than once I have journeyed far to watch their troupe perform in distant parts of our country.

And so I asked her, "Do you still play, Helen?"

She lowered her lids like a blushing, young girl and answered, "Not so much since my beloved Harmodius has crossed the Styx." We remained silent for a moment in respect to her dead husband.

"Would you grace us with a tune?" I asked. She raised her eyes, still large and beautiful despite the creases that extended from their corners, and said, "Yes, but only if you will accompany me with your lyre."

I bowed low and watched through the door as she took her instrument from a chest in the house and returned with the hint of a bittersweet smile on her face. It was wrapped in cloth and she handled it with reverence, carefully exposing it to the night air. I have not been so gentle with my own lyre. Though I have some skill in the more elaborate *cithara*, I am fond of my old friend, its tortoise shell now worn and scratched from my rough handling. "And what tune is it that you would like to hear?" she asked when she took her place on the bench.

"Play for us the song of the mournful lark, for I recall it is that melody that I first heard you play in Athens and the one I will always remember you for."

Helen closed her eyes and smiled, remembering how wonderful life could be. She brought the wood to her lips and was soon absorbed in a time past when she and her husband traveled our fair land and gave pleasure and amusement to those who would partake of their entertainment. I plucked along for a minute or two following the lead she created with her woodwind. The notes lingered in the night air and then disappeared like fireflies in a summer meadow; we smiled to hear them and hoped that she would continue forever for the notes she turned soothed us, like an invisible ointment that freed us from our mortal concerns. As her melody turned more complex, it left my fingers in quandary. I ceased my effort to stay with her and, unnoticed, returned my instrument to my bag. I leaned my chair back against the tree under which I sat, content that my old friend was lost in another world that brought her happiness, a world from which I would not make her return.

"I believe it was not by chance that you brought us here to spend the night with this women," Parmenides commented softly, his face turned upward with eyes closed. His head rocked slowly and rhythmically on his shoulders. "It is a strange melody, this one. It evokes images of both joy and sadness. Is it of her own making?" he asked. I acknowledged that it was.

"It brings to mind the life of a man, any man, for each man's life is filled with some joy and some sadness," he continued. "We can only pray to the gods that they bring us more pleasure than the other." Helen continued to play as if she heard nothing but the notes that escaped her instrument, which I am certain, was the case. If she noticed that I no longer added my notes to her tune, it was of no concern to her. I have seen other musicians in a similar, trance-like state. They play impervious to any mortal distraction, as if possessed by the gods.

I offered a thought I had once heard, first spoken, men say, by the poet Hesiod...

> *"They were all of one mind. Their hearts set upon song and their spirit is free from care. He is happy whom the Muses love. For though a man has sorrow and grief in his soul, yet when the servant of the Muses sings, at once he forgets his dark thoughts and remembers not his troubles. Such is the holy gift of the Muses to men."*

Epi, Cimon and Parmenides raised their cups in agreement. "It is unfortunate," I added, "that Xeno finds no reason to sit with us and be calmed by the gift of song."

As the music had its healing way with us, I turned to Episcles. "Young man," I said, "I guess by your look that you are about the age that Theagenes would have been had death not befallen him in the quarry."

"Indeed you are correct," Epi replied with enthusiasm. "I was but one year older than Theo and knew him well as a boy before he left Thasos for the fame that was to be his at the great games, though we were not so close after his return many years later. Of course he befriended no one when he came back. It is a shame, but it is true."

Helen's melody brightened and turned Epi's thoughts away from Theo's death and toward the happy, carefree days of his youth. Each Thasian smiled wistfully but then Cimon added with a glint of sadness in his eye, "Do you remember when he stole the statue?"

"Who could forget," Parmenides answered.

"And the punishment that followed," Cimon added gravely and they all became sullen. "He was lucky to escape with his hide attached. I for one found innocence in the boy's act, but the elders, empowered in no small way by Theo's own father, were not so willing to forgive his youthful undertaking. Tell the story, Episcles, for I'm sure our friend Simonides would like to hear the tale."

I filled their cups with more wine and Epi began his narrative as Helen's notes continued their dance into the night air.

CHAPTER FIVE

Episcles Remembers the Theft

When we were young boys, even before we began our formal training in school, we worked with our fathers like all young Hellenes. We followed them to the fields, the forests, the docks, and sometimes even to the mines. There, we carried water amongst the quarrymen who labored hard under the hot sun chipping away at the large blocks of stone that were of great value throughout Hellas and even in other parts of the world. Theo's father was a priest, but not elected by us, rather by his Theban countrymen. It is odd that he was able to come to our island and assume the position like he did, but no one objected. Nonetheless, because of his father's position, Theo had no cause to callus his hands like the rest of us who were roused early in the morning and left our homes with our fathers. Theo could have enjoyed a life like Xeno's, but he would have found no pleasure in it. Some might say that was his boon, but not Theo. To him his parentage was his bane for he longed to join us in manual labor and escape the mystical and favored household that he was born into. Theo longed to test his strength and to use his muscles.

My father was a stonecutter. Every morning, we would march up the road with other men and their sons, and we would pass the house of Timosthenes, Theo's father. We boys would find a stick or some other object to kick as we made our way, and we laughed as we raised a cloud of dust on the road. My father paid no attention to the young boy who always sat on the front step of his home watching us as we passed, but I remember the forlorn look on Theo's face. The rest of us boys considered Theo and the merchants' sons the lucky ones, and we never understood why he looked so sad every morning. Theo saw it from a completely different perspective. He envied us the opportunity to work the mornings with our fathers while his own father spent the time at the temple in prayer. Theo was more inclined to use his body than he was to exercise his mind. I do not mean he was not a smart boy. He was, but he had little use for the idleness of daily worship in the temple.

One morning as we followed the carts on our way inland to the quarry, I smiled and waved at him hoping to cheer him up. He sat like a frog on his doorstep and only frowned. We cannot be happy when our friends are not. I knew what he wanted, and so I jerked my head twice in the direction we were headed, and I waved my hand in short motions from my hip. I formed the words 'Come with us' with my mouth. Without moving his head, Theo glanced to his right, then left to see if anyone was watching. He smiled, and like that same frog he mimicked in his compact stance on the doorstep, he leapt quickly onto the dusty road and followed us to the quarry. My father never noticed until we had reached the work area and he and the other men began unloading their tools from the cart.

The cart driver was the first to spot Theo when he halted his team of oxen and set his brake. Climbing down from his seat he said jovially, "And look whom we have with us to-day." The men turned around and saw Theo standing in the center of the path twenty paces behind us.

"It's the priest's son!" one exclaimed.

"And from the look on his face, he thinks he has the strength of Herakles!" another said, and they all laughed. Theo stared at the men defiantly, uncertain whether they would welcome him or turn him back down the road.

"Well, boy," my father finally said, "You've come this far with us, you may as well spend the morning here and be of use." Theo walked forward to the back of the cart. "Here, take this skin of water. The men will be thirsty. You can help Epi."

Theo pointed at the heavy bronze pick that rested on the wheel. "I'll take that," he replied.

His answer brought more laughter from the men, but that laughter receded as the five-year-old boy struggled, unsuccessfully, to raise the heavy tool to his shoulder. "You are not ready yet," my father said to him kindly, "Perhaps someday, though your father is apt to condemn us all to Hades for our unknowing part in your escape this day from the temple." The men laughed again, and Theo reluctantly took a skin of water and walked with the workers and me into the pit.

That is how we knew Theo as a boy; he was happiest working with his body, rather than his mind. And my father was right: Timosthenes was not pleased with the men that they had allowed his son to spend the day in the quarry and had not ordered the child to return to his own father at the temple.

Several years later, I was 10-years-old and Theo was nine, we were both required to attend our school and had been doing so for some time. Our teacher was a wise old man, dead now. We called him Peta because he was never seen without a hat. If it wasn't on his head to protect him from the rain or the hot sun, it hung on his back from a short strap. If I ever knew his real name, I cannot recall it now. It was through Peta's teaching that Theo learned to use his mind as well as his body.

Peta taught us our letters and our numbers. Though he was a poor musician, Peta even struggled to teach us the lyre. The instrument in our classroom was always out of tune and sounded harsh and sour, not at all like your own, Simonides, or like Helen's *aulos* that continues to touch our minds and bodies with its pure and soothing notes. Our learning was centered on our study of the Great War with Ilium. Peta sang us the songs of Homer. He taught us to count soldiers and weapons, and bags of grain and sacks of gold. Peta's gnarled fingers formed words with letters in the sand that recounted the heroic deeds of our ancestors. We all paid close attention, but it was most often Theo whose eyes remained opened wide, particularly when Peta told us of the deeds of Achilles and Odysseus, and those of Herakles and his labors. When each story ended, Theo begged for more. He was the last to leave the classroom, always asking Peta question after question while the old man shooed him out the door. Theo memorized every syllable, like we all were required to do, but while most would forget from one week to the next, Theo's mind latched onto these stories of ancient men and gods and refused to release them from memory. We would play at war in the afternoon sun, and Theo always declared himself Herakles to lead our band of pretend combatants against any whom would resist our power and the righteousness of our deeds.

I was but a babe and therefore have no recollection of the time when Timosthenes came to Thasos, but his influence upon us Thasians is most conspicuous by the reverence he instilled in our people for Zeus's son, Herakles. Our veneration is no more evident than in the small temple he instructed us to build, and by the bronze statue of Herakles that stands before it in the *agora*. It is a thing of powerful beauty for the sculptor caught the naked hero in mid-flex.

As Theo grew, his body matured much faster than those of his peers did. While some of our classmates were tall and lanky and others short and squat, Theo was the perfect blend of lithe speed and restrained power. Most of us had meat stretched over our bones; Theo's bones were wrapped in thick muscle even as a youth. We waited for the day when our parents told us our bodies would 'catch up' to Theo's. It never happened. I am no weak man from my lifetime in the quarry and I was strong as a lad, too, but I was a shadow to Theagenes as a boy, and even more so when he returned to Thasos from his travels and victories.

One afternoon, Theo and I, with a group of our friends, were returning from our hours in the classroom with Peta. As we approached the *agora*, we noticed a group of girls waiting for their mothers who chatted near a vegetable stand while their daughters sat giggling on a bench not far from the statue of Herakles. As boys, we were self-conscious of our youth and we slowed our pace and looked for an alternate route so that we would not have to pass near the girls. Even as we did, Theo yelled to us, "Come on!" and raced ahead of us toward the statue. With the girls watching, and with our mouths agape, he flexed his arms and struck a pose identical to that of the statue. What should have been comical wasn't. With the afternoon sun glistening off Theo's tanned body, it was difficult to tell the statue from the boy, for that was the size it was sculpted, and the color of the bronze metal was a perfect match for his brown skin. Theo held his pose long enough to quiet the girls. His eyes were turned towards the heavens the entire time. If I had been bold enough to do what Theo had done, I would have been the goose for weeks. No, only Theo could do what he had done without becoming the object of laughter. So impressive was his feat that day, that the entire crowd gathered at the moment in the *agora* went silent for those few, brief moments until Theo broke his pose, walked back in our direction and simply said, "Let's go." The group of us walked proudly with him as the young girls watched. Slowly, the men and women returned their attention to what they were doing before this brash youngster stopped time with an action they couldn't help but watch.

A younger boy not yet in school found his way into our group when Theo ran to the statue. As Theo rejoined us, the younger boy, Alcamenes by name, yelled, "Watch me!

Watch me!" He raced back to the statue and attempted to strike the common pose of Theo and Herakles. Alcamenes was tall for his age and thin. As he stood there with his *chiton* drooping from his narrow shoulders, the onlookers reacted to his comical pose with mocking laughter. Alcamenes was confused, but when one of the girls cried out, "Look, mother, Alcamenes is Herakles!" an uncertain grin came to his face. But the grin did not last long when Theo shouted, "No, only Herakles is Herakles, but if any human can follow his path, it will be me, Theagenes of Thasos, not this stick of a boy." The children in the *agora* cheered Theo, and the adults laughed at Alcamenes. The little boy's smile turned to a frown. He ran back to his mother's arms holding back tears of shame. Alcamenes did not forget the event for you see, he was the older brother of Xeno.

Seven days later, the incident occurred which would change Theo's life forever, and unknowingly send him on his path to glory.

As Timosthenes strolled through the *agora* in the dawn light that day, he was the first to see that the statue of Herakles was gone from its pedestal. His response was not a timid one and he ran through the streets of Thasos screaming as loud as he could, "It's gone! It's gone!" Up and down the streets he ran awakening everyone with his cries of alarm. After passing through the entire village, he found himself breathlessly sitting on the steps of his small temple still gasping, "It's gone."

One by one, all citizens, young and old, gathered before the temple. Theo's mother, Selene, stood with a comforting arm around her husband's shoulders. It was you, Parmenides, with your friend Iphicles who finally asked, "What is gone, Timo, that causes you such grief?"

Without lifting his head, Timosthenes pointed to the empty pedestal. "The statue of Herakles... it is gone." Indeed, the bronze statue had disappeared, but none of us noticed its absence until that moment, distracted as we were by Timosthenes' anguish.

"We will be subject to the wrath of Zeus and his son," Timosthenes wailed. "We must find the statue. It is our duty."

Parmenides encouraged Timosthenes to compose himself. We doubted that the statue had walked away on its own accord, and it would have been no small task for any two men to haul it away without drawing the attention of someone in the village. There had to be an explanation for its disappearance that did not defy the laws of nature. With Timo still shaking like a dry leaf in the wind, Parmenides addressed the assemblage and asked, "Does any man here have knowledge of what may have happened to the statue?" The crowd murmured, but no man or woman stepped forward with any information.

"I swear to you," Timosthenes shouted, "Thasos will be condemned by the gods for this evil sin unless the statue is returned to its proper place and the perpetrator punished!" We fear our priests only when they are angry with us. Timosthenes' anger continued to build like the billowing, dark clouds of a summer storm and a wave of apprehension seized the people. They implored Timosthenes to pray to the gods in his special way to spare us their anger. But you

Parmenides above all others showed reason in that moment of panic.

"Calm yourself, man! There is an explanation," you told the priest and then said to us, "We must search the city, hovel by hovel, to find Herakles." But even as the crowd began to disperse on its quest to find the statue, young Theo walked to the steps where his broken father sat sobbing under the comforting arm of Selene.

"Father," he said, "I have the statue." Every man, woman and child in the *agora* froze as if he had been struck and turned to stone by the Gorgons' glare that shot from the eyes of Timosthenes as he angrily raised them to his son in disbelief.

Everyone heard Timo's response. "That is not possible, son, for no two men have the power to move that statue. Where is it?" he yelled to the crowd ignoring his son. "And which men among those gathered here are accomplice to the theft?"

A puzzled look came to Theo's eyes for he had yet to learn the word 'accomplice' from Peta. He answered, "Come, father, I will show you."

We followed Theo, who had taken his father's hand, as he walked through the *agora* and down the street toward his home. Theo led his father to the small courtyard behind the house. There it was, standing slightly askew, the heavy bronze statue of Herakles. Timosthenes was furious and pulled his hand from his son's grip as if he had been holding a rotting piece of flesh. "Why is the statue here?" he demanded of his son with unrestrained indignation.

I shivered behind my own father whose hand I held tightly in mine. While there was little room in the courtyard for the group who had followed the priest and his son, my father and I were among the few who were able to walk behind the house to see the statue and witness the events that transpired there upon its discovery.

To his father's question, Theo shrugged his shoulders in his childlike way and replied, "Because I wanted it here so I would not have to walk to the temple every day to pray."

Timosthenes' face reddened and in a sudden, catlike movement, he knocked Theo to the ground with the back of his hand. Selene gasped and raised her palms to cover her mouth. "Timo!" she cried through her fingers. No human, not even his wife, could quell his wrath.

Timosthenes turned to the crowd and demanded, "Who among you is guilty of this crime? Step forward now or rot in the Underworld with Hades as your master!" No one in the frightened crowd moved as each looked from one to the other hoping that some one would admit to abetting the boy in his theft of the statue.

Theo regained his legs and stood directly before his father. A small trickle of blood flowed slowly from his nostrils. With a defiant pride that inflamed Timo even more, he said, "Look to no one else if you are looking to place blame, father, for it is only your son who carried the statue to his own house." Before Timosthenes could respond or strike out again, Theo moved to the statue, took a deep breath and bent to lay the heavy bronze on his small back. A path parted through the stunned crowd as the boy strained to haul it from the courtyard back to its pedestal in the *agora*.

His steps were short but sure. He stumbled only once but caught himself with a flailing arm and regained his balance. No one dared to help him, not even I, his friend, though I am ashamed to admit it now. I was frightened for him no less than I feared divine retribution on me for the simple reason that I was the friend of a boy who stole a sacred statue. Theo's muscles, all of them, flexed hard like steel as he worked his way down the dusty road. With great effort, he managed to slide the heavy bronze statue from his shoulders and stand it erect upon its original place of honor.

It was a feat of strength that none had ever witnessed before, nor would again. Timo was right in one respect: no two men could have moved the statue. Indeed, no two men in our village could have done what little Theo had done by himself. Theo's action could have easily inspired reverence within our community, but men cowered before his father's rage and denied Theo the praise he deserved. As I saw it, if Theo had sinned, it was offensive to no one other than his father. Timosthenes should have been proud and forgiving in response to his son's harmless behavior. I know my father would have considered the action an innocent transgression, but Timo saw things differently. His son had violated the sanctity of what Timosthenes perceived as a consecrated image. True to his threat, Timo would see that the boy was punished, and he did not wait for the privacy of his own home to quench his wrath. His justice was twisted and far exceeded the chastisement that might have been appropriate for the crime, if it could have been called a crime at all.

Timosthenes roughly grabbed his weakened and sweating boy and tied him with rope to the base of the statue.

Beneath the feet of Herakles, Timo whipped his son mercilessly with a stiff branch handed to him by none other than young Alcamenes. I have been punished and chastised myself as a boy, as have we all, but I have never seen a whipping, not to slave nor animal, that compares with the ferocity of the beating that Timosthenes inflicted publicly upon his son. The awe inspired by Theo's feat was replaced with horror as scarlet welts opened on his smooth skin and flowed freely with blood that stained the ground beneath him in bright red puddles. It is a wonder that the white of Theo's bones was not exposed. I shiver when I remember what I saw that day, and I apologize for my weakness in telling this tale that should be one of joy but ends as one of terror and deep revulsion.

Timo left the boy tied to the statue for the entire day. As nightfall approached, he warned the citizenry to leave the boy where he was and to offer him no comfort or sympathy saying that Theagenes had offended the gods themselves and would have to bear the consequence of his crime alone. Not even the mother was allowed to show mercy to her son though she shed every tear in her body and pleaded desperately to her husband to free the boy so that she could attend to his ugly wounds.

When morning came, Theo was gone. His bonds had been broken, not severed, and lay in a heap at the foot of the pedestal. Whether or not he was aided by his mother, grandfather or anyone else was never revealed for fear of further retribution by Timosthenes. The fact remains that Theagenes left Thasos and did not return for 15 years. Many thought him dead, perhaps drowned in the sea in his effort to escape the island and the misguided rage of his father. But as time passed, our memories faded and when we spoke of Theo, we only spoke of his stunning theft of the statue, not of the price he paid at the hands of Timosthenes.

In years to come, we heard stories of a young boxer and *pankratiast* who had been crowned in many competitions. One of our merchants had seen him fight and win at Delphi and returned to tell us that Theagenes had made good his escape from the island and was now winning fame and glory in the crown games. Despite the fact that his father unwittingly chased him from our island—and not a man among us stepped up to prevent it—we began to call him our own. Whether he liked it or not, he was Theagenes of Thasos. We made him our champion...He was my friend when we were boys.

CHAPTER SIX

Simonides and the Thasians engage Khepri

By the time Episcles had finished his story, Helen, too, had stopped her playing. Unnoticed, she had left her secret and private world and returned to the present moment. Like me, she was enthralled in the tale of the young Theagenes and the statue of Herakles. I glanced in her direction and saw a single tear fall from her cheek. You could almost hear it above the silence that had befallen us when Episcles was finished. While the others stared at the coals and the dying embers, an unsettling look passed between Parmenides and me as I recalled the story he had told me the previous night in the forest.

The scars of his childhood beating were still visible upon the back of Theagenes when I met him many years later. Only once did I dare ask him the source of the disfigurement. He did not answer, and only glared at me with fire in his eyes. He held the look of an enraged bull but refused to comment and kept his anger caged. His expression held the defiant look of a proud and desperate animal attacked but not beaten by a pack of wild dogs. I never inquired again. Now I knew, and I understood why the mere question painted such a hateful countenance on his otherwise handsome face.

I forced a bittersweet smile and we all bowed gratefully to Helen as she left us in the courtyard. Despite our exhaustion from the day's trek and the late hour, I suspected each of us would have difficulty finding sleep this night. I was wrong. No sooner had we taken our places upon our sleeping mats than through the window, we heard the sound of Helen's *aulos* again. She played a tune I had never heard before but it is one I will not forget. A nightingale had found its way through the dark to the olive tree that swayed above us in the courtyard and began its tune. With no effort, Helen created an accompaniment to the bird's sad song. Though my heart is soft, I am not one to show my feelings with tears. Lest my new friends see me, if any were still awake, I turned my back to them and tasted the salt of my emotion as it ran freely in response to the duet that Helen and the nightingale wove in reply to Episcles' woeful tale. Within minutes, the Thasians and I were fast asleep.

Rest had taken the edge from the dark mood that accompanied us to our beds the night before. Even Xeno, not privy to the Epi's retelling of a tale that I am certain Xeno knew well, woke in good spirits that were free from the bitterness that hadn't left his face since our first encounter. I came to learn during our journey that Xeno was most often an unhappy person and had no inclination to hide his annoyance at the world and those things that happened which were not in his favor.

We gave thanks to Helen for her hospitality and bid her goodbye. "The Pythia's words to me, gentle friend, suggest that our paths will not cross again," I told her. "I pray that the gods give you long and happy life. The Muses continue to bless you. May they do so forever." Helen's eyes moistened and she fell into my arms. I held her tenderly for a moment while my companions walked away down the road in silence. "I must be gone," I said releasing her. We smiled and I turned and followed the Thasians.

Our pace was steady and we made the coast by Aulis on the night of the third day's march. We supped lightly and retired immediately to accommodations we had acquired at an inn near the center of the town. The harbor was occupied by more ships than would normally have been the case. Rumors abounded that pirates were on the prowl on the far side of Euboea and this influenced the merchants to seek safe harbor until the triremes secured the waters from the would-be felons. As is often the case, one man's bane is another man's boon. The innkeepers smiled while the merchants filled their establishments and spent their *obols* and *drachmae* on food, wine and accommodations, and even women. We were fortunate to find an open space, and with so many vessels in the harbor, the situation boded well to find passage north to Thasos.

It was noisy in the town that night, and Hypnos crept slowly to take me in his gentle grasp. As he did, amidst the snores in the room and the boisterous merrymaking in the street outside, I reflected upon what new tales I had learned in the past days about Theagenes. I continued to struggle with the story that Parmenides had told me. I believe deeply in the gods and always have. Their methods are often a mystery to man, but I believe in them nonetheless considering the alternative risky, if not blasphemous. It was difficult for me, however, to accept as fact that a man of my time could have been the son of a god conceived in shadow and mystery. Those are events and tales of antiquity and not meant to happen in the present day. Yet if any mortal man could have been of Herakles' seed, it would have been Theagenes. I was confusing myself, and, in a very uncomfortable way, frightening myself as I involuntarily questioned the way of the gods as suggested to me in Parmenides' recounting of Theo's conception. The troubling and heretical thoughts refused to leave me. I groaned.

I considered the theft of the statue. That act, too, as told by Episcles, supported Parmenides' strange tale of Theagenes' supposed divine birth, but I was struck by the severity of his father's punishment. It left no doubt in my mind that the act influenced his violent actions in the stadium for he was not known to show mercy to his opponents. Those things that occur to us in our youth are carried with us to our grave. The seed for Theagenes' vehemence had been planted in him at a young age. It was a lesson he would not forget. I do not remember falling asleep, but I do remember awakening. I was still tired.

Early the next day, we made arrangements for our voyage with an Egyptian merchant who was bound for Thasos with grain. His name was Khepri. We were to learn from his crew that he adopted the name because, like the scarab beetle, he had born many children and through his hard work had raised them from dung to relative wealth on the banks of his Nile River. We never learned his real name. Khepri knew my work and because of it, he said he would be honored to give us passage aboard his boat. He advised us to be ready to depart on a moment's notice but from all reports, it was likely they we would not sail to Thasos for at least two days. He hoped the winds would turn favorable for our journey while the triremes cleared the path of the Macedonian pirates.

Khepri invited us to dine with him that evening in the tent he had erected not far from the water's edge. "I travel with my own accommodations," he told us, "and am never at the mercy of other men for a place to lay my head." We accepted his generosity. With nothing to do but wait, Epi and Cimon decided to bath themselves for the water remained unusually warm in the strait between the mainland and the large island Euboea. They asked us all to join them, and we did, even Xeno. The closer we got to his home, the more agreeable Xeno's demeanor became.

The sky hung like a dirty white cloth above our heads, so low that it seemed we could reach up and disturb it with our hands. A light mist fell and gathered in the heavy growth of our unshaven faces. The chilled air in the sunless sky made the water feel all the warmer in contrast. Not one of us removed his garment but each dove headlong into the sea and replaced the salt from his sweat with the salt of the Aegean. Our garments would stiffen later in the day, but at least the pungent smell of our toil would be washed from our clothes and our bodies. The water was calm and Poseidon allowed his nymphs to keep my body afloat with not much effort from me. It had been several days since I had the opportunity to truly rest and collect my thoughts, and I enjoyed the reverie I found on the beach at Aulis, particularly after my sleepless night at the inn.

As I lay floating on my back in the water, the mist began to lift, and the tide turned my feet toward the shore. Slowly through the morning hours, the clouds began to part and I could see the blue of the heavens. My gaze drifted to the nearby summit upon which stood the temple of Artemis. I breathed a silent prayer for the young children whom she is sworn to protect. I wondered, ever so briefly, why she had not personally interceded to prevent the beating of young Theagenes. I concluded that the answer was beyond my comprehension and was not meant for me to know.

The tide moved me gently to the beach and deposited me on the sand before it turned and left me there to dry in the sun that had now dispersed the remaining clouds with its warmth. My eyes closed and I fell soundly asleep to be awakened several hours later by the laughter of children as they carved pictures in the wet sand. No doubt the sun had reddened my face while I slept. I sat up and gazed around me and found that my companions, still asleep, had been smart enough to find the shade of a nearby tree. I chastised myself for my foolishness and lack of foresight.

The lazy day had refreshed us all, and we walked into Khepri's tent that evening with great anticipation for news, good company, conversation and good food and drink. We were not disappointed. Though small, his accommodations were plush and reflected his success as a businessman. The walls of his tent were made of coarse fabric to keep out the weather, but they were dyed in bright colors and patterns to keep his spirits high when he traveled far from his homeland and his large family. No ordinary posts held the roof above our heads, but ornately carved and painted pillars of a light wood that was easy to transport and move about. His home away from home was designed for the comfort of his body as well as for the peace of his mind.

"My new friends," Khepri greeted us jovially as we entered his tent, "You do me honor this night by sharing my humble meal. I hope you will find it enjoyable, for soon we sail for Thasos. This will be the last such meal until our feet touch the ground of your island. Please, please," he waved his arms dramatically toward large and wildly colored pillows, "take a seat and rest your weary bones. As I recall, you've come through the mountains from Delphi. No small journey, particularly for such as yourselves." He bowed slightly toward Parmenides and me.

"We have shed our weariness on this beautiful day," I replied, "We took advantage of the clearing skies and rested, and are greatly refreshed as we look forward to the final leg of our voyage."

His eyes opened wide and they, with his shiny, white teeth stood in brilliant contrast to his dark skin. "I shall not delay our pleasure then." Khepri clapped his hands sharply, though not sternly, and two very big, very black men entered from the rear of the tent with two very large trays. I had seen such men before in my travels and knew that they were from lands beyond the realm of the pharaohs. Two similarly black and bare-breasted women appeared with cups and bowls and pitchers of wine. The trays were heaped with fruits and vegetables. Barley bread dripped with golden honey. Khepri was pleased with the delighted expressions that came to our faces and he rolled back on his pillows shaking with laughter, his arms attempting to contain his stomach as it bobbed with his amusement. "Let us drink and eat and talk," he commanded.

"So it is to Thasos that we travel together," Khepri said as we filled our plates from the platters extended to us by his slaves. "A once beautiful island that has turned brown under the weight of famine. It is for that reason that I travel there with my cargo of ripe Egyptian grain. I help Thasos; Thasos fills my pockets." He shrugged his shoulders as if he had given us the secret to a happy life. "Strange that you have need to go to such a desolate spot in the Aegean, though why is none of my business."

"Not so strange as you might think," Parmenides answered, "for the four of us, excepting Simonides, call Thasos our home. It is true: we sit amid the waters of the Aegean like Tantalus in his eternal pit of wine. Poseidon and his brother refuse to bring the rain, and so we have sought council with the Oracle at Delphi and return now with her instructions."

A warm breeze from the sea fluttered the flaps on the entrance to the tent behind us. "And what do you think, Parmenides? Has your god counseled you wisely, or is the message as cryptic as many I've heard?"

"We have gone to the Pythia twice, now. As you note, her message is rarely as clear as most men would prefer. We are considering her words and how to act upon them. It is for that reason that Simonides has joined us," Parmenides bowed slightly toward me and I smiled to give him assurance.

"We met him four days ago at Delphi not long after we left the sanctuary. If wisdom comes with age, then he is a wise man and we welcome his counsel." They all laughed appreciatively except for Xeno who diverted his gaze to one of the black women and raised his cup for more wine. "I am certain the priestess has given us the answer. It is up to us to discover its true meaning," Parmenides concluded.

"Well spoken," Khepri responded and raised his cup in a toast of acknowledgment. He deftly changed the topic of our discussion and said, "I remember a Thasian youth from many years ago. I had cause to sail to Piraeus and trade with Athens. While there, one of my Athenian friends remarked that he was bound for the games at Nemea. Never having attended one of your great spectacles, I accepted his offer to journey with him. Business in Attica had been exceptionally good that summer, and I allowed myself the distraction. Of all the events, I found the *pankration* most intense, and I remember the winner of the *athlon*, a Thasian whose name I have heard repeated many times since ... Theagenes. He was magnificent, this Theagenes, a bear and a bull combined in a single man's body. And what about you Thasians? How many times have you seen this hero of yours compete in the arena?"

The younger men deferred to Parmenides for the answer. "Unlike you, Khepri, we have little cause to travel and can't say as we've seen him in competition."

Cimon added, "In truth, he left our island as a boy and only returned many years later never to compete again. We do not know him as an athlete but remember him fondly as a youth."

Xeno visibly tensed at the very sound of the athlete's name, much like he did when I first spoke it at Delphi. I could feel the tension build in the tent among the Thasians, Parmenides, Episcles and Cimon on the one hand, and Xeno on the other, but I do not think that Khepri noticed. For the moment, I assumed the lead and steered the ship to calmer, less turbulent waters, or so I thought. "Have you attended other games," I asked our host, to which he replied in his ever friendly way, "Only one other time, the Isthmian games near Corinth, the following spring."

"And did you enjoy them?" I queried.

"Did I enjoy them?" he responded rhetorically. "Yes, I suppose I did to a certain degree, but not so much that I follow them with passion as do you Hellenes. I find there are more important things that require my attention than the frivolous games and contests of athletes. In all due respect, friends, I find the Hellene obsession with athletic venture most amusing. Things of more substance weigh in the balance." I raised my eyebrows rather than my voice. While I have come to agree with the Egyptian to a large degree, I will never consider sport frivolous. My expression did not pass unnoticed and Khepri responded to it, "I trust we can continue this discussion as friends with no offense meant from one to the other. If not, there are other things upon which I am certain we agree and can talk about without conflict."

I laughed, not offensively, and replied, "No, no, Khepri. I would be pleased to continue our discussion on this subject. That is one thing that I hope you recognize as true: we Hellenes are not afraid to express our thoughts in public, nor do we condemn those who may disagree. We welcome differences in opinion on all topics at all levels within our society. If such were not the case, we would not have the art of Athens and the militaristic might of Sparta living in relative harmony and occupying the same country. While one man may call himself an Argive and another may call himself a Boetian, all men here call themselves Hellenes." Khepri acknowledged my retort with an amicable nod of his head.

"And you others?" he asked, "Are you of the same ilk as the wise Simonides?"

My Thasian friends bowed in deference to my words, and Parmenides added, "Although we may disagree on specifics, we are of the same mind that all men should be free to express their thoughts and opinions without retribution from any man."

Khepri raised his cup again and not for the last time in what would evolve into a long, but enjoyable evening of conversation, "I applaud your openness, Hellenes!" We all enjoyed a hearty draft and Khepri invited me to continue. "Please explain to me, Simonides, this Hellenistic fascination with sport."

I smiled to myself thinking there are patterns of life that remain constant. Judging by the spectators I've seen at the games—whether at Olympia, Nemea or anywhere else—fascination with sport is not a characteristic limited to men of Hellas, for the visitors to our games come from the farthest lands we know of! There are things that never change. Among them: whenever three or more men convene—no matter their origin, no matter their calling in life, regardless of their ages—at some point, the conversation turns to the games.

"Sport to us, Khepri," I began, "is not the frivolous activity you have inaccurately referred to it as. I suspect that other men in other lands might tell you the same, although we Hellenes are proven to be more serious about it. Athletic competition is a perfect reflection of life... and death. In each competition, the winner is born; the losers die. This is true every time opponents meet in the gymnasium or in the stadium. Life and death are at the heart of our crown games at Olympia, Delphi, Nemea and Corinth, and even the smaller games where a man might host competition as part of the funerary banquet in honor of his departed brother. Life and death," I repeated, "There is nothing trivial about either." Khepri tactfully yielded with a polite bow, and I continued.

"Man is born to die and his immortal fate will reflect the life he has lived on this earth. The greatest hope is to rise as a god to Olympus, like Herakles; the worst, to fall even beneath the House of Hades to the pit of Tartarus, like Sisyphus, damned to push his stone uphill which forever will roll back down again. Athletic competition is like battle where all men struggle to live but too few succeed. The gods give us life and they send us death to take it away. Our games honor the gods who grant us both.

"The Olympian games were given to us by Pelops, murdered by his father and fed to Zeus himself, but returned to life with an ivory shoulder by the grace of the gods. The Nemean games were initiated by the Seven Heroes on their way to Thebes to honor the death of the slain babe Opheltes, called the Beginner of Doom. Sisyphus, damned for kidnapping the god of death, gave us the Isthmian games to remember the drowned child Melikertes; and Apollo himself founded the games at Delphi in remembrance of his victory over the python, the monstrous beast created by the Great Mother.

"We honor the gods and we honor our ancestors by our observance of sport. Each competitor's loss is death, and each man's victory celebrates life. It is pure and simple. Athletic competition reminds us of who we are and that our very existence is as fragile as a fine piece of pottery.

"As a young boy, I attended many games with my father. Captured by the magic of words, I composed my first poem well before I reached manhood. It was a long and tedious thing in honor of a young athlete from my own home in Ceos, who had met an unexpected death, but the words were mine and I was pleased with them. I cannot explain how the words and the tune came to me, only to say that as I watched the funerary games staged by the dead athlete's father, I saw beyond the violent confrontation of two *pankratiasts* and into their hearts and souls. That night at the banquet, I sat in the shadows with my friends and heard the father call for a song to praise his deceased son. As one man looked to another and no one stepped up, I walked fearlessly into the light and recited the words that had come to me as I watched the contest. Before I started, the men smiled as if the young boy before them meant an innocent joke, but when I finished, they applauded me, and many even tossed me coin. The feeling was invigorating, more so when I saw my father beaming from the other side of the room. It amuses me that I still remember the words. 'For Strekiades we rouse a song of triumph,' I sang. 'As to be a glorious reward of his labors, for we know he would have achieved just recompense at Isthmos for his strength in the games of Nemea and beyond... ' My own young classmates who emerged from the shadows to watch my conquest cheered wildly when the final words left my lips and I lowered my head.

"It was at that moment I learned my personal talent was of considerable value to some champion or his bene-factor. I embarked on a profession that was to reward me handsomely for work that came to me without effort. I was always prepared to earn a heavy pouch of drachma writing praise for those who would stand victorious in the games. I traveled from town to town bestowing honor on the vic-tors with my epinicions, at a fee of course. And why not? These men had made their countrymen proud and famous, and everyone was willing to pay for my services. I found no shame in using my ability to enjoy the comfortable life I've lived.

"But the songs that you may know me best for, I would have gladly done for no fee, and in some cases I did. My hab-its and perceptions changed in the year my path and that of the Thasian Olympian crossed. Where once I hungrily fol-lowed only the champion who fought for personal accolades, my course changed after my days with Theagenes, and I now looked upon man and his achievements from a new perspec-tive. As we journey to Thasos, you will learn why.

"You Egyptians and the once powerful Medes to the east revere the education of man but reserve it only for a special few. We Hellenes educate every man with no regard to his origin or status in life. Educated men build strong nations. When the Spartans defended the pass at Thermopylae, they didn't do it because they had to, they did it because they wanted to; they did it to protect their freedom, and the freedom of all of Hellas. This way of thinking comes from each man's education. You Egyptians school your selected few in letters and in numbers. We school all men in both of these but we do not sacrifice a man's health and physical strength to his mind. No, Khepri, we enrich his soul and his heart with music, and we strengthen his body with sport. In Hellas, we educate to produce the *kalos kagathos*, the man whose superior intellect is balanced by the strength of his body and the beauty of his soul. Thus, all men in Hellas partake of sport. Are we passionate for it? Yes, there is no denying that, for it is an important aspect of every man's well being. Is it a frivolous obsession? No, it merely completes the total development of each man in our society. We are satisfied with the result, and we take collective pride in watching one man's mastery of his skill, be it in boxing, running, wrestling, racing or any other athletic endeavor.

"I must stop for fear of offending our host," I concluded.

"Not at all, Simonides. I respect a man who is firm in his belief and is willing to express it with eloquence. Our land and our people are different from yours. I can assure you that our pharaoh would not tolerate such open expression; at the very least, you would lose your tongue for it, if not your head! But he would make you rich beyond imagination if you agreed to use your talent with words to compose songs that glorified him and him alone."

We learned that night that our Egyptian host was a worldly man who had traveled far and witnessed things that even I had not. It was because of his broad exposure to ideas of men and races at the edge of the world that he was so willing to listen to me without the need to disagree, as is often the disposition of other men I have encountered. I listened attentively while I enjoyed the wonderful delicacies his slaves brought to our table. "Though their purpose is not always clear," Khepri concluded, "the gods make all men different."

"And had they not," Parmenides added, "life would not be as full and rich as it is."

A man I took for the helmsman of Khepri's vessel came into the tent and bowed, noticeably uncomfortable for interrupting the merchant's dinner. "I am sorry to disturb you and your guests, sir," he said apologetically, "but the winds have turned and remain steady. They favor us. We make sail with the morning tide."

"As you see fit," Khepri responded with a wave of his hand. The captain bowed low again and retreated into the night. Khepri turned his attention to me and said, "We have many hours before we depart. The night has only just begun and there will be plenty of time left to rest. Please grace me with a tale of your grand games at Olympia. While I'm told the games I witnessed in Corinth are the best attended of all due to their proximity to Athens, they say that the greatest competitions are held at Olympia. Is this indeed true?"

I told him that it was and proceeded to relate the story of my first encounter with Theagenes...

CHAPTER SEVEN

The Poet Meets the Boxer

In the year of the 75th Olympiad, there was great anticipation throughout all of Hellas on two counts.

On the one hand, word had spread of a young man,
a boxer and *pankratiast*, who would rival the great Spartan champion Lampis. Since the previous Olympic games,
Lampis had bested the defending champion, one Euthymos
of Lokroi, at Nemea and at Delphi. While those who followed the sport expected another battle between these two
for the Olympic *athlon*, they could not dismiss the stories
of a young Thasian, Theagenes, who it was said had not lost
a single match for two years. Though he had yet to fight
in the crown games, his record was impressive. He boasted
that the reign of Euthymos would come to an inglorious
end, that Euthymos would fail to survive the earlier rounds
be they against Theagenes, Lampis or even some boxer of
lesser renown. Theagenes predicted it would be Lampis
that he would pummel at the games in the final contest,
and not Euthymos.

On the other hand, Hellas shivered under the ominous
cloud cast from the east by Xerxes, known to his people as
the Great King. Xerxes had not secreted his plans and made

it known that he would avenge his father's defeat by our hand at Marathon. They say he made it his only purpose in life. As dark as that cloud was, we Hellenes seemed to think that it would pass or dissipate. We tried to ignore it and escape its shadow. We clung to the belief that the Medes, like the rest of the world, would honor the *ekecheiria*, the sacred truce that banned warring in times of the games. It was a foolish thought, and I think now that we should have known better; we paid dearly for our naiveté.

On my trek to Olympia from Megara where I had been visiting a friend, I took shelter from an approaching storm in a farmer's barn. Night had fallen, and the sky was dark as pitch. As he often does in the heat of *Metageitnion*, Zeus opened the heavens with blinding flashes and a torrent of rain, and shook the very ground itself with his thunderbolts. I sat nervously with the farmer's dog, a large but friendly creature with short fur and long ears that found his way to the relative comfort of the barn as well. We trembled together seeking warmth from each other's body as hard, cold raindrops attacked the roof and sought to find their way to us through the thatch. I had never been in such a fierce storm and prayed that I would survive it unharmed.

I was startled when another burst of lightening in the turbulent sky revealed two motionless silhouettes in the open doorway. They heard my gasp and no doubt saw the fear that came to my face in that brief moment of illumination. The dog growled. The light flashed again, just enough so I could see by the color of their cloaks and the length of their long, curled locks that they were Spartans. You can always recognize a full *Spartiate* by his scarlet cloak and his long hair, for the Spartan men believe that the color masks the trail of blood that might seep from their wounds in battle, and long locks make any man more terrifying to face in combat—and more handsome to confront in bed. How long they stood there like statues, unnoticed by the dog and me, I do not know, but after observing my gutless reaction to their presence, they stepped into the room and the rain dripped from their long cloaks that reached midway between their knees and the ground. Puddles formed at their feet.

"Fear not, old man," the one said, "We have traveled the day and, like you, only seek shelter from the wrath of Zeus as he throws his bolts with unusual fury this night." Each removed his *tribon*, unashamed, if not proud of his nakedness save for a thin strap of leather wrapped around his waist that held a dagger. They shook their cloaks fiercely as the dog would its fur had he been caught in the downpour. They seemed unconcerned that the shower of cold drops flew in my direction. Their bodies were chiseled, the result of many years in the *agoge*.

"Your dog?" the same one asked.

"No," I answered, "The creature probably belongs to the farmer and his family."

The next flash of lightning was so close that my hair bristled. I was blinded, but in that brief moment between the burst of light and the roar of thunder, I felt the dog fall limp at my side; then he was gone. As my eyes adjusted, I saw a small flame casting light from a fire made of dried straw and small pieces of wood, and I watched as the Spartans carved up the unfortunate dog for their supper. Such was the speed and agility that their training afforded them. Their butchery was so expert that the dog never uttered so much as a whimper to announce his passage from life to death. In a short time they had spit the meat and propped it over the fire. Their crude culinary preparations created a pungent smell that was not pleasant, particularly when I considered its source.

"Hungry, old man?" the older one, who offered what few words were exchanged, asked me as he reached out with a steaming bone from which burnt dog flesh hung in stringy strands. I shook my head no, timidly, content to eat the few figs that remained in my bag. He shrugged his shoulders with little concern, and the two Spartans began to rip the smoking meat from the bones and stuff it hungrily into their mouths. The meat was not greasy for the dog was thin at the time of his quick and painless death, and they ate it heartily. They washed it down with water they had collected in their inverted helmets, which they had left outside in the downpour. When they finished their meal, they collected straw from the empty stall and made places to rest. I suspected they would wait out the storm and leave; I sensed they had no intention to spend the entire night as I was prepared to do. The *agoge* teaches them to survive on the land and with little sleep. Spartans this far away from home are always on the move and rarely stay in one place for long. They are like phantoms.

"As we'll share the dryness of this barn for now," the one said, "it makes no sense that we remain strangers. I am Leon, an *ephor* of Sparta, and my young companion is Demaratos."

I bowed and said, "I am Simonides, the poet."

Leon laughed, "You'll soon have more work, poet. Before the moon is full, the clash of armor will be upon us again." Demaratos remained obediently expressionless.

"And where are you bound, Leon? It seems you are far from your home in Sparta."

Leon rolled to his side and rested on his elbow while Demaratos found more dry wood to put on the fire. The room was smoky, but the open door and window cleared enough out that it was better than the alternative in the rain outside that continued to fall heavily. The Spartans showed no mind to the discomfort; my eyes burned and watered. "We travel to Olympia to speak with the priests of Zeus and to our Spartan brothers gathered there to compete in the games. We bring words from our kings, Leonidas and Leotychidas, though the message is directly from the one, Leonidas."

"Are you free to share these words with a harmless poet, or is your message such that it is meant only for their ears?" I asked.

"It is meant for the ears of all free men of Hellas," he answered with no hesitation, "for our land is in great peril. Xerxes has assembled the Medes again and they are on the march. We have heard accounts that their army has already crossed the Hellespont on a bridge made of a thousand vessels. Our spies report that they number as locust that cover the sky and blot out the sun, and like those evil creatures, they destroy everything in their path while they suck our rivers dry. They say that Xerxes rules the world save only for Hellas. He is set on changing that and avenging the defeat of his father and countrymen at Marathon by the hands of Miltiades and the Athenians. Leonidas fears that the immediate defense of the land may fall solely to the men of Sparta, and it is his concern that takes me to the priests at Olympia. The *ekecheiria* has been passed on the bronze quoit, and all men move toward Olympia in peace to partake of the festival. All men, that is, but Xerxes and his Persian horde who pay no regard to the truce." Leon spit into the red embers, and sparks rose in the air and died. He took another draft of water and wiped his mouth with the back of his hand.

"Our kings have dispersed the five *ephors* throughout Hellas with a plea to ready our armies to face the Persian onslaught. I have been dispatched to Olympia to persuade the priests to delay the festival until the threat from the east has passed. What think you, poet? Will Hellas rise to its own defense or will the games go on?"

"This man, Xerxes, who calls himself the great king, should at least feel shame at violating the sacred truce that bans our countrymen from making war. No man, friend or foe, has ever broken that truce. Our fate is in the hands of the gods," I told him with some resignation, "and I do not believe they will fail us in our time of need."

Leon laughed sardonically and pulled his cloak closer to his body. "This man Xerxes knows no shame! You have evaded my question, Simonides, but your answer smacks of exactly what I fear. We must take our destiny into our own hands. As Leonidas has told the *ecclesia*, 'The gods give every bird its food, but they do not throw it into the nest.'" He shook his head with such disgust that his long locks whipped around and lay forward on his chest. I couldn't help but tremble thinking I had offended him; I wanted no quarrel with a Spartan.

"Words to consider," I whispered. He watched me closely and with some suspicion, as if I spoke on behalf of all men of Hellas. I could tell he knew that his mission to Olympia would be fruitless, but men like this are not easily beaten or turned aside from their duty.

After a short while, the storm had passed and a soft, damp mist floated into our barn. Leon rose to his full height and, with his squire Demaratos readied himself to leave. He nodded toward the door. "We have no more time and must be on our way to Olympia. Safe journey to you, Simonides, and may the gods indeed protect us all, but if they don't, Sparta will."

I stood up and dusted my *chiton*. I offered him my hand in friendship. He took it firmly and said, "I leave you with a final word, the very message that Apollo's Pythia gave our emissaries: '*O ye men who dwell in the streets of broad Lakedaemon! Either your glorious city shall be sacked by the children of Persia, or, in exchange, all Lakonia must mourn for the loss of a king, a descendant of great Herakles. For Xerxes, mighty as Zeus, cannot be withstood by the courage of bulls nor of lions; strive as you may, there is naught that can stay him, till he has got for his prey: your king, or your city.*'"

I felt his grip tighten as he spoke the chilling words. Without waiting for a response, he and his squire disappeared into the darkness and I was left in the smoky barn with the dismembered carcass of the dead dog, its bones picked clean.

The closer my steps brought me to Olympia, the more crowded the path became. For every one man or woman I passed moving toward me, away from the city, a thousand or more converged upon it. In all, they say that more than 40,000 people from all over the world attended the festival that year; such was their number that they were impossible for a single man to count and surprisingly so in this time of peril when each man knew the peace was threatened. But for all the people that made their pilgrimage to Olympia, I learned later and even saw with my own eyes that ten-fold, no, twentyfold that number crossed the Hellespont with Xerxes accompanied by a fleet of ships that formed a moving wall on the sea such that no man has ever seen, all intent on destroying Hellas and subjugating it to the great king as the Medes were known to call their ruler.

I was dismayed by the lack of urgency and concern at the rumors that found their way to the swelling city, rumors that spoke of a million-man army moving toward us, an army that flattened the land and drained the rivers. "We come to sacrifice and pay homage to Zeus," one man told me with a smile, "He will protect us." Easily enough said, but again, my faith was being tested as I struggled to understand the balance of divine intervention: what would the gods do and what would they expect their subjects to do in defense of their own homeland. Would the gods come to our rescue and wage their personal war on our behalf, like they did at Ilium in a time that no living man has been able to remember and recounts only through stories that have been passed from father to son for generations long since forgotten? They say that Xerxes worships Ahura Mazdah whose sign is the winged disc and whom the Medes call the Lord of Wisdom. Was this to be a clash of the gods and not men? As I marched toward Olympia, I was often drawn back to the words of the Spartiate: 'The gods give every bird its food, but they do not throw it into the nest.' Did the gods defeat the Persian host and Ahura Mazda at Marathon? I tried to avoid the question for fear of my own damnation, but I knew the answer was 'no.' The Athenians defeated Darius at Marathon. Men of courage turned the tide of battle, not the unseen hand of a bolt-wielding giant. Leon's words echoed in my head: 'May the gods protect us, but if they don't, Sparta will.'

Khepri and the Thasians listened patiently, but I feared I lost their interest as my tale of the Olympic games wandered to other issues that I could not separate from that year of the 75th Olympiad.

"I'm sorry," I said as I stared, almost blankly at the flame that burned from a single candle which sat flickering before us on a table. "Surely I bore you with thoughts that have no relevance to your interests, Khepri, and you have been such a fine host." The black slaves brought us honeycomb with which to sweeten our tongues. Khepri continued to surprise us with culinary pleasures and insured we lacked nothing in his tent this night.

"Not at all," Khepri answered, "Your story takes a turn in a most interesting direction, for as you tell it, it occurs to me that the games that year had great influence over the future of Hellas."

"Indeed they did," I replied.

"Then please go on. We have no where to go but Thasos, and then, not until the morrow."

My friends chewed casually on the sweetstuffs as I continued my story.

Amid the rumors of war, I thought long and hard on the *Ekecheiria*, the Sacred Truce, for to me this was, above all other things, at the heart of our contests. All Hellenes swear to one another that during the games, there will be no warring or conflict between us, only the competition that takes place on the stadium floor at Olympia. The games bring universal peace to our world, and now the Persian intruders would desecrate that peace. What evil possessed them and their king to violate what they and all men knew kindled harmony throughout our land? The more I pondered that question, the more irritated I became. Was there any other time in the course of history when all men were entrusted to lay down their arms and be brothers regardless of their race or their beliefs? Had there ever been another time when all men put aside their differences and weighed their worth in friendly strife? I thought not, and I seethed to think that Xerxes would take it upon himself to strike Hellas in its moment of tranquillity. Did he perceive our peace as our weakness? "Great King?" I asked myself. "I think not."

The games would begin in a few days, but I still had a ways to go. The mood was festive despite the imminent danger. Musicians paused on the side of the path and played their songs for passersby to drop an *obol* or two on the blanket spread before the performers for that purpose. Food and drink vendors had erected small booths even this far from

Olympia, and their business was brisk. I paused on the side of the path and wiped my brow. "A drink?" a vendor asked. I nodded and reached for his cup. As I did, I could see the mass of people parting perhaps a full *stade* before me. The travelers moved to the side of the path as if a large boulder had dislodged itself and was rolling steadily through the crowd and in my direction. I waited and watched curiously. The crowd grew silent as it pulled back to the sides of the footway, and soon I could see that it was no natural danger that caused the people to move from the path. The two Spartans I had met several nights earlier in the barn and another man who towered above them strode in my direction. Leon's look was stern and the three moved with purpose down the path, away from Olympia, with no regard to any man who was foolish and unfortunate enough not to clear the way. They made no apology if one chanced to roughly shove an inattentive pilgrim aside. It was only by chance that Leon happened to glance in my direction as he approached; their collective gaze was generally straight and true, with other, more important thoughts on their minds than the people moving in the opposite direction to watch the games. When he saw me, he stopped and his companions followed suit. I dared not speak, and the crowd seemed to cower and pull away from me as if I were diseased, or maybe charmed to attract the attention of the warriors.

"Ready your pen, poet," Leon commanded me, "and not for the victors at these games, but for the brave men of Sparta who will protect your land while this mass of children gathers at the feet of Zeus. Days from now when the priests carve up the oxen at the altar, think of us and know that we Spartans are doing the same to the Medes." He nodded once, with finality, turned in unison with Demaratos and the other man and continued down the path. The crowd gathered its wits and moved on, and the noise of casual conversation swelled again.

"You know those Spartans?"

"What?"

"Those Spartans. Do you know them?" the vendor repeated.

"Not really," I answered, "Though I spent the night in a barn with the two. The large, powerful one, I know not at all."

The vendor raised his eyebrows and laughed, "That is the one everyone knows. That, my uninformed friend, is Lampis."

I replied with some sense of recognition, "Ah, the boxer, the champion of Sparta and of late, the would-be champion of the world."

"It seems to me," the vendor commented, "that his reign will end before it begins for he appears to be headed in the wrong direction."

Though I had never seen Lampis before, like most men who follow sport, I knew of him. He appeared every ounce as powerful as the stories implied. Leon and his squire were no small men, but built powerfully and honed in the *agoge*. But this man, Lampis, was a half-a-head taller than either, and the breadth of his shoulders and the stone-like muscles that covered them seemed large enough to bear the weight of the mountains that loomed before me beyond Olympia.

The image of Atlas carrying the world on his shoulders flashed through my mind.

"I wonder why he travels from Olympia?"

"If I was to guess," I answered, "I would say he returns to Lakonia where I'm told the men of Sparta prepare to march against the Medes."

"I may not be as sure as you are. As you can see by the cart behind me, I have much food and drink that I bring to the games. I have rested here for a full day now and offered drink to all travelers. Many Spartans have passed my stall. Those three are the first I've seen heading back toward Lakonia and not toward Olympia. Perhaps others will follow," he gazed west and shrugged his shoulders, "but I think not. It is only those three I see who have returned parting the crowd like a strong wind through crops." I considered his observation while I finished my drink.

"If Lampis does not return," he added, "The men of chance will have to reconsider their bets. I think more money is apt to be made on the Thasian, Theagenes, if Lampis does not compete. You know of Theagenes?"

"I have heard of him. Though he is better known as a *pankratiast*, his skill with the *himantes* has spread like a fire through dry brush. It is sure to be a disappointment if Lampis is not at the games for the two to face each other for the *athlon*. Perhaps Euthymos will stand a chance to repeat as victor." I handed the cup back to the vendor, paid him for the drink and shuffled into the crowd that continued to surge toward Olympia.

Two days later, I crested the hills to the east of the city, and Olympia lay shining in the plain before me, the sun reflecting brightly from each temple and building. Not nearly the size of Athens, it is impressive in its own, glorious way. Dust rose from the hippodrome as charioteers ran their teams to prepare for the races that would occur on the second day of the games. The hippodrome pointed toward me like a long, fat finger that extended from the sanctuary. Parallel to it and between it and the Hill of Kronos, where spectators would gather for a glimpse of the races, was the stadium, a thin, 200-meter sliver, dwarfed by the horse track. In contrast to the bland, earthen color of the stadium and the hippodrome, the sanctuary and its buildings were surrounded with vibrant green trees and plants, finely groomed, which shimmered in the sunlight. The entire complex was protected at its western boundary by the *potamoi* Kladeos who flowed in his serpentine way from the hills to the north. The line of nine treasuries is easy to spot, but the most predominant structure, beyond the massive hippodrome, is the venerable temple of Hera which she shares with her husband, a building of such perfect harmony that it puts the universe in order just to gaze upon it. Near it was the altar of Zeus where sacrifices would be made.

Long before memory could be considered fact, it was said that Herakles was the first to celebrate these games in honor of his great grandfather, Pelops who won his bride by defeating Oinomaos in a chariot race. Herakles' mother, Alcmena was the last, mortal woman with whom Zeus, his father, had ever slept. It was here at Olympia that the mighty Zeus struck the ground with a bolt to show his son Herakles where the altar should be set. They say that soon, a new temple to Zeus alone will be built in the sanctuary, a structure that will have no equal throughout the entire world. It will be raised to honor Zeus as the supreme judge of all men in all things. I hope that I can live long enough to see it, but 'soon' is a strange word that means different things to different men. Today, the temple remains but an image in our minds.

Within Hera's temple is the bronze quoit, the Diskos of Iphitos, inscribed around its circumference with our most Sacred Truce, the truce of God, and also a table made of ivory and gold upon which were spread the olive branches made into crowns that would be presented to the victors at the games. I tell you, to gaze upon that city is to glimpse the invisible heights of Olympus itself and the wondrous things that reside there.

The city had mushroomed with the thousands who had traveled to witness the spectacle. Long lines of eager spectators flowed like mountain streams to the valley. Most people would sleep in the open air, for the gods always grant warm weather for the games; only one bolt has Zeus cast at Olympia, and its only purpose was to mark the site at which his altar now stands. The wealthy merchants and dignitaries erected their extravagant pavilions, and bright colors continued to erupt like an ocean of spring flowers creating a patchwork of reds, blues and golds that were raised in contrast to the white buildings and the virescent vegetation that surrounded them. The air was filled with expectation as it always is, and the gaiety of the crowd grew louder like the buzz of bees as you approach their hives in the forest. The excitement was contagious. All men smiled, seemingly confident that the truce would be honored. If any gave thought to the impending advance of the Medes, none voiced his concern. Though only Hellenes can compete, visitors strolled the temporary metropolis from the farthest lands, men with dark skin, men with slanted eyes, men from every corner of the earth converged to be a part of this grand celebration. You might think that havoc raced through the valley and disrupted its serenity every four years as thousands descended on Olympia, but such was not the case. True, it was noisy, but the *Hellanodikai*, those from Elis, who organize the games, imposed a structure on the growing city. The tents and pavilions were erected in straight rows so as not to undermine the symmetry of the sanctuary, and roads were planned for vendors and entertainers. The athletes themselves were allocated a special area that would provide them with the undisturbed rest and privacy each would need to compete at his highest level of performance.

The vendors were particularly pleased with the attendance; those who had brought ample supplies of their goods would leave with full and heavy pockets. I myself anticipated a productive week at Olympia for patrons of the athletes always paid me well for my epinicions.

Xeno interrupted my story with a question spoken in feigned innocence but no doubt aimed like a dart to annoy me. "And what about the great Pindar?" he asked, "Does he stand in your way as you approach these patrons with your hand extended for *drachma*?"

"If you ask me if Pindar and I compete for the purses, Xeno, I tell you 'no.' There is enough business for ten of us, and we often have more work than what any sane man can manage. Further, I approach no one, for they seek me out. My work speaks for itself and I have no need to advertise it like a common salesman in need of customers for his baubles. I have met Pindar, only once. I found him a pleasant and engaging man. I respect his work as he respects mine. There is no rivalry between us. We leave that to the men in the gymnasium. You are correct in one assumption, young man," I continued, "My words have made me a wealthy man, but be certain that the words I write are born of the passion I have for that about which I sing." The smirk left his face and was replaced by a look of interest as if the thought had never entered his mind that my work is a clever man's way to fleece his uneducated brothers. "I need make no excuse that I have gained some notoriety that extends well beyond Hellas... Like Pindar," I added pointedly and regretted saying it as soon as the words escaped my lips. The words were boastful and I find men of such character over-bearing and generally not capable of proving their ill-chosen words with action. I refrained from further comment with a wave of my hand, and I could see that Xeno's interruption had irritated our host.

"Please continue," Khepri insisted, "Your story is most informative and interesting. Don't you find it so?" He looked to Parmenides and the others for support, and they, excepting Xeno, nodded enthusiastically.

In that year of the 75th Olympiad, I, too, had reached my 75th year. Through those 75 years, I had composed hundreds, if not thousands of paeans, epinicions, odes, and other works written for the glory of god and man, and intended for the entertainment of all men so that they might know of the great deeds of their brothers.

A month prior to my journey to Megara, I made arrangements to meet Hiero, the Sicilian king's brother, and to stay with him in his pavilion at the games. Hiero's white steeds would race for the *athlon* in the hippodrome. Certain of his victory, Hiero requested my presence in his temporary residence at Olympia, and I agreed knowing full well this man's extravagant tastes and his appreciation of luxury. I looked forward to the days of comfort that awaited me at the games as Hiero's personal guest. His pavilion was large and expansive, and I had no difficulty finding it for, as I suspected, none other was quite like it. It was set up not far from the hippodrome so that the master could be close to his team of horses.

After a full and sumptuous meal that first night, I accompanied Hiero to the stables so that he could make certain that his team had been properly groomed and bedded for the night. I considered the task unnecessary for had that not been the case, those responsible for the well-being of the steeds would have paid with their own hides. He called each animal by its special name, and they responded affectionately to his touch. The horses carried the names of the four winds: Boreas, Eurus, Notus and Zephyrus. They were beautiful animals and I gazed upon them wondering if the teams of Helios and Selene could be any finer.

"Now," Hiero said with a broad smile, confident and satisfied that his 'children' were properly cared for, "a unique treat for my friend from Ceos." Showing its respect to the gods and the athletes whose presence would honor them in the official ceremonies that would commence on the morrow, the tent city had quieted. The sounds of sleep were more predominant that those of laughter or conversation. Hiero led me through the dark streets. We moved south from the hippodrome down the avenues between the tents, bypassing the *altis* altogether, and headed toward the river that we followed north. Fog drifted across the water from the west and floated like a layer of spilt milk over Olympia. I often wonder why birds cease their chatter in fog.

Hiero obviously knew where we were going, and he moved through the decreasing visibility with confidence. In a short time, I could see an orange glow where the darkness before us was illuminated by the light of many candles. "Aha!" Hiero exclaimed, "We have arrived." Within minutes Hiero and I joined a handful of others, mostly athletes, in the swimming pool. The most recent addition to Olympia, the pool and the adjoining baths were generally reserved for the competitors and their trainers. The guard at the entrance guessed correctly that I was neither. He passed a skeptical look to Hiero and then waved me in. My friend had clearly made previous arrangements for my admittance, and I suspected it was secured with the guard by means of his purse, and not by his fame as a charioteer. "Don't be concerned," he told me as he disrobed and prepared to enter the warm water. How could I not be, I thought as two men left the pool and headed for the tubs in the baths. Their bodies were brown from the sun, from head to foot, and their muscles tight and compact. I on the other hand appeared as a child's doll: brown arms and legs the color of sticks and a round, white torso like a mother's fresh pastry.

"Let us relax in the pool and then cleanse our pores in the tubs," Hiero said. "I smell like my horses do after a hard race, and you, Simonides, carry the odor of the labor from your journey." Hiero slid into the pool effortlessly, like a javelin in water; I plunked in much like a large rock. I saw the smiles from the others who we joined as waves from my entry rolled the surface of the water. "So what do you think?" Hiero asked as we waded chest-high to steps at the far end of the pool, "Have not the *Hellanodikai* done well with this addition?"

We reached the steps and sat down; the water was just beneath my chins. "Indeed," I answered as the warm water enveloped me with its soothing hands. It was scented and flower petals floated on the surface.

"We'll wait our turn for the tubs, but I think it will not take long at this hour. Most athletes have retired. The stress of the competition is not so much for a charioteer like me as it is for others. I'll admit it: it is my team of horses that does the work. I'm along for the ride." He laughed good-naturedly.

"Good that you give them the credit they deserve. Others have not been so generous with their praise in the past as if the driver ran the race and carried the team of horses on his back," I responded. Hiero smiled and stretched his body fully on the steps.

The moon was barely visible above us through the veil of fog that moved from the river and settled over Olympia like a magical, protective cover from heaven. Hiero squinted as if to see through the mist and said off-handedly, "I was visited this morning by Pindar." He waited for my response, but I remained silent. He continued, "Yes, young Pindar offered to write my epinicion for my certain victory in these games. Actually," Hiero laughed, "he had already composed it and shared several verses with me. It was very good and it pleased me." Hiero glanced in my direction and waited, hoping his statement would elicit a response, but I gave him none. "Still," he added, "I found his presumption impertinent though I did not tell him so. I thanked him for his confidence in my abilities but told him I had made other arrangements. You have endeared yourself to me and my brother," he said as he ran his fingers through his wet, wavy hair.

I hid my pleasure from him. "And why is Gelon not here with you?" I asked.

Hiero shrugged his shoulders. "He fears the condition of the state should he leave. He allows me to play the citizen while he plays the despot." Hiero slid lower into the pool and submerged his head and sat that way for a full minute before he rose slowly to seize another breath of the damp air.

It is true that the lives we lead as citizens are free from the concerns of the man in power who is often the target of others who would usurp his throne. I do not envy the men in political office. As a young man, I may have thought differently, but I know better now and am thankful for the lot the gods have cast to me.

A singer sat not far from the pool under an olive tree and he played his *cithara* with great skill. I smiled to myself when I heard him sing one of my own songs, an epinicion to young Glaucos of Carystos who won the boys' boxing years ago but never achieved success in the gymnasium as a man. I vainly took pride in my own words and melody, sung by another with deep passion. I knew and respected the art of young Pindar, and I immediately recognized his work when the singer began his next song:

> *Whose memory is so dim that he will e'er forget*
> *The son of Eunomos from the hills of Lakonia*
> *Whilst Lampis stood victorious over his van-*
> *quished Opponent at Nemea...*

No sooner had the name Lampis left the singer's lips when the water at the opposite end of the pool erupted violently as a large man rose quickly and moved his hand over the surface splashing water over the startled singer and those in close proximity. The young entertainer fell back off of his stool and was lucky to save his instrument from crashing into the low stone wall behind him.

"I'll not hear that name," the perpetrator roared like a wounded beast as he stood waist deep in the pool. "Do you understand me?" he hurled his question at the singer who lay sprawled on his back; the youth was too frightened to respond.

That, my friends, was my first glimpse of your Theagenes, for Hiero whispered his name to me following the outburst. Theagenes could not contain his anger at the mere mention of the name, Lampis. Stunned, I held my breath, not so much from the unexpected outburst as from the visage of the body that rose from the pool like Poseidon. From my reckoning, he was nineteen years old then, but he was no young boy. He was a lion contained in the body of a muscled, 25-year-old man. Another, older person, who I learned later was his trainer, stood and put a hand on Theagenes' shoulder which was level with the top of the trainer's head. "Calm yourself, lad," the trainer said, "It's only a name."

"To you it's a name," Theagenes bellowed, "To me, it is the object of my journey to Olympia, and now the coward has fled like a woman." Theo slammed his open palms on the water making a loud, smacking noise that sent large drops flying in every direction. His wild eyes looked directly from one athlete to the other gathered in the pool, and for some strange reason locked with mine when he shouted for all of us to hear, "Yes, you all heard me: he is a coward and has left the games to shiver with his Spartan friends in the shadows of Lakonia. If any man doubts that or challenges my words, I will meet you in the gymnasium and our fists will determine the truth, not our mouths."

Never in my life have I ever heard such venom directed at a single man, particularly not at a Spartan. As ferocious and imposing as this Theagenes appeared, I had no doubt had the Spartans I met the night of the storm heard his accusation, they would have attempted to deal with him no differently than they had the helpless farmer's dog, though I suspected that Theagenes would not have fallen victim to the Spartans as swiftly as the animal had.

He climbed out of the pool and took a threatening step toward the singer who flinched and pulled his instrument close to his chest as if the action could somehow protect it from Theagenes' wrath. "Rabbit!" Theagenes said in disgust as he stretched out his arms and waited for his trainer to dry his body. As he stood there dripping with his back now to us, I swear to you Khepri, I have never seen such a perfect man in body whose every muscle appeared carved from bronze in flawless symmetry. At the same time, I had doubts about the strength of his spirit for I thought his outburst inappropriate and demeaning to the character of a champion athlete. I remembered Lampis and the other two Spartans whom I crossed paths with earlier that same day. Their presence alone was as intimidating as any words they might have spoken, but in truth, they appeared no match for this man though I am certain they would not cower before him or any other man.

For that single moment when our eyes locked, even in his anger, I could see them sparkle in the dim light of the candles; there was something intangibly good in this man hidden behind his swagger, but he refused to let it escape. His trainer dried him thoroughly with linen and then applied a thin coat of oil to his smooth skin, painfully plucked clean of body hair.

Hiero said softly to me, "Now you know why I drive in the hippodrome and avoid the gymnasium. I have no desire to incur the wrath of such as him."

Theagenes heard the whisper and turned toward us. He wrapped the cloth around his thin, rippled waist and approached us on the edge of the pool. "Do you have something to say, old man?" he directed at me.

Hiero shook his head briskly, 'no,' but I have no tolerance for insolence and could not stay my tongue. "If it enhances your reputation, young man, to intimidate such a harmless old codger as me, please proceed in your disrespectful way. If not, I suggest you quell your anger for it will do you no good here or in the competition you will face. For every great man," I concluded, "there is one better. I suggest you consider which one you are before you accuse this Lampis of being a coward."

His nostrils flared and he opened his mouth but held the words that sat steaming on his tongue. He stared for a moment and then calmly said to me, "I am here, Lampis is not. His actions speak for him." Yes, they do, I thought without saying it.

As Theagenes turned to leave with his trainer, a man sitting on the edge of the pool, dangling his legs in the water said in a deep but unthreatening voice, a voice without fear but with some resignation, "Stay your tongue, Thasian, for none of us here is capable of doing it for you. Listen to the old man," he continued, "Lampis left by his own choice, but I can assure you and all gathered here at Olympia that he is not a coward and did not leave to avoid a fight with you." His long locks betrayed his origin: he was a Spartan. His muscular and compact frame suggested he might be a wrestler. Though powerfully built, he would be no match for the angry Thasian.

Theagenes glowered at him. He pointed his finger at the Spartan, narrowed his eyes and said, "Believe what you will, Lakedaimonian, but I swear to you this. When I have been crowned with the olive wreath, I leave with one purpose in mind: to find the coward. Be it in the stadium or on the side of a muddy road, I will have my match with Lampis and will straddle his fallen body when it is done." He turned and walked away, his rage seething visibly from his powerful body.

When Theagenes was gone, the Spartan looked at Hiero and me and said, "When a man's emotions take control of his brain, he loses at love and at war!" He lowered himself into the warm water and glided smoothly to sit on the steps with us. "I am Kleo," he said.

"A Spartan?" I asked. He nodded.

"Then perhaps you can explain to us why Lampis has indeed left the games while other Spartans such as yourself remain for the competition. Mind you, I do not share the Thasian's belief that your countryman is a coward, but I do wonder why he is gone while you and others remain."

Kleo laughed in such a way as to betray his own lack of understanding as to why men make the choices they do. But he was not without comment. He dunked himself fully in the water and re-emerged with the same grin on his face, unable to wash it away. "Gentlemen," he said, "I believe it is simply a matter of faith."

I looked at Hiero and he raised his eyebrows.

"Perhaps you failed to notice the huge crowd that has gathered here for the festival," he observed rhetorically and mimicked the look on Hiero's face. "Despite rumors from the north, my countrymen and I remain at the games because we have faith that one of two things will happen. The more unlikely of the two is that the Persian generals will respect and honor the sacred truce. It is as well known to them as it is to all men."

"More likely," Hiero interrupted, "that Xerxes attacks knowing full well that Hellas will not violate the truce." The men who remained in the pool at this late hour gathered to listen to our conversation, impressed, as I was, with Kleo's willingness to risk his own neck with a retort directed at Theagenes. Reluctantly, all of us murmured our agreement with Hiero.

"If it is doubtful, as we all agree, that Xerxes will allow us this most sacred of our festivals," I said, "Then I ask you again: why are we all still here, particularly you Spartans who are always alert for an opportunity to test your skills at war?" We stared dumbly at each other as we faced the reality each of us tried to dismiss.

"Faith," Kleo repeated. "We have faith in the divine will of our gods. We have faith that between Zeus and Ahura Mazdah, Zeus is the more powerful. We have faith that Zeus will protect his people, particularly at this most holy of times. He has done it before, and we believe he will do it again. As for us Spartans who remain... there will always be war for us and any others who choose to partake of it. Those of us who remain, remain to honor the gods as we believe it is our obligation to do." We grappled with his explanation, and I for one said a silent prayer to Olympus hoping that Kleo was right: the gods would protect us.

"And what then of Lampis?" I asked. "Is he a coward or is he a man of little faith?"

The wrestler smiled again, and his grin was infectious and relieved the tension that had gripped the pool and all in it. "Like I told the bully Thasian, Lampis is no coward and fears no mortal man."

"Then according to your logic, friend Kleo, he must be a man of little faith," I offered with no malice.

"I am certain that Lampis has great faith, but his faith is in his king, Leonidas. Let me explain," he offered. "We have two kings, Leonidas and Leotychidas. One, Leotychidas, though a fine warrior himself, follows the priests from temple to temple and makes his journeys to Delphi. His faith is in the gods. The other, Leonidas, the lion's son, though a man who prays often and publicly follows the men and spends his days in the *agoge*. His faith is in himself and in his men as much as they are willing and prepared to harvest what the gods lay before them. Leonidas makes no sacrilege but is convinced beyond doubt that it will be men, inspired by the gods to greatness, who stem the tide of the Persian advance, not the gods themselves who will refuse to soil their hands in the melee. As men have faith in the gods, so, too, does Leonidas believe that the gods have faith in men!

"As word of the Persian advance has reached us, Leotychidas and the priests took council with the Pythia. He returned with her words: only the death of a Lakedaimonian king will satisfy the hunger of the gods and influence them to turn Xerxes from his mission in Hellas.

"Three days past," Kleo told us, "the *ephor* Leon met with all Spartans gathered here at Olympia. Our *ephor* explained that when Leotychidas returned with the oracle's words, the *ecclesia* met to set the course of action. When the vote was taken, it was clear that more men put their faith in the gods; the games would go on, uninterrupted and with full Spartan support. That, my friends, is why my countrymen and I remain in Olympia, firm in our faith that Zeus himself will deal with Xerxes and his horde. We stay to bring honor to Lakonia and Olympus while our countrymen who remain in Sparta celebrate our own sacred festival, the *Karneia*, to honor the soldierly way of life that we hold so dear."

The water rippled as Kleo submerged himself again and surfaced with that ever-present and confident smile upon his face.

"But what of Lampis?" another athlete asked, "He has left despite what you have said, that your council has decreed that Sparta will attend and participate in the games."

"Listen carefully, friend," Kleo replied, "The *ecclesia* decreed that any Spartan could attend and participate in these sacred games, not that they had to. The *ephor* made that clear to us when we met before Hera's temple in the *altis*. His personal plea came from the lips of Leonidas himself who said in four days he would march north with however many men chose to go with him. Leonidas would fault no man who paid tribute to the gods at the festivals, but in his own heart, the king is convinced that the gods command him and his Spartiates meet the Persians before they sweep into Hellas. Whether or not Leonidas believes he is the Spartan king who must die as the Pythia has foretold, I do not know, but I do know he will not shy away from any destiny the gods might have chosen for him.

"Lampis is a Spartan knight, a personal bodyguard of Leonidas. I suspect that Lampis and the 300 knights will all march with Leonidas for I have seen none of them here in Olympia. The Spartiates will do whatever their king decides."

"If what we hear is true," Hiero said, "that the armies of Persia number as the stars in the sky, it is a fool's mission with no chance of success. Better to muster the *hoplites* in Attica as soon as the festival is finished, there to give the Medes another taste of Hellene thunder. We all remember Marathon and it can be done again." Other men in the pool nodded their approval.

"Perhaps you are right, sir, inasmuch as 300 men have little chance against a million, but if they can hold the Persians, only for a day or two, it will give us the time to complete our homage to Zeus as we have always done, and then to muster our men as a single nation to face the coming storm. As these games have always united Hellas in peace, maybe this time, they can unite us in war. No, friends," Kleo concluded, "Lampis is no coward." As he climbed the steps out of the pool, he said one last time with the impish smile that refused to leave his face, "It is about faith, gentlemen. I for one put my faith in the gods, but my heart goes north with Leonidas and his 300 knights. If you think him crazy, I remind you of a tale from games past when an old man wandered the stadium in search of a place to sit and watch the events. Having circuited the entire stadium, he finally came upon where the Spartans had gathered. Seeing the old man's plight, several young Spartans, and old ones too, stood and offered their places to the weary, old man. Sitting down, the grandfather commented loudly enough for all to hear, 'It is such a tragedy that all Hellenes know what is right, but only the Spartans do it!' Who is right? Only the gods know for sure." Kleo walked up the steps to the side of the pool toward the doorway that led to the baths. We sat in silence for no man was willing to suggest otherwise.

Before Kleo passed into the darkness a young man called after him, "And to where do Leonidas and his 300 Spartans march? Will he make his stand at the Isthmus in Corinth?"

Kleo stopped to face us. "We have word that Thessaly will collapse before the weight of the Medes. A stand in Corinth saves only Lakonia and Arcadia. Leonidas and his Spartans fight for all of Hellas, not just the Peloponnese." He raised his face to the milky darkness and pointed to the northeast, "To the Hot Gates, to Thermopylae. That is where Leonidas and his men march to make their stand."

CHAPTER EIGHT

The Olympic Games

I do not wander like a lost child in the forest as I tell my tale, Khepri. I will satisfy your curiosity. In the telling, however, I am obligated to explain the events that wrapped these games like the cold, heartless coils of a serpent, circumstances that few men were willing to acknowledge though all men feared. It is difficult for a man to look at dark fate with hard-nosed defiance and unbiased clarity. Perhaps it was his pragmatism and not his lack of faith in the gods that made Leonidas and his contingent unique among other men. Too often, we give the false appearance that every thing is fine, that bad and evil things are not there even when they are so close we can see our reflection in the deep color of their eyes. We turn away and hope that it will vanish when we look back. Leonidas was unwilling to turn his face from destiny or to close his eyes to the danger that approached from the north. I continue...

The following morning as even more people flowed in from the hills, the crowd gathered at the *Pelopeion* where the *Hellanodikai* sacrificed a black ram to Pelops. I passed near enough to see that the animal's eyes were as black as its thick wool, like pitch, and it seemed to glare at the crowd not in submission, but rather, in defiance as if it was not willing to give up its slothful life for something it did not understand. Its struggle was in vain and it fell to the swift blade of the priest who drew his knife expertly across the animal's throat. The ram's blood poured to the ground and mingled with that of its ancestors from all games past. With stained but sanctified hands, the procession made its way through the parting crowd to the nearby *bouleuterion*, the council building. The *Hellanodikai* waited solemnly for all the athletes to gather. Priests stood watch over the dismembered pieces of the sacrifice that seemed to move by the number of flies that gathered at the altar to take their small pieces of the dead animal. Their number was so large that I could see the tiny scavengers swarming around the altar like a dirty cloud of black smoke as I worked through the crowd toward the stadium. When I could stand the sight no more, the sacrifice was lit calling the contestants to muster, and those flies not consumed by the flames flew off in search of other victims.

Some 500 hopeful participants arrived from all points in Hellas and stood before the *bouleuterion.* I had managed a good vantage point from the Hill of Kronos behind the stadium, but from that distance, I was unable to find my host, Hiero. Yet it was impossible not to see the young Theagenes whose shaved head glistened in the sunlight and rose well above most.

At a signal from the priest, the crowd hushed. In one voice, the contestants swore to Zeus *Horkios* the enforcer of oaths that their training had been true for ten full months, that they would follow the rules of the games and that they had abstained from sexual relations for a full moon and had partaken only of vegetables during their abstinence. From the looks of those I had seen, from a distance, as well as close up, I had no doubts that what they swore to was true. In their turn, the *Hellanodikai*, robed in black, swore that they would judge all events with no bias or prejudice, that the winners would earn their *athlons* based solely on merit and no other concern. With the oaths taken, a second priest at the altar lifted his arm, and I was startled at the sound of a hundred horns that lifted their voices behind me at the top of the hill upon which I sat. They were powerful, true, and unwavering in the notes that fled joyously from them; their strength and power reflected that which we would soon see on full display in the games. At the final note, the *Hellano-dikai* led the multitude before them in a hymn to Zeus. We sang the very same words first sung by the ancient heroes for it had given them victory over their enemies at Ilium.

> *I will sing of Zeus, chiefest among the gods and greatest,*
> *All-seeing, the lord of all, the fulfiller*
> *Who whispers words of wisdom to Themis as she sits leaning towards him.*
> *Be gracious, all-seeing Son of Kronos, most excellent and great!*

As one man, we raised our voices to the sky and sung so loudly that I am sure we were heard with clarity on Olympus itself. You have never heard such a sound of jubilation delivered by so many voices with such deep awe and reverence. If for nothing else, it is for that moment that all men should take part in the games as spectator or contestant. There is a unity among the diverse crowd assembled in Olympia that cannot be duplicated anywhere else on land or water. I tell you, at that instant, all men of Hellas were a single organism of common flesh and blood. It thrills me yet to think of that moment of joy. When we finished our song, all men embraced, each turning to those near by. Some were with friends, but it made no difference. I held in my own arms a pock-faced man whom I had never met in my life, but we hugged firmly and patted each other on the back as if we were lifelong brothers. Indeed, in that instant of time we were.

The priests let the swell take its own course, content that the gods were pleased as Hellas prayed and cheered in unison to the omnipotence of its divine benefactors. Minutes passed before the noise subsided, and no one interceded to quiet the crowd. Slowly, the deafening din receded, and a man emerged from the *bouleuterion* with a silver vase.

He placed it upon a small table before the entrance to the building. Inside the vase were 40 small stones for that was the number of contestants who would compete for the crown in the *stade*. Twenty of the stones were white, and the others colored. One by one, each man approached the table and knelt before it saying his own, silent prayer, some, I am certain, to Hermes that their steps in the race would be true and swift. As each runner pulled his stone from the vase, he disrobed leaving his *chiton* at the foot of the table, and was then directed either to the right or the left depending upon which stone he pulled from the container.

The contestants were separated into two groups for the two heats that would determine which men would compete in the final race for the crown.

When the last stone was drawn, the crowd cheered deliriously and with unrestrained pleasure; the games we all awaited were about to begin. The crowd parted as the *Hellanodikai* moved slowly from the *bouleuterion* toward the stadium, and the forty would-be champions followed the judges. The athletes' nakedness came alive as the sun reflected from the oil on their lithe bodies. While the procession moved in measured steps, the spectators scrambled, ant-like, to find a place to observe the day's events, the *stade*, the single-course foot race and the *diaulos*, the double-course foot race.

The natural tendency for man is to walk. Though all Hellenes are taught to run from birth, few overcome the instinctive and less tiresome predisposition to walk. For those few that do, they appear at a more comfortable gait when they run than they appear when they walk. I noticed this as the contestants proceeded to the east end of the stadium. The runners' bodies appeared stiff and awkward as they struggled to maintain the slow pace of the *Hellanodikai* who led them to their starting point. These men ached to free their bodies in fast, fluid motion. Their lives are focused on these fleeting seconds in time when each would unleash his speed to fly down the smooth, dirt stadium of Olympia to the finish line, matching the core of his life against the fastest men in all of Hellas. Each was here to demonstrate his mastery of the simple act of running. The thought is over-powering and for that reason, I hold the athletes who

compete at the games in great respect, notwithstanding the
insolence with which the young Theagenes greeted me the
night before.

I'll not bore you with the details of the two, preliminary heats that determined those twenty runners who would
compete in the final race to win the Olympic crown except
to relate one incident to show you that we do not take these
competitions lightly or, in your words, Khepri, frivolously.
You'll recall that when each athlete takes his oath, he swears
to follow the rules of the games. As the runners took their
places for the second heat at the starting line behind the
husplex, each was tight like the pulled string of a bow, his
senses sharp as he anticipated the fall of the wooden gate.
One runner, a man from Crete who had a long, thin neck
snapped and leapt forward before the gate was released. He
fell to his knees in shame while the crowd hissed its dis-
dain at his fault. Two *Hellanodikai* promptly ushered him
to the foot of the hill where we sat. He was bound in cord
and whipped with thatch. The beating was not physically
brutal, though I'm sure it brought some pain to his back.
More, it was humiliating, and the shame was far more painful than the blows to his hide. Such is the fate for any who
would seek unfair advantage over his opponents, though
certainly this man's intention was not to cheat or gain unfair odds, but only to time his start with the opening of
the gate. Today, I oddly remember a story told to me by a
friend who counseled with the Athenians during the Great
War. The wise Themistocles urged quick action against the
invaders. In response to his plea, a Corinthian general said,
"At the games, the runners who start before the gate drops

are beaten." My friend told me Themistocles was quick to respond, "Those left behind win no crown." It is a fine art to time your actions well, being neither too soon, or too late. The consequence can be unacceptable in either event.

After a short rest, the 10 top men from each of the heats were ready for their final race. They took large quantities of water and some had been wrapped in wet blankets to keep their bodies cool. The moment had arrived for these twenty men who had dedicated their lives to be the best they could possibly be. The world watched, eager to see who would claim the crown. One by one, the runners were called to the starting line, each one's name and home announced by the *Hellanodikai*. The information was passed quickly from spectator to spectator so that we all knew whom the participants were. My eyes were drawn to the runner from Kroton for I had seen him race before. Like his rivals', his body was lean and taut, but he moved to the line with a noticeable bounce in his step as if he struggled more than the others to contain the burst of pure energy that would propel him down the course. From where I now stood, I could see old marks on his young back, which suggested that he might have had his share of false starts.

There was no wind that day. These twenty would create their own gust as they exploded from their starting point. The ancient priest that remained at the altar of Zeus at the east end of the stadium waited until the name of the final runner reached him. In that way, he could be sure that the thousands who waited now, holding their breaths for the race to begin, knew the names of all runners. A large bull stood proud and tethered on the pile of ashes on the

altar. There was no doubt when the sacrifice was made, for
the huge beast fell to his knees as his life-blood drained
from the deep cut applied to his throat. In a short time, he
crumbled to the large fagot beneath him, and the priests
lay upon him with special, consecrated knives and dismembered his once powerful body. The beast never uttered a
sound but accepted his fate in silence as if knowing his
death was made in honor of the mightiest of gods. His demeanor was different than that of the ram.

The priest had a clear view to the end of the stadium
where the runners waited for his signal. My eyes moved
quickly from the priest to the Kroton, and back. The crowd
was silent and waited. The priest dipped his torch in a vessel
of consecrated oil and raised it fully over his head, waving
it, unlit, from side to side. The runners prepared themselves. It was time, and each drew his muscles tight like
the bow of Odysseus in the instant before the great archer
released his shaft. The priest lowered his torch and fire was
applied. All of us, spectators and contestants alike, could
see the black smoke rise from the fired torch. In one even
motion, the priest raised the flaming torch directly over
his head, and a trumpeter, behind me on top of the hill,
blew a single, loud, powerful note to begin the race. As the
note resonated through the valley, the *husplex* was released,
the gate dropped and the runners leapt from their starting
stances and exploded down the length of the stadium.

The strongest were a full step ahead of the others within
seconds, and I and spectators near me gasped as the Kroton
stumbled and struggled to regain his balance while he saw
the backs of all nineteen of his competitors pull away from

him. In a race that lasts no longer than 30 beats of a resting man's heart, I knew his initial error would be disastrous for this man who had trained so long to be the first to the finish line at Olympia. But as my heart plunged for him, I saw that he was made of tougher stuff than I and the thousands of others who resigned his position to last in the race. Within 50 meters, all runners had found their pace. It was blistering. Arms and legs pumped smoothly but almost violently as blood rushed through their veins at breakneck speed. At 100 meters, halfway through the race, the Argive led his competitors, but all could see that the runner from Kroton had actually passed half of the field and the distance between him and the Argive had grown noticeably smaller. What courage pulsed through his heart to spur him beyond his physical limitations and to achieve what appeared impossible? He had won the crowd to his side. As the distance between him and the Argive continued to decrease, the roar from the spectators increased. The noise was so loud it froze thought in all that could hear it. We clung only to the image of the twenty athletes racing down the course.

I would guess that you have never seen a man run with the grace, the power and fluidity of a horse. I can tell you that this man, the one from Kroton, did. He caught and passed the Argive with less than ten strides to the end of the stadium and his momentum carried him to the base of the altar of Zeus where the priest waited with the flaming torch. The man's name was Astylos.

The crowd's approval was unrestrained as all men were on their feet cheering wildly. Astylos struggled to maintain his balance. His muscles burned from their exertion.

He stood at the foot of the altar, hunched over, propping his hands on his knees. He didn't even have the energy to turn and watch as the runners who finished behind him fell to the ground in abject disappointment, but still knowing they had been defeated by the stronger man. There was no glory for second place. Only one man was the victor, the others had failed, but in their failure there was no shame for each had given his best effort, his heart and soul to the task he faced.

The winner's trainer approached him shortly, smiling broadly like a happy child and as breathless as his champion. He carried with him his *aryballos* and *strigils* with which he gently scraped the oil, sweat and dust from Astylos's body before his runner could accept the fired torch from the high priest. The multitude waited for the trainer to complete his chore while the athlete rested. When the trainer had finished, Astylos turned to the priest who waited patiently with the torch.

"You have run for your life, Astylos, and won. All Hellenes share in your victory." The crowd bellowed and thundered as an attendant tied purple ribbons around the winner's forehead, arms and legs. These would mark him as a victor for the remaining days of the festival and make him recognizable to everyone who saw him. "Yours, now, is the greatest honor: to complete the sacrifice of an entire people to the highest of their gods." The priest handed the torch to Astylos who waited while the wine was poured into the sacred cup that the priest now held. We all began to chant, "*Sponde! Sponde*," in anticipation of the libation and sacrifice.

Some say the victory in the single-course is perhaps the most prestigious of the games at Olympia. Not only would the victor receive his crown of olives at the temple at the end of the festival, but he had also won the right to complete the sacrifice to Zeus. No other athlete at Olympia could claim such honor. Astylos raised the torch above his head and stared at the flames momentarily as all eyes focused on this single man. With his arms raised, he walked slowly and deliberately around the altar and the sacrificial pyre. The voice of the appreciative crowd raised slowly, a heavy rumble at first that swelled into a delirious sound of joy as Astylos set the torch to the wood. When he did, we prayed while the priest poured the blessed wine onto the pyre and into the flames. The dry kindling at the bottom caught quickly and rose with a life of its own to consume the bull and take it to Olympus. Those close to the altar backed away from the intense heat. The smell of the burning fat drifted through the *altis* and men waved their hands to draw the smoke to their nostrils feeling that it made them even more a part of the victory and pulled them to the bosom of Zeus.

The first event was completed and the winner would be crowned at the conclusion of the games at the temple of Hera with the other victors. It was a good way to begin the games for the race held unexpected suspense when Astylos stumbled, and this unintentional and potentially disastrous act intensified the satisfaction of both the victor and those in the crowd that could not predict the outcome until Astylos's foot crossed the finish line a single step in front of the Argive's.

There was little drama in the running of the *diaulos*, which Astylos won as well. In fact, this was the third successive Olympic games where he won both races. And because you have witnessed the games yourself at Nemea and Corinth, Khepri, I will not recount each event at these games; this evening is too short for me to sing the praises of all the victors and provide you with the details of each. Still, I am drawn to one event, the result of which has tied me to these Thasians and compels me to journey with them to their island. I will share with you the details of one more event, and that event is the *pyx*, boxing.

I spent my time at Olympia leading up to the *pyx* attending all competitions, but I was not remiss in visiting the holy sites to pay due homage to the gods during the day; at night, Hiero and I wandered from party to party reveling with the victors. Always, my eye was sharp to find Theagenes. He was not difficult to spot, but I saw him at no other places than at functions he was required by the laws of the games to attend. Never did I witness his presence at the evening celebrations. I felt his focus and commitment to the task at hand. As dedicated as I perceived all the athletes to be, I saw deeper commitment etched on the face of Theagenes. His countenance was fixed and firm and displayed little emotion despite the anger that he had no intention to conceal at the baths.

I will tell you on the second day, with no surprise, my host, Hiero, did win his race. He cut a fine figure aboard his white chariot pulled by a team of all black horses. They ran faster than the winds for which they were named, and skillfully avoided the many spectacular crashes that sent

two charioteers home to their funeral pyres. As my bene-
factor, Hiero, and justly so, expected me to compose his
epinicion to be performed at the celebrations and banquets.
I failed him. Although I had every intention of fulfilling
my contract to him, you will soon learn that I did not. He
has never accepted my apology, and Pindar now takes my
place of privilege and honor in Hiero's entourage. I hold no
ill will against either, for my failure was of my own doing
and by my own choice.

On the morning of the third day, the crowd gathered
early at the altar of Zeus for the traditional sacrifice of the
100 bulls brought here for this special purpose from the
city of Elis. As you have not seen such numbers of men that
were gathered at Olympia, you have not seen such a large,
but not unruly herd of beasts in any one place at a single
time. Those that performed the sacrifice did so expertly and
in short order. No time was wasted as each bull was dispatched quickly and carved up in pieces. You could smell
the blood as it flowed freely around the altar and soaked
the ground in dark pools. The fat was burned at the altar
and the meat was reserved for the large feasts to be held
that night throughout the swollen encampment that surrounded the city.

By mid-morning, a Spartan had proved victorious in
the *hoplitodromos*. He carried his shield with ease as he out-
distanced the other twenty-four contestants through two
lengths of the stadium. His victory was not unexpected;
two lengths, one up and the other down the stadium,
was child's play compared to the miles he had run with
shield and helmet during his years of training at the *agoge*.

Watching him heft the shield he had been given by the Hellanodikai for the event, I sensed it was like a feather compared to the one he carried into battle with his Lakedaimonian comrades on the plains of the Peloponnese. Oebotos of Achaea claimed the victory, but on further investigation, the *Hellanodikai* determined that the Achaean's trainer had substituted a much lighter shield for the measured one reserved for the race. Claiming ignorance of his trainer's ruse, Oebotos escaped the punishment of the *Hellanodikai*. His trainer, however, was whipped, fined and expelled from the games, a broken man whose career as a professional trainer was finished because of his own greed. Hence, the victory belonged justly to the Spartan.

Boxing always attracts great interest at our games, but maybe even more so at those games of the 75th Olympiad. Due to no gossip from me, word had spread rapidly through Olympia that Theagenes had called Lampis coward. Derisive words do not set well at our games and are considered offensive. Because Theagenes had violated this unwritten but understood protocol, the crowd swung heavily in favor of the defending champion, the Lokrian Euthymos. Most men hoped to see Euthymos hand Theagenes his head on a platter, and gathered that afternoon to see it happen.

I marvel at the courage of boxers. The sport favors the large man with muscular arms and strong shoulders. While many contestants displayed those characteristics, there were others who did not. Some were even shorter than I am with large girth, though none displayed the softness of a man who does not test his muscles, all of them, on a regular basis. My mind's eye weighed the physical tools of some against those of Theagenes and Euthymos and concluded that it was only superior courage and confidence that brought them to this place. The mental fortitude of the smaller men had served them in the past, for they would not be here to compete on this greatest of all stages had they not tested and proven their skills in countless matches since the last games.

Some say that the *pankration* is the most brutal of all sports because a man can strike blows as he does in boxing, but he can also kick like an angry mule. There is a strong case for that, for the heel of a man's foot can land with the force of a blacksmith's hammer. But from what I've seen, a *pankratiast* can elude the viciousness of receiving blows by grappling and wrestling during the course of his contest. The boxer must always stand erect and face his opponent; he cannot hide nor rest while pinning his opponent's arms to his body like a wrestler.

I find that boxing demands more of its participants than any other sport. I acknowledge with no dispute that each athlete is a specialist in his own venue of competition and each who wins at these games can be called the best in his realm of expertise. We can say, "He is the best runner," or "He is the best man with the disc," but our subjective assessment can only be verified by the competition itself. Despite our subjective opinions and analyses, the runner who crosses the finish line first has earned the right to be called the best regardless of who thinks what; the athlete who tosses his disc the farthest has earned the right to be called the best thrower. So, too, with the boxers ... the last man standing has earned the right to be called the best and to wear the crown. But the boxer's path is more brutal and more demanding than the path of any other competitor's, save only the wrestler's and the *pankratiast's*. The wrestler and the pankratiast are similar in their own right, but from my observation, the boxer is the greatest athlete. A sprinter runs for thirty heartbeats and as he crosses the finish line his lungs burn and his muscles ache. The javelin thrower calls upon his strength and agility for one brief, explosive moment. The charioteer relies on his driving skills, but it is his team of horses that ultimately carry him to the end of the race. The boxer walks to the stadium floor never knowing if he will be gone quickly or if he will endure for an entire afternoon. His fate is literally in his own hands, but he cannot pace himself as a runner. He must fight his hardest in each match to increase the chances that it will not be his last.

The boxer has one goal and a single means of achieving it: he must use his fists and only his fists to beat his opponent into submission. There is no time to rest or to catch one's breath. Some think that the *himantes*, the leather straps that a boxer dons on his fists, will soften the blows he delivers to his opponent. I think just the opposite. If you strike a rock with your bare fist, your hand will swell painfully and bleed; if you wrap your hand in cloth, the cloth will absorb much of the impact of the blow. I say that the leather straps of the *himantes*, wrapped cleverly around the knuckles and wrists, protects the wearer and allows him to deliver more force with less damage to his own weapons, his fists. All sports of combat are brutal and dangerous, but boxing exposes the participant to more physical damage than the others. As I gazed upon the group of participants, I saw that more than half displayed ears that resembled squashed vegetables more than they resembled human organs to receive sound. Yet here they were once more in pursuit of their dreams. I respected them, but their disfigurement told me it was unlikely that any of these could escape the damage Theagenes and other unscathed boxers were prepared to render. Their cause had little hope of success.

With Helios riding at his zenith and his team of fiery horses pouring its heat on the spectators and contestants, the thirty-six boxers who would compete for the crown gathered on the stadium floor. The mass of spectators rushed to the Hill of Kronos for the best possible positions to observe the afternoon war. My vantage point was as good as any for I was the guest of Hiero. His servants had erected a small shelter to shield us from the sun, and we sat on comfortable chairs unlike most men who had to stand all afternoon if they were to witness the event without obstruction.

"Have you completed my victory ode?" Hiero asked with a broad smile and clapped my shoulder as I lowered myself into the seat he had reserved especially for me.

"Not yet, great charioteer," I answered. "Words to commemorate your victory flow slowly like honey from the comb, not like common water from a mountain stream." He laughed appreciatively.

Hiero's interest in this competition was keen for with Lampis gone, he was convinced that the man who would take the boasts from Theagenes' lips would be Euthymos, the defending champion who had spent time training in Sicily at Hiero's facilities. Indeed, as I gazed on the contestants, I saw only one man who appeared to have the physical stature to match that of Theagenes, and it was Hiero's friend. I remembered his victory in the games at Olympia four years prior. It was most unusual, for in that year, the number of boxers was odd, and Euthymos proceeded to the final fight by drawing the odd lot through all preliminary matches; he was an *ephedros*, the athlete in waiting, and as such had great advantage over his competition. He fought but a single match, the final one. I cannot recall his opponent's name, but the man fought fiercely through five exhausting matches before he took his place in the last opposite Euthymos. In the fight for the prize, he managed to push the Lokrian to the limit, inflicting upon him a broken jaw, but his preliminary bouts took their toll and the eventual champion outlasted the tired pugilist. Older and wiser, Euthymos carried himself with strength and power. He glowed with a confidence meant to intimidate his opponents. The competition would be a memorable one even without Lampis on the list.

Hiero nodded toward the stadium before us. "And where do the odds fall, poet?"

I raised my hands in ignorance but offered, "They say the young bull will outlast the stud."

"Is that what 'they' say?" he responded. "I say you are listening to phantom voices in your head, my old friend. Real men of flesh and blood with knowledge of the sport tell me that the young man's anger will blind him to the task at hand. His defense will fall and Euthymos will see it when it happens. And what do you say, Simonides?"

I thought for a moment and answered, "You may be right, but I have seen anger in combat come to a man's rescue. Having seen Theagenes at the baths… I think the young Thasian will emerge victorious."

"Well said. Perhaps a friendly agreement then. If Theagenes wins, I double your fee for my song. If my Lokrian wins, I'll pay you only with my heartfelt thanks." He smiled and offered his hand to seal the deal and waited for my response.

Hiero's wager was a sizeable sum of money that tempted me greatly. I studied the combatants again with a critical eye. For a moment, I considered not accepting the bet but then blurted out, "Done." We shook forearms firmly and sat back to watch the outcome.

The pairings for each match were drawn by lot. Mixed within the same silver urn from which the runners drew their stones days earlier, were 36 beans, one for each competitor. The beans were marked with letters and other symbols: there were two 'alphas', two 'betas,' and so on. The fighters were paired by the symbols on the beans they drew from the vase. After all have drawn their lots, the fighters make a circle, none knowing at that time who his opponent will be. With the final bean drawn and the circle complete, the *alutarches*, under the direction of the *Hellanodikai*, walks around the circle, examining each man's symbol, and pairs the men for their first test. Hiero and I breathed more easily when we saw that Euthymos and Theagenes had avoided each other in the initial round of fights. The single, silent prayer that rose from the spectators was answered. Zeus had bid the sisters of Fate that Lachesis would keep Theagenes and Euthymos separated until the final match was determined assuming, of course, that both fought their way to that ultimate confrontation. With Lampis gone, I was confident that both would.

Ten matches were conducted at one time, as 10 were the number of the *Hellanodikai* who would judge them. A match was finished when one man conceded by raising a finger, or when he was fairly pounded to the ground from which he had no more strength to rise. A match could be over in minutes, or it could endure for hours.

The ten pairs walked to the open space on the stadium set aside for this purpose and faced each other with muscles tensed and fists clenched in tightly strapped *himantes*. The eldest *Hellanodikai* raised his arms and when he loosed a bird to signal that the contests could begin, fists and arms began to flap more wildly than the wings of the bird that soared gracefully and moved quickly away from the noise of the crowd.

My eyes remained fixed on Theagenes who fought in the first group; Euthymos would wait until he and his opponent were called to fight by one of the *Hellanodikai* in the next round.

Theagenes was paired with one of those short, stocky men, a Theban who, I had heard, claimed Herakles in his lineage. Before either man struck a single blow, the Theban employed an unexpected stratagem, perhaps, but unlikely, the only scheme he could employ to topple Theagenes who stood above him nearly two, full heads. The man stepped quickly back two paces and spread his arms wide like the crucified man I suspected he was about to become. His stomach protruded beyond his chest, but there was no mistaking the power that he could deliver from his massive arms. Theagenes lowered his fists in disgust as the black-robed judge stepped between the two boxers. No, the Theban had not conceded the contest. He declared *klimax*, a strategy generally reserved to conclude a match that had continued for an exceedingly long time. I have not seen it often, but as I considered the physical differences between the two combatants, I concluded that the Theban had opted wisely. One of two things would occur, the most improbable of which, he could win. If not, the match would be short and swift, probably not painless, but the Theban would avoid the punishment he would no doubt receive from Theagenes if the match continued for any length of time.

In *klimax*, each man stands defenseless before his opponent and the two take turns delivering their most powerful blows while the other is denied the effort to avoid it.

The crowd hissed and expressed its displeasure with the Theban's declaration. Still, it was the man's right. After a brief discussion with the two contestants, the *Hellanodikai* retreated and Theagenes spread his legs and planted them firmly. With his arms at his sides, Theagenes awaited the Theban's first blow. Standing there like that, he appeared as a bronze colossus, fearless in the face of any adversary.

I am not a boxer, but given one chance to topple this giant of a man, I would have struck upward on his chin with as much power as I could muster. The Theban had other thoughts, and as I watched him deliver his blow, it occurred to me that his motivation for declaring *klimax* may not have been the most inspired for it appeared not born of courage and cleverness, but rather of stupidity. He crouched low as if he were a toad and leveled his right arm at Theo's groin. A blow there was strictly forbidden, so I wondered at his antics. Keeping his arm straight and locked at the elbow, the Theban pulled it down, back and up... down, back and up, describing a circle in the air. The speed of the rotation increased and with no warning, like the squatting toad he appeared to be, the Theban leapt high into the air and brought his closed fist down hard on the crown of Theagenes' head. Even though there were other matches in progress, all eyes turned to watch the Theban with great curiosity; the crowd erupted in laughter as he delivered his blow.

Theagenes never budged, and his knees did not buckle or waver. Whatever advantage the Theban hoped to gain from his unorthodox, first strike, failed to accomplish the intended result. He withdrew one step and gathered himself to await the counter-blow from Theagenes.

With no preamble, Theagenes pointed menacingly at his opponent with his left arm and cocked his right arm from his cheek, much like an archer would pull his bowstring. With lightening speed, his arm flew forward, straight as a battering ram, and his fist landed squarely in the center of the Theban's chest. The smack of the leather *himantes* straps on bone was loud and audible, as the thin layer of skin on the Theban's chest did nothing to soften the strike. He stumbled backwards, fell on his buttocks and lay sprawled on his back gasping for air. The force of the blow had stolen the Theban's breath and he writhed like an inverted turtle struggling to regain it. He rolled to one side and made a feeble effort to rise but could not. The pain that shot through his chest as his arm sought purchase on the ground was excruciating, and he collapsed unconscious to the earth. I was to learn that Theagenes' blow broke the hard bone that protects a man's internal organs and the splintered shards of ribs had punctured the Theban's lungs. He would fight no more that day, nor ever again. His trainer rushed quickly to kneel at his side and waved for assistance. Nothing could be done to relieve the boxer's pain and the trainer followed solemnly as two men took hold of the Theban's legs and dragged him from the field of combat.

The presiding *Hellanodikai* raised Theagenes' arm and escorted him to the designated waiting area. Theagenes took a seat and watched the remainder of the first fights with no great interest. It mattered not to him who remained as victors, for he was prepared to defeat them all. The initial bouts were completed within an hour. No man won faster than Theagenes, and he rested as the others fought to completion. Though never knocked from his feet, even Euthymos received more than one heavy blow that rattled his brain and one froze him briefly in a state of confused disorientation. He managed to recover quickly and dispatched his opponent with a hard punch to the man's forehead that rendered his opponent unconscious and unable to continue the fight. Euthymos was breathing hard as he sat down not far from Theagenes. Neither looked at the other.

As soon as all of the initial pairs had completed their first match, the judges filled the silver urn with the lots, this time only 18, as half the field of competitors had fallen.

Lachesis continued to smile and kept the two favorites apart.

I enjoy the sport, but I will concede that the brutality of the event exceeds the grace, power and agility that these athletes possess. The afternoon wore on. Although a bear of a man from Attica had tested Euthymos, Theagenes fought each opponent quickly and expertly so that no match lasted longer than the time it takes to walk two stades. In that way, he was able to earn a few minutes of rest and keep his eye on Euthymos. Boxing results in many injuries, and all competitors drew blood from their opponents, most often from the orifices of the head: the nose, the ears, the eyes and most certainly the mouth. More than one man finished the day with fewer teeth in their proper places. Due to his size and superior defensive skills that were founded on his quickness—the only man more formidable in the stadium than a big man is a quick, big man, and such was Theagenes—Theagenes was cut far less than his opponents or any other competitors in the stadium. Perhaps those he faced saw his reaction to the first man who did manage to land a solid blow to his mouth that drew a thin trickle of blood.

Theagenes' third opponent was a man of medium height who possessed quickness that rivaled the Thasian's. I overheard a man nearby me comment that the boxer built his muscles in the quarries close to Athens; this explained his exceptionally large biceps and thighs. Look no farther than young Episcles there, and you will see what I mean.

By the third match, the number of contestants was odd, and so one man was *ephedros*. I grimaced and Hiero smiled as the Lokrian drew the odd bean for the third, fourth and fifth matches that led up to the final contest. How can this be, I thought, for he was only required to fight one match in the last games at Olympia? It was uncanny that such luck would fall his way, but the gods had decreed it so!

Your land of the Pharaohs crawls with the cobra, so too do the wet lands at the farthest ends of the earth that Xerxes called his Empire. It is a creature that delivers death faster than a man can blink his eyes. Many years ago, I met a strange merchant from a distant place in the Mede Empire, and he carried with him, in a cage, a weasel-like creature that he would pit against the cobra for entertainment. Men would place their bets on the cobra for it was sleek and known for its lethal movement. No man would back the furry weasel believing the rodent to be at a disadvantage merely because it moved on four legs. I saw it myself in the *agora* in Athens. The creature was quick and cagey. It would circle the cobra and wait for its moment. Though the snake struck many times, it never found its mark.

Theagenes reminded me of this odd creature, for his success was not due solely to his size and strength, but to his quickness as well, and his ability to make good decisions without hesitation. Like the animal from the east, Theagenes circled his opponent and deftly dodged attempted strikes but for one time, when he moved directly into the path of the Athenian's lucky punch. The blow glanced off the side of the Thasian's face but caught enough of his lip to draw blood. At the sight of the scarlet drops, the Athenian stepped back as in shock that he had wounded the mighty Theagenes. Theagenes felt the wetness with his upper lip and raised his *himantes* to wipe the area. He saw the red smears on the leather straps and tasted the saltiness of his own blood. I sensed it was of no consequence to Theagenes who had undoubtedly bled before in his countless battles, but when he looked up and saw the Athenian standing with his arms at his sides and a mute look of surprise on his face, Theagenes struck like the weasel would the cobra. He delivered the blow to the man's left shoulder with such speed and power that the Athenian's arm was dislodged from its shoulder socket and hung uselessly at his side, the limp fingers dangling well below his knee and seemingly held to his hands by the *himantes*. As Theagenes prepared to finish the task, the Athenian raised two, functional fingers on his right hand and conceded the match without further physical damage to his lopsided body.

Well into the day, only the two rivals remained: Euthymos, who had only fought the first two matches, and Theagenes. I stared at Theagenes with awe and some respect knowing that he had survived almost seven hours on the stadium floor. Though he defeated most of his opponents quickly, his opponent in his last fight before the final fought well, and the bout lasted for twenty minutes. Theo pummeled his opponent with a never-ending rain of blows, yet the man, a Boetian, refused to submit and continued to rise to his feet each time he was knocked violently to the ground. More than once, the *Hellanodikai* asked, almost pleaded if the man was ready to submit. He waved them aside and gave them no notice and continued to move forward into the hail of Theagenes' blows spurred on by the crowd who acknowledged his courage with wild cheers. Mercifully, Theagenes ended the fight with a series of three, solid blows to the man's head, swollen now to the size of a pumpkin. He fell for a final time, senseless, and crawled to the edge of the stadium where he collapsed unconscious.

Euthymos appeared the fresher of the two for he had rested nearly four hours since the conclusion of his second match, which lasted nearly an hour. During that fight, he and his opponent moved from left to right and back, each trying to gain an advantage from the sun. Watching that peculiar dance, I imagined a runner sprinting through the countryside for an equal time. I knew that the runner's chest would burn like fire, just like that of Euthymos and his opponent, but for the same hour, the boxers kept their arms raised high in defense and struck out many blows and received a sizeable portion, one from the other. It was a brutal test of endurance, for every muscle and every organ in their bodies worked wildly and their labor was not restricted solely to their chests and legs like the runner's was. As well, it was a test of their mental acuity, their determination and their will to win. I grieved that one of the finalists would lose and secretly hoped it would be the Lokrian so as to secure my double payment from Hiero.

But at last, a disappointment to no one, Theagenes and Euthymos faced each other in the center of the stadium. They talked only with their eyes.

"And so, our wager is still alive," Hiero nudged me and smiled. With bravado he added, "I'll give you a final chance to cancel our bet. I have great confidence in Euthymos. He has worked his muscles well during his time on the stadium floor and has sharpened his skills. He is well rested and as *ephedros* has studied the Thasian through three matches. He is ready to take down the bear cub."

My attention remained directed at the two boxers and I simply shook my head 'no.' I am certain that Hiero expected me to make him a similar offer to void the bet, and he probably would have accepted it if I had. True, Theagenes had expended more energy, but to my eyes, he appeared to have more left in his muscles to consume. There had been no evidence of the Thasian's anger all afternoon, only his strength and endurance. He appeared in full control of his emotions and his mind was focused sharply on the task at hand. Both men were covered with dust that clung to the sweat that ran profusely from Theagenes and the sweat and dried blood that did the same from Euthymos. Heat had settled in the valley, and it amused me to think that I was sweating more than Theagenes.

Even though he was well rested, Euthymos had been forced to work hard in his two matches and he needed the respite, but the hot sun may have taken its toll as well. I could see that his right eye remained swollen shut and obscured his vision. The blood from his nose and mouth had congealed and the flow had stopped hours ago, but the now ruddy streak extended from his head even to his groin. One of the many red welts on his sides had turned an ugly, deep blue; it had to be tender and painful. I could see no way in which the Lokrian could vanquish the Thasian.

Forty thousand voices roared when the *Hellanodikai* signaled for the final match to begin. It was as if two armies, and not just two men, were about to clash.

Rather than assume a defensive posture, Theagenes remained upright with his hands clenched at his sides. Whether or not Euthymos suspected some trickery, I do not know, but he crouched low and circled to his left so as to afford himself a better look at his opponent through his one, good eye. As Euthymos moved around his opponent, Theagenes remained still; he did not even turn his head to follow the man who was intent on removing his skull from his shoulders. In a short time, Euthymos had completed a full circle around the Thasian and faced him again. Neither man had thrown a single punch. Euthymos stayed low in his crouched stance and repeated the maneuver a second time, probably thinking that at some point, Theagenes would turn, cat-like, and attempt to deliver his first blow. It did not happen, and once again Euthymos had moved a full circle around Theagenes with neither man striking out against the other.

The spectators on the hill, myself included, knew not what to make of Theagenes' unusual strategy. Unlike the others, I was not inclined to add my 'hiss' of disapproval at the lack of action for I knew that soon enough, the battle would be joined. For now, the dance continued. After three complete circles around Theagenes, Euthymos stood up straight and turned toward the crowd with his arms extended like a supplicant in the temple. Theagenes' quiescence swayed the crowd to side with his opponent and it began to chant, "Euthymos, Euthymos."

"It appears that your man is not prepared to fight," Hiero said to me above the noise. It was at this moment, with Euthymos's back to him, that I expected Theagenes to strike. It would be a dastardly deed, but one that would be sure to bring him victory, and there was no rule against it.

But I breathed more easily when he did not, for the champion should win with honor and not deception.

Again, Euthymos faced his opponent and crouched low. This time, however, much to the delight of the crowd, when he was behind Theagenes, he delivered a crushing blow, that landed loud and hard between the Thasian's shoulder blades. Theagenes staggered forward one step, regained his balance and reassumed his upright posture. He allowed Euthymos two more undefended strikes, one to his abdomen, a wallop that doubled him over, and one to his head that knocked him off his feet. He was inviting disaster with every undefended blow. Perspiration and blood splattered on the white garment of the nearest spectator. Without declaring *klimax*, Theagenes had unexpectedly given his opponent three clear opportunities to deliver his most powerful blows. He staggered to his feet, blood flowing freely from the corner of his right eye. The crowd quieted, shocked by the strange direction the final match had taken.

Theagenes pointed his right index finger toward the face of the Lokrian and said loudly enough for those nearby to hear, myself included, "You are not Lampis. I have given you three opportunities to win this match as Euthymos. You have failed. Now I attack you as I would have assaulted the Spartan had he not fled these games like a frightened girl." The spectators from Lakonia shouted all sorts of derogatory things; others joined them. They shook their fists in the air, and one even threw a sharp stone that struck Theagenes on his thigh and drew blood. Those nearby quickly restrained the man. The nasty wound was more of a gash than a cut. Such an act had never occurred at the games, and the *Hel-*

lanodikai were confused and did not know how to respond. Should the match continue? Should Euthymos be disqualified by the actions of a zealous man he didn't even know?

Theagenes answered the unspoken questions from the crowd of spectators when one of the *Hellanodikai* asked if he was prepared to continue. "Back away," he ordered the officials with a wave of his wrapped hand. As they obeyed, he turned to face Euthymos and cried, "Defend yourself, pretender to this crown of olive. Only if the gods are with you, can you hope to survive. If you must rely only on your own skill and courage, you will not."

Theagenes' comment was ominous. Each contest in every event is a celebration of life over death, though it is rare that a man actually dies in these or any games. It is a symbolic celebration where the victor lives and those he defeats die. Still, Theagenes did not hide his purpose in the tone of his voice or in the fire that flashed from his eyes. After giving Euthymos a more than fair chance to win the match, or at least to inflict three, debilitating blows, Theagenes no longer saw Euthymos before him; he saw Lampis whom his heart was bent to fight for the weeks and months leading up to these Olympic games. He felt robbed of his personal victory by the premature departure of the Spartan, and now Euthymos would be the target of his wrath. Perhaps Hiero was correct, I thought; maybe the Thasian's anger would blind him more than the Sicilian's swollen eye did him. Every man in Olympia waited to find out as the maelstrom commenced with the fury of Charybdis. I held my breath and wondered if even Odysseus could escape the violence of the storm before me on the stadium floor.

Theagenes dominated Euthymos in a match that lasted into the fading light. Even Helios seemed reluctant to drive his chariot behind the hills to the northwest until the outcome was certain. I must report, Euthymos was not without his moments of brilliance that lured the crowd into thinking that perhaps he could win the fight after all. I could see that the gash in the Thasian's leg affected Theagenes in two ways: he lost much blood which weakened him as the match drew on; it also hobbled him and disrupted his balance and dulled the quickness he used to dispatch his earlier opponents. But each time Euthymos would deliver what would be considered a paralyzing blow to any normal man, Theagenes answered from deep within himself with a counter-blow that matched the fury and violence that boiled like harpies from the one he had just absorbed. None of the earlier fights could compare to the havoc wreaked by these two men upon each other, and the spectators cheered appreciatively. Whichever man survived was indeed the greatest boxer in the world. As good as they say this Lampis was, it was difficult for me to imagine that any human was as tough of mind, body and spirit as either of these two.

Each man was bloodied and panting heavily, trying to draw the one breath that would afford him the strength to outlast the other. But after an hour that saw each man knocked to the ground more than once—and Euthymos more often than Theagenes—Theagenes' fist landed squarely on the left eye of Euthymos, blinding him completely as the flesh around both eyes was now swollen like the eggs of large birds, and red and flaming with pain.

Euthymos stumbled forward and fell to the ground, his balance affected by his inability to see. I thought of Polyphemus, the blinded Cyclops, and victim to the clever Odysseus. I prayed that Euthymos would stay on the ground and concede the fight to the giant that loomed above him, tired and marked himself, but still dangerous and threatening.

The chants of the crowd were split between two names, but neither was Theagenes. On the one hand, they cried "Euthymos, Euthymos!" On the other, the Spartan contingent had enlisted others to yell out much louder than their numbers would suggest they could, "Lampis, Lampis!" I was frightened by the effect the sound of that hated name could have upon Theagenes. Inspired to reach deeply for his last breaths of energy, Euthymos rose to one knee, gathered himself and struggled to rise to his feet whereupon he flailed aimlessly with his arms hoping to strike a lucky blow. It did not happen. Theagenes easily dodged the aimless arms of his opponent and delivered a thunderous right hand to Euthymos's mid-section that knocked what little air he had into the wind. Bent over, gasping and teetering, but refusing to fall again to the ground, Euthymos was totally exposed to the left hand that Theagenes delivered with murderous force to the side of his head. The Lokrian's knees buckled and he crashed to the ground like a giant tree that falls and shakes the earth. He lay there motionless save for the ever so slightly rising and falling of his chest as his body struggled to fill itself with air.

The *Hellanodikai* moved timidly forward to examine the fallen boxer. Even with his eyes swollen shut, the judges could tell that Euthymos had lost consciousness. The match was over; mercifully, it would last no longer. One *Hellano-dikai* raised Theagenes' heavy arm into the darkening sky.

The spectators voiced no joy, nor did Theagenes express any outward satisfaction at the result. His trainer rushed to greet him as he moved slowly from the stadium floor. Despite its eagerness to feast, the crowd remained hushed and watched silently as his trainer helped Euthymos to his feet. The fallen champion stumbled unsteadily and fell again, but managed to assume an awkward sitting position on the ground. It pains me to say he looked foolish. The crowd left him there and slowly abandoned the Hill of Kronos turning its back to Theagenes in silence.

This evening would be the grand feast, but at that moment there was little gladness in Olympia. One man stood victorious, but at what cost to his opponents? This man Theagenes had not merely out-boxed his challengers with superior skill and endurance, he punished them as if each had a part in some conspiracy contrived so the Spartan, Lampis—would who not fight—could maintain the reputation he had earned in the past year throughout the land. What personal price had Theagenes paid, what cost to his integrity as a human being? We cheer the respect two combatants extend to each other even in the heat of combat, but in these contests, the ultimate winner showed none for his opponents and thus gained no honor in return.

I lost sight of Theagenes as he walked slowly from the stadium toward the *altis*. I sensed that the victory to him was as hollow as an empty water gourd. I glanced back a final time at Euthymos and returned with Hiero to our quarters to prepare for the evening feast.

CHAPTER NINE

The Journey Continues

I had lost track of time, and the night was late. We had all satisfied our hunger in sumptuous style, though I did more talking than I did eating, and we owed great gratitude to our host. I was satisfied that my tale, though far from finished, had entertained Khepri and my Thasian companions. Xeno watched me intently but never betrayed to our host his apparent hatred for the subject of my story. More likely, because of Theagenes' ill demeanor as I related it at Olympia, Xeno took some satisfaction from the story though I am certain he would have been happier had Euthymos beaten Theo senseless.

Khepri stifled a yawn and said, "Forgive me, Simonides, it has been a long day for this merchant. Had it not been for your exciting story, I fear I would have succumbed to sleep long ago."

I smiled to relieve his embarrassment and said, "The hour is late and we must all rest for our journey."

"Unfortunate, but true," he responded. "But I must know: how did Theagenes conduct himself when he received his crown? Surely there was controversy at the presentation?"

I rose from my pillows and stretched. "The answer is not a simple one, but I am certain you will find it even more interesting than my story of his victory in the stadium; the same will be true for these men who claim him as a countryman. If it pleases you, I will continue the tale tomorrow as we sail north to Thasos."

"Indeed you shall," he said, "and that alone shall be your fare for the voyage."

I bowed appreciatively and departed with my companions.

We rose from our mats early and met Khepri at the dock. His boat was larger than most merchant vessels in the harbor attesting to the success he had enjoyed through his years of prosperous trade. It was a sturdy craft and promised us a safe and comfortable voyage to Thasos. A crew of five sailors manned the boat, and two of those shared duties at the rudder. Five other men, all dark, accompanied Khepri from port to port to haul cargo on and off the ship. Most merchants do not travel with such men; rather they hire them at each port as necessary. I favored Khepri's approach. His laborers appeared happy men and not discontent in the manner of most slaves who were handled like beasts of burden and resigned to a life of servitude far from their homelands. Khepri had learned to regard his workers in such a way that their deportment expressed open appreciation for the tasks to which they were assigned. They bore no marks of cruelty so often seen on the backs of such men. All the while that they worked, these men sang songs. Similar songs I recalled from Piraeus, but they were coalesced amid the other noises that surround the large Athenian harbor so they were vague and indistinct. Here at Aulis, I listened closely, for the meter of their songs was much different than what we Hellenes know. Their music made me smile for it expressed great energy and happiness with the labor they were engaged in. Though I could not understand the words, the syllables blended well with the melody and the driving rhythm made my heart beat faster and lifted my spirits.

We would not encounter open water for a day. Our journey would take us to the north and west, up the gulf from the Euripos Strait that separates the mainland from the large island of Euboea to its east. The phenomenon of the water's flow is strange and unnatural for it changes direction and speed with great frequency. No man has yet to provide an explanation, but some say it happens most often when Selene is but a sliver in the sky. The strait separates the north and south arms of the Euboean Gulf, and the water flows between them from one to the other at different times and on different days. Khepri's crewman had studied the phenomenon for years and the previous night had determined that today, the water would flow into the northern gulf creating a current that would push us toward our goal with the help of what wind raced between the island and the mainland. There is safety in a position from which one can see land on both sides of the vessel. We would enjoy it for such would not be the case when we rounded the Cape of Artemisium and headed into the Aegean in a day or two.

The small harbor was busy as other ships prepared to depart as well, but due to the size of our broad sail and the skill of Khepri's crew, we were soon on our way catching the current of the water as well as the wind and out-distanced them all. We watched, as they became specks on the water behind us.

The ride was smooth and gave not the slightest reason for a man to take ill, though I noticed the color slowly receding from young Xeno's face leaving it pale and ashen. I could see him struggle to hold his small breakfast of bread and fruit, and when it was obvious that he could not, Khepri escorted him down the high platform upon which we sat at the rear of the boat and ushered him forward. Khepri's timing was precise. As they reached the prow, Xeno leaned forward and out, toward the island side of the boat, and spewed a colorful but foul-smelling eruption of undigested food into the vessel's wake. Parmenides, Cimon, Episcles and I took guilty pleasure in the young man's misery. One of the crewmen wrapped a rope around Xeno's waste and anchored it on a heavy barrel filled with grain.

"Sometimes a forward position can put a newcomer at ease," Khepri commented as he returned to the platform to join us. "He'll be fine."

An occasional spray from the bow rose high in the air, even to our position, and I found the wetness and the taste of the salt water refreshing as I licked it from my lips.

The crew was in total control of the vessel and worked with the elements to insure us a safe and rapid passage to our final destination. "Is it always so smooth and uneventful?" Episcles asked once we were well on our way.

"Not always," Khepri conceded. "You will not think it such if we should encounter a storm, or worse yet, pirates when we enter open water." He saw the look of anxiety come to Cimon and Episcles and added to calm them, "But fear not. My seamen understand the weather and watch for the signs that their gods give them. We expect no adverse weather, at least for now. As for the pirates, none dare pass the Cape at Artemisium for they know that they would be trapped in this narrow gulf where an Athenian trireme could make easy work of capturing them, or worse yet, ramming them to the bottom of the sea. I suspect we'll see our naval guardians on the other side of the cape tomorrow or the following day. As for tonight, we'll sail to ground in a sheltered port we know well on the north end of the island before we round it and head into open water." Khepri stared at the land as it passed by us, then at his sail. "Your gods are kind," he said, "We're making good speed and can reach our objective well before nightfall if all goes well."

Khepri had made this journey before and we watched his crew as they managed the craft with ease and kept it moving without deviation up the center of the channel. There were enough clouds in the sky to protect us from the sun so we remained on the upper deck though we could always move into the hold for protection against any elements the gods might toss in our path.

The farther north we moved, the more my mind wandered to events that occurred in the waters before us not too many years past. Late in the afternoon, the channel narrowed before us and we turned away from the mainland and toward the island Euboea where we were greeted by the calm waters of a peaceful harbor with wide beaches covered in white, chalky sand. As we veered toward our destination for the night, I stared west at the cliffs that plunged a hundred feet from the mainland to the rocky shoreline below. Not far from the land that loomed on our left like a dark curtain in the distance, the ancient Phocians built a wall to protect their land against northern invaders from Thessaly. Up above those cliffs overlooking the Malian Gulf, Leonidas and his 300 Spartans clashed with the Persian Immortals while in the very waters we would cross tomorrow, on the north side of the island, Themistocles and his Athenian triremes battled the Persian fleet at Artemisium. I stared at the bulk of our vessel, slow and cumbersome, like a giant turtle, and wondered what sound it made when thrust with the battering ram of a trireme. How long would it stay afloat? I strained to hear the distant sound of wood as it snapped before the bronze beak of a trireme; I heard nothing, but I knew the sounds were there, like ghosts who would not abandon their earthly shells. They remained here in these waters much like the spectral sounds of combat that would refuse to abandon the cliffs above us on our left. They would haunt this land forever. I could smell death like I did years ago at Thermopylae. I thought of fallen leaves, dry and brittle with a musty aroma; that is what death smells like to me. It would never leave this place. The images I saw above those cliffs were painted forever in my mind. Perhaps my breath came shorter, or my eyes misted from the recollection of what I had seen. My physical reaction did not go unnoticed.

"Relax, Simonides," Parmenides said to me as he rested his hand on my shoulder. "Within minutes your feet will find the firmness of the land." I shook unpleasant thoughts from my head knowing that I would share them on the beach with Khepri and the others when we supped in the evening. I smiled and nodded as if to confirm to Parmenides that my body was only reacting to the long hours aboard the ship.

Khepri's crew captured the momentum the tide and wind afforded us and steered us toward the beach. In a simple and coordinated motion, they lowered the sail, and the vessel rotated sideways to the shore and slowed to the pace of a walking man. A half-stade from the shore, we felt the underside of the boat scrape the bottom; the rudder had already been pulled. The vessel tilted slightly toward the island.

"We have arrived at our first port," Khepri announced. "The tide will continue to recede for many hours. As the channel fills again, early in the morning, we will float out of the harbor and be on our way again. For now, we make camp."

Khepri himself extended a ladder from the side of the boat into the water. He was the first to descend, and the water reached only to his waist. Satisfied, he beckoned me to follow. The crew had already retrieved a portion of his tent-works from below decks, along with the necessary items to prepare our evening meal on shore. I turned to grasp something, a cooking pot, to relieve their burden, but Khepri waved his arms to gain my attention. "I'll not allow it, great poet." He commanded. "I've made my bargain with you: Your fare is your story, and I think you have much left to tell. I treat these men well for their service. They will do the work for you are my guest."

Parmenides took the pot from my arms, "You go ahead," he suggested, "We'll help with what we can."

I lowered myself into the warm water of the small, secluded harbor and waded with Khepri to the beach. The others followed shortly, and soon the tent had been raised and the cooking fire struck. The aroma of a fish stew drifted among us reminding me that we had not eaten since our early meal. I heard my own stomach make a rumbling noise in anticipation of the evening's sustenance. "Have no concern for our safety," Khepri commented. "This beach will be ours alone tonight for no other ship that sailed this morning will reach this spot tonight. Any ship traveling in the opposite direction will find harbor on the north side of the island."

The moon rose brightly that night as the last light of day passed from the cloudless sky. The land was so illumed by Selene's silver chariot that a man could walk upon it freely with full sight of any obstacle that might be in his path. The heavens were filled with the sparkling torches of the gods. We dined on the open beach that grew even larger as the tide continued to ebb; I saw that our ship, though still in the water, canted slightly toward the sea as if it yearned to free itself from the soft sand upon which it sat. The land rose behind us, and my eyes were drawn to the clear silhouette of the rough hills that stood in contrast to the smooth, level beach, which cooled our feet. I easily spotted the star that remains motionless in the heavens, Polaris, which guides Apollo to the comfort of his Hyperborean brothers. Those hills beckoned to me and I knew that if I sat atop them, I could look west, across the channel and spot the Trachinian Cliffs that guard the Hot Gates. It was there where three Spartan men I met ever so briefly and their comrades summoned every ounce of courage within their brave hearts to withstand the insurmountable odds that the King of Persia raised against them less than 10 years earlier. Would I be here now, I thought, had the lion not been sacrificed at Thermopylae?

"It is a beautiful site, is it not?" Khepri asked when his bowl was cleaned.

I answered only with a wistful smile.

Not understanding the depth of my thoughts, for he had no way to know them, Khepri stated, "It is time, Simonides, for you to continue the tale. We know Theagenes as a great boxer, and you have explained how he won the competition."

Episcles interrupted innocently and enthusiastically, "This is true, Khepri, but he may have been even stronger in the *pankration*." He turned to me and said, "Tell us, Simonides, after the boxing competition, did Theo have the strength to compete in the *pankration*?"

"I suspect he did, young Epi," I answered, "but he refused to compete further at these games." I sighed and added, "He left like a thief in the night."

Xeno had waited for days to hear words of derision slip from my tongue to attack the object of his anger. He was quick to comment and became more animated than he had been since we embarked from Aulis. "And there you have said it, poet. The great Theagenes was but a common burglar!"

"Not quite so." I answered. "Even a poet can choose his words poorly, and in this case I have." I glanced in the direction of the hills behind us and said, "Selene will bless us with her silver light for many more hours. The hills behind us beckon me like Circe and I must heed the call. You, Xeno, more than the others must join me, for there is no other place from which to continue my tale than at the crest of those hills." I opened my arms to Khepri and the Thasians, "Please join me, if you will. If not, it will only be Selene and I who contemplate past events this night." No one there could have known why I was compelled to mount the hills on the cape. Still, the passion in my voice lured them to follow as I turned and walked toward a path I could clearly see that worked its way effortlessly through the rocks and up the slope. Khepri and the Thasians followed.

The days of rest had strengthened my legs and I, the oldest of the six who climbed, made my way to the top with no difficulty. As I had hoped, we crested the hill and walked two stades across a flat plain to the far side where cliffs, not hills plunged precipitously to the rocky shoreline beneath us. Even from our height, we could hear the waves in the distance as they beat against the rocks below. The narrow channel flowed to the west into the Gulf of Malis; to the east, it followed the headland of the island past Artemisium to the Aegean. The brilliant moon cast its pure light on the world, and the water shimmered as it reflected Selene's lovely visage.

Overwhelmed by the sight, I fell to my knees and pointed to the cliffs that framed the southern edge of the Malian Gulf. "There," I said solemnly, "On those heights are the Hot Gates where men of exceptional courage gave their lives to defend the freedom we Hellenes cherish above all other possessions." I extended my right arm to the eastern channel that bordered the northern edge of Euboea. "And there, while Leonidas bled at Thermopylae, the Athenian triremes attacked the Persian navy while the gods sent strange winds to shatter Xerxes' boats on the beaks of Themistocles' triremes or on the giant rocks that line the northern coast of the island. Here was our freedom defended."

"Each man preserves his own freedom," Xeno remarked, "And it cannot be said that Hellas owes its freedom to these events."

His statement offended me and I rose, angrily to say as much. "Each man preserves his own freedom, Xeno, but together, men define and maintain their way of life and protect it from those who would take it away, a concept you Thasians know nothing about." My brief tirade was sharp and pointed. "If I offend you, so be it. Though I've not been to your island myself, I have heard it said that Thasos is protected by strong and high walls of stone that no man or army can penetrate; yet you opened your gates to Xerxes like lambs to the wolves. Did you offer any resistance, any at all? Did you detest your life that much that you would allow another to impose his own upon you?"

Parmenides was the first to speak, "No, Simonides, we did not. Many of us, including these two here, Cimon and Episcles, fled to the interior mountains of the island, and the Medes did not follow for they were content to force their presence only on the harbor. Shamefully I agree: others among us welcomed the invaders." He looked directly at Xeno. "You were even more a boy then than you remain today. And your brother, too, had not more than 14 years. I can find no fault in you as a boy, but your family...." His voice faded, reluctant to utter the final words. "Your family," he forced himself to conclude, "made a small fortune by serving the Medes and satisfying their every whim. While we huddled in the woods, your family, and others like it, bartered with the sons of Persia. You have spoken your childish mind, Xeno. Your family indeed preserved its personal sense of freedom in willingly accepting the hand of the Medes, and truly Hellas owes no debt to Thasos in its fight for freedom. Your act of submission was an act of preservation, that much cannot be denied, but it was a selfish act for your own, personal benefit, and not an act on behalf of all men who call themselves Hellenes."

Khepri filled the void of silence that followed. "You Thasians, then, must be a forgiving people," he said, "for here you are together, with no malice from one to the other. Three men who fled to the mountains and one who lives in luxury from saving his own skin." He patted Xeno's shoulder and concluded in a conciliatory manner, "We merchants are known for our sense of preservation as well as our eye to exploit the woes of other men. The flaw in our characters serves our purses, but I admit it may not be something to take pride in."

Xeno appreciated the Egyptian's mollifying words, but I was not so willing to let Khepri's water douse the fire. "From my point of view, you should be ashamed of your actions in that regard, particularly you and your family, Xeno." I could even feel the heat and passion of the events that occurred ten years ago brush my face as I gazed again across the water to the cliffs on the mainland. As they did, they steeled my heart against the little men like Xeno. I call them driftwood for they are incapable of making their own ways in life; rather they are pushed and pulled by events with no will or desire to resist and set their own course. It is a miserable way to travel through life.

"My presence here among you," I continued, "relates directly to those events of years past, and it is because of those events that your island feels the burden of famine. The Pythia has told you such even though you are blind to the truth of which she speaks. I bid you sit with me here and gaze upon that holy site across the strait while I tell you of one Thasian who knows the depth and meaning of the sacrifice that was made there."

CHAPTER TEN

Thermopylae

Though I had faithfully and enthusiastically attended each Olympiad for as long as I can remember, I only attended one other after that one, the 76th, and solely with the hopes of renewing my friendship with Theagenes. Though I saw him win the *pankration* that year, no words passed between us, only a single glance of recognition as I stood in the crowd at the presentation of awards. That knowing look was enough for both of us.

While the games were profitable to me, money is not the sole or primary reason for which I attended. I have other venues to make my life comfortable through my writings. The games, all the games from Olympia to Nemea and beyond, simply provide an easier market in which to vend my talents.

No, my motivation to attend the games has never been based exclusively upon my ability to make money. As a young boy, I saw my first games with my father. It was there that my soul was bound inextricably to the courage and valor of these men who publicly risk life, limb and reputation for the glory of their names. I follow the games because I love the athletes and I love to mingle with them.

I still remember the boxer from Opuntian, Rexibyos, who won the crown at the first games I attended. His statue made of fig wood still stands in the *altis*. He winked at me when I was a little boy sitting atop my father's shoulders for a better view!

More than once I have seen Milo, the great wrestler of Kroton who won the competition through five Olympiads. Milo conducted himself with dignity each time he received the crown. I respected him for his talent and for his humility at the award ceremony. Nonetheless, he tricked me! I learned that Milo was a vain man. Tales of his conceited antics became legendary. I talked with his trainer once, an old man with disfigured ears named Pythagoras. Pythagoras trained Milo not only in the art of wrestling, but in the art and grace of handling himself as a worthy victor. He told me many years ago that it was important for Milo and all athletes to suffer and endure the great pains that accompany their regimens, but to avoid the pride that often comes with victory. Pythagoras believed, as I do, that our heroes should be the noblest of men and purest of character. In this respect, he had failed with the wrestler. Alas, Milo is not the only Olympic champion who has allowed his success to muddle his mind.

I feared that Theagenes, for all his physical prowess and success, lacked the character that should be expected of a true Olympic champion. Everything I had witnessed told me so, and it pained me to see such a gifted man belittle himself by his regrettable actions both inside and outside the stadium. My personal journey with Theagenes began the night of his victory over Euthymos...

It was a night of celebration that drew all men closer together and caused them to forget, at least for a few hours, what had happened in the *pyx* that day. The great sacrifice to Zeus had been completed and the meat from the offerings freely distributed throughout the city and the encampment that surrounded it.

The feasting that night was magnificent, and I am certain no man hosted a finer banquet than my friend Hiero did. His guests included the entire field of charioteers who had raced the previous day. Charioteers are a more sophisticated sort than the other athletes at the games, for their competence in their sport is not so much dependent upon their muscles, but more so on their brains. They rely upon their wits and their ability to manage and coordinate up to 16 hoofs pounding at breakneck speed. A charioteer can only be successful if he can teach his team to operate as one, single organism working in concert to drive quickly and safely around the frantic Hippodrome. To be a charioteer, a man needs courage—and money. No other sport requires the equipment of a charioteer. They are wealthy men.

The wine flowed freely as the evening festivities proceeded, and I could tell there was less water in it than what most men were generally accustomed to. The conversation remained amicable and the infrequent taunts of one charioteer to the other were taken in jest and with no harmful intent. Libations were bountiful and continued well beyond what was generally prescribed for such a banquet and coming together of notable men. No man's thoughts lingered on the outcome of the *pyx*; this was not a time for pensiveness but of celebration free from the burden of deeper notions.

As it did throughout the entire city and encampment, the sound of camaraderie and merriment increased as the stars and constellations rotated through the sky, and then a peaceful quiet took hold as one stellar hero after another slid behind the nearby mountains. I saw eyelids strain to remain open as the day's activities took their toll on the tired and now inebriated celebrants. No one noticed when I took my leave of the banquet, determined that I would find a quiet place to contemplate the epinicion I was hired to compose for my host. I smiled at the thought that in his state of merry inebriation, Hiero had already paid me for the undone work, and it was a handsome sum as a result of Theagenes' victory over the Sicilian. The streets and pathways were empty as I made my way north through the *altis* toward the Temple of Hera. I would pray to the Muses in this sacred grove to inspire my creative energy so that I could compose a work worthy of Hiero's victory—and of his money.

Just beyond the *Pelopeion*, I took a seat on a small, stone bench facing Hera's temple, first to pray, and then to contemplate Hiero's victory and organize my thoughts and words. Unlike many supplicants, I pray with my eyes open, for the signs the gods give us are not confined to the images they weave solely on the tapestries in our minds. Each man has his own way that brings comfort and contentment to this task. I sat very still and made no sound, perhaps I appeared as a statue, like those of heroes past whose stone visages watched the pathway. Deep in reflection, I caught the slightest of movements, perhaps 50 paces to my right, where the treasuries lined the street. It was very dark. The full moon of Karneia would rise soon, but for now only the soft glow of the flame that burned within the temple provided any illumination. I dared not turn my head, but managed to scan the treasuries one by one seeking the cause of my distraction. I saw movement again in the shape of a large, stooped over form that crept suspiciously from the front of one building to the next, pausing briefly to avoid discovery, though from what I could see and sense, there was no one else in the streets, only me and the form I observed attentively. Undetected, I sat motionless and watched the hulking figure take the temple steps two at a time and scamper from pillar to pillar, pausing briefly at each like a mouse scurries through a maze of table and chair legs in search of scraps but always alert to human discovery. When it reached the entrance to the temple, the shape disappeared inside.

My curiosity had diverted my creative efforts and I was determined to discover who this man was and what purpose he had at Hera's temple so late at night. If his cause was noble, he disguised it well.

The olive branches to be presented to the victors on the final day of the celebration were arranged on a gold and ivory table inside the temple. Until that final day, no man, other than the *Hellanodikai*, was allowed within the temple walls. I was certain the phantom I saw enter the building was no *Hellanodikai*. If he were, he would have no cause to skulk. I made no sound to alert the object of my interest as I walked furtively up the temple stairs. Standing in the doorway behind a pillar, not yet prepared to violate the law myself, I squinted through the dim light cast by the candles and recognized the man I followed as your very own Theagenes.

Atop the altar at the far end of the room were spread the olive branches, twelve of them formed into crowns, one for the victor of each event including the three boys' events. There was no prize for second place. Silently, and perhaps stupidly, I crept into the chamber and approached the giant Theagenes whose back was to me. Now two of us had broken the sacred law. My sandaled feet made no sound on the stone floor, and I took my position less than 10 meters behind him and continued to watch. Theagenes stood before the altar and studied each crown even though they were identical in appearance. He moved from one to the other but did not touch them, and I was inclined to think he was merely contemplating the feat he had accomplished. I hoped that in doing so, he could recognize the importance of it and perhaps acknowledge his inappropriate behavior as an Olympic champion. One man, staring at his prize in the solitude of the temple without the distraction of the crowd that would fill and surround it in just a short time. A sense of guilt took hold of me, and I considered leaving as silently as I had entered so as not to disrupt his reverie and meditation.

Then, in a single act that I deemed as utterly blasphemous, Theagenes turned to his right and reached for a crown. I could not prevent the reflexive gasp that escaped my throat. His hand froze before his fingers touched the object of what I thought at that moment was his greed. I saw the muscles in his shoulders flex and rise like mountains. He did not turn but whispered in a feral and menacing way, "Who stands behind me had best stay where he is or prepare to defend himself, for no man will stand between me and what is rightfully mine." He spun around to face me with the same agile movements I witnessed in his matches. His bare fists were raised, more in a position to strike than to defend. When he looked down and saw that it was only I, he dropped his arms to his sides and placed them on his hips. We stared at each other in the shadowy light, neither uttering a word. His eyes glistened as the candlelight flickered from his quick movement. "I remember you, old man, from the baths, the defender of cowards."

I did not respond as I deliberated my course of action as well as my choice of words.

"Why do you sneak up upon me in the darkness unless, of course, you do not value your life?" he asked brusquely.

"I mean no ill will, Theagenes," I answered with some temerity in my voice. "I was meditating outside the temple when I saw a figure steal inside behaving like a man who has no good purpose in mind. It seems I may have been right from the looks of the action you were about to take."

He stared at me a moment longer and then took one of the crowns and placed it carefully in the satchel that was draped over his shoulder. I was unable to conceal my shock at his irreverent act. "Think what you want," he said matter-of-factly, "I only take what is mine."

Like a dumb animal, I refused to move from his path as he walked down the steps. He stopped before me but was reluctant to place a hand upon me. "I have no cause to harm you. What is your name?" he asked.

"Simonides," I answered and continued, "I have neither the will nor the capability to stop you, Theagenes, but I cannot let this theft go without revealing the culprit to the *Hellanodikai*."

"As you wish, Simonides. Do what you will, but for now, remove yourself from my path, or I can do it for you. The choice is yours."

With no desire to be man-handled by the Olympic boxing champion, I told him I would not stand in his way, but I asked only for him to tell me what he was up to. Theagenes was correct: the crown belonged justly to him, but his manner of taking the *athlon* like a common thief was as unorthodox as it was unacceptable. The act begged explanation and I found it reasonable to demand one.

"I have obligation to no one, Simonides. If I am not mistaken, you must be the same Simonides who writes the epinicions so often sung at these games."

"I am he," I responded, and asked again, "Can you please tell me what you are doing here and why you are taking the crown with you now instead of waiting for the ceremony that is planned?"

"You were at the stadium today?" he asked. I nodded. "Then you saw my victory. Hard fought as it was, the victory is empty. Euthymos was a pretender whose time has past. The real challenger to the crown is Lampis, not the Sicilian. I will not place this crown upon my head until such time that I meet the Spartan in combat. He has left like a woman. I will follow, and when I find him we will fight on his terms before the army he has fled to join. I fear neither Lampis nor his countrymen. If the Spartans are the men I think they are, they will welcome the challenge I bring to their champion. When I am finished with him, I will bid him place this crown on my head with his own hands, that is, if his arms have not been broken in our contest." He patted his satchel. "That, then, is my objective, Simonides. I leave now to find Lampis and his countrymen."

I dared to raise my arms before the giant.

"There is another way, Theagenes. There are other games where you and he will undoubtedly meet to determine who is the better man with his fists. I beg you, for your own self-worth: protect your reputation. Return the *athlon* to its place on the altar. No one will know that you were here this night. Accept the crown with an open heart on the morrow, and accept it gratefully and with humility. You will meet Lampis again. Do not be so offended by his absence that you make a thief and fool of yourself before all of Hellas. You will be recognized at these games as the best of all boxers..."

"No I won't," he interrupted, "Even if I allow the *Hellanodikai* to place this crown upon my head, I will know what everyone will be thinking: Theagenes was victorious only because Lampis did not compete. I say the man is a coward, and I will track him down like a runaway dog. I will have my contest with him so that the world knows it is Theagenes, not Lampis, who is the greatest boxer. Now move, Simonides, I must be on my way."

I was certain his course of action would destroy his reputation. Resigned nonetheless to his brazenness and afraid of his muscles, I stepped aside and asked, "But where will you go? Where do you intend to find him?"

He paused and answered, "I've heard it said that he is with his king, Leonidas, and that they march to Thermopylae. That is where I will go. I will follow Lampis to the Hot Gates." Theagenes walked swiftly passed me toward the doorway.

"Please wait," I cried passionately, "I will join you on your journey and bear witness to the contest myself."

"I have no time to wait for you," he called over his shoulder.

"Then I will follow."

"Such is your privilege." The sound of his steps echoed through the temple as he disappeared into the darkness outside.

I cannot say how my mind worked that night or why. Perhaps it was the wine from the celebrations, or more likely some undetected influence by the gods themselves. The logical thing for me to do would have been to return to the comfort of Hiero's lodgings and to rise early the next morning and report the theft to the *Alutarches*. Perhaps I could have called for assistance that very moment and perhaps Theagenes could have been restrained or detained. But those things did not enter my mind. One thought consumed me: I will follow this man to Thermopylae, and I will bear witness to his fight with Lampis. No epinicion could rival what I would compose for the winner, whoever it might be. That single fight would have more emotion in it than any fight ever in the history of sport. Perhaps even Leonidas himself would act as judge of the contest. The allure of the event over-powered my sense of reason. I had to be there. In that instant, no thought of Xerxes or Persians entered my mind. All I could see were the two boxers facing one another within a circle of red-cloaked Spartans, hair blowing wildly and voices raised maniacally in support of their champion. If I did consider my obligation to Hiero, I disregarded it with the thought that I could honor him at a later time. Not completely understanding my own motivation, I raced from the temple to follow Theagenes. Selene had crested the mountains to the east, and I could make out Theagenes as he made his way through the deserted streets. His path would take him within a stone's throw of Hiero's encampment. I ran after him as best I could and overtook him as he approached my lodgings.

"Please," I begged uncharacteristically, "I will get my things and come with you." He seemed not to notice when I pulled on his *chiton*, nor did he acknowledge my presence. I released the fabric and he continued east at a steady pace without saying a word.

I moved quickly to Hiero's quarters. Not a man there remained awake. Loud, drunken snores filled the tents that comprised his encampment. A handful of servants were attempting to clean up around the sleeping bodies. They looked at me with some surprise and I raised my index finger to my lips to quiet them. It took only a moment for me to grab my belongings and secure my satchel. I was back on the avenue in mere seconds and took my bearings in the last direction I saw Theagenes moving. I could still see him, barely, perhaps a stade beyond me, about to depart the tent city and head into the rugged hills beyond. I dared not shout 'Wait' for fear of awakening others who were deep in wine-induced slumber. I followed the course Theagenes had set, the moon in my face. My shadow followed me and gave me comfort; I glanced back at it every now and then to insure I was not alone.

His longer stride, stronger muscles and deeper commitment to the task he had set for himself increased the distance between us with every step – I knew that. Still, I was unswerving in my resolve to follow him to his ultimate confrontation. I found a rhythm to my pace that at least limited the lead that Theagenes continued to build. I suspected he did not know that this old man was following him. Not once did he look back.

In a few hours, the sky lightened to the east, and as it did I realized for the first time, that I had lost track of Theo's bobbing head. How long I had been walking in a tired stupor without seeing him in the distance before me I don't remember... it may have been five minutes, it may have been two hours. My body was weary, but I ignored its cry for rest for our common destination had been made clear: Thermopylae. I fought the urge to stop. In my travels, I had never had reason to visit Thermopylae. I heard, however, that the springs that flowed from the ground there were warm and soothing and brought relief to many a man whose limbs had been knotted and twisted by unknown demons. My friends told me that if man traveled to the northern reaches of our land, he would have two choices: travel over water by boat, or walk through the narrow pass that separated the cliffs from the sea at Thermopylae.

I attempted simple calculations in my head. It was six days since my path had crossed with Lampis and the Spartan *ephor* shortly before I arrived in Olympia. Knowing their reputation on the forced march, they would have joined Leonidas and his vanguard and probably have arrived at Thermopylae two, maybe even three days ago. My mind wandered back to that chance meeting on the road to Olympia when Leon said boldly to me, *"Ready your pen, poet, and not for the victors at these games, but for the brave men of Sparta who will protect your land while this gaggle of cowards gathers at the feet of Zeus. Days from now when the priests carve up the oxen at the temple, think of us and know that we Spartans are doing the same to the Medes."* I had no knowledge of the position of the Persian host, but I believed it could have been possible that the sacrifices at Olympia and Thermopylae were coincident, just as Leon had predicted. At Olympia, I knew for sure that oxen had been set to the sacrificial knife. I wasn't as certain, despite the Spartan's confident boast, who would be the offering at the Hot Gates.

I approached a fork in the road as the first beams from Helios exploded over the mountains and blinded me. I raised my hands to shield my eyes from the glare. I was prepared to take the right fork, which would have led me to Corinth and the Isthmus, but before I took more than 10 steps in that direction, I heard a loud whistle from the rocks well above me and to my left. As my eyes adjusted to the light, I made out the silhouette of a large man who could only have been Theagenes. He was waving from the ridge, perhaps four or five stade from my position at the fork. He signaled to me, I reckoned, to follow, but as I waved back in friendly greeting, he turned and continued his trek north with no obvious intention to wait for me. Frustrated, I took the path to the left with some trepidation. His plan could only be to cut the journey in half by taking a more direct route to the northeast. That route was only feasible provided he could secure passage across the narrow strait that joins the Gulf of Calydon to that of Corinth. He, and therefore I would travel through Achaia in the northern Peloponnese and cross the strait into Aetolia where we would continue moving northeast, to the west of Parnassus, then down the slopes of Kallidromos to the Trachinian Cliffs where sat Thermopylae in a narrow pass on the seaward side of Locris. His plan made some sense but the time he would save could only be guaranteed if he found quick passage across the strait. If the trip would have taken 10 days through the Isthmus, it would take no more than five, maybe even four across the strait. In either event, I believed I had no choice but to remain on his heels as best I could.

I followed the goat path north and saw no other man. At times I thought I heard men and animals scrambling in high pastures, but never did I see a one. The birds were my companions and once I even favored myself to think that a grand eagle soared with me as my guide and protector, but after an hour, he had turned his mind in other directions. The night was cold and the ground was hard as I sat down to rest. I covered my head with my garment. I was tempted to pity myself, for only two nights before, I lay among soft pillows covered with silk, and I filled my stomach with every exotic delicacy I could possibly want. Doubts crept into my mind. Had I embarked on a mission of folly? I had no glimpse of Theagenes since early in the day and now wondered if that had been some ruse of the gods, or had the renegade pugilist just led me astray to abandon me in these cold hills. The wind rippled through the trees and I swear I heard laughter. Was it the *Oreads*, the nymphs of the mountains, come to tease me and mock my foolishness for following Theagenes on this journey whose end was as uncertain as the flight of a startled deer in the forest?

I had enough *maza* to keep my strength up and there was always a stream of fresh and cold water near to the path to quench my thirst. What I lacked now was not nourishment, but the confidence that I had made a wise choice when I followed Theagenes from Olympia. Uncomfortable with the thought that woodland creatures stood just beyond my vision and watched me intently as they licked their chops, or worse yet, that unearthly beings were plotting to take me prisoner, I moved on so that I would not be taken in my sleep.

As the light began to fade on the second day, I descended from the hills to the shoreline and admitted to myself that I had been deceived: Theagenes had no intention to wait for me even if he did come this way. I had no reason to feel betrayed, only duped by a man who had no allegiance to me or anyone else. I fell in a lump on the ragged shoreline of Achaia. I could make out the opposite shore tempting me with its nearness, but it might as well have been on the opposite side of the world if such a land existed. Oh, Tantalos, I said to myself, I feel your eternal pain and suffering. I spotted a lonely hovel a short distance up the coast from where I sat immersed in self-pity. A thin column of smoke wafted above it. As bedraggled a tenement as it might be, I would gladly accept its protection from the cool sea breeze that would soon roll in from the water. I contemplated my predicament. I had been fooled and found myself alone on the rocky coast with no way to the other side. I was a fugitive and I could not return to Olympia or Sicily. I could only imagine the ire that erupted from Hiero when he learned that I was gone and had not composed his epinicion, particularly since he had already paid me for it.

Deep in troubled thought, I was startled when a small stone landed next to me as if it had fallen from the sky. When I looked up into the darkening heavens, I heard laughter behind me and turned to identify its source. It was no nymph or satyr, as I feared.

"What has taken you so long, poet? If your words came as slowly as your steps, you would no doubt starve." It was Theagenes and I found myself more relieved than angered by the thought that he might have tricked me and left me to my woes. "We are in luck," he said without waiting for my reply. "The fisherman who lives in that hut has given me his boat, and has even offered us his supper. He is a bashful man and will not come out to meet you."

Thankful that I was no longer alone, I said, "Then I shall go to meet him and offer my personal appreciation for his generosity." I felt some shame that I had doubted Theagenes' willingness to wait for me, but that feeling waned quickly, overwhelmed by my relief at companionship.

"If you must," he replied off-handedly as he stooped to place a steaming pot on a flat rock.

I entered the hut and saw a young man drawn up in the corner, his arms raised to his head. "Please, sir," he begged, "You are welcome to take what is mine, but please leave me in peace."

I shook my head and placed two drachmas on a small table, the only piece of furniture in the shanty. "We are not thieves," I said and walked back to join Theagenes on the rocky beach.

"Eat heartily, Simonides, for we leave as soon as we are finished." The fish stew the young man had prepared was unseasoned and very bland, but it filled our empty stomachs. I was grateful for it. So grateful, for that matter, that I returned to the hut and tossed two more coins on the table while the young man cringed in the corner.

The boat was small and intended for not more than two men and their catch of fish so it suited us well. The night air remained calm and we did not raise the small sail. Theagenes grasped the two oars and began to pull effortlessly while I seated myself astern and manned the rudder. The moon had not yet risen and the water, land and sky had become one. Still, I fixed my gaze on the North Star and steered a steady course toward it. The gentle rock of the boat caused me to doze and before long, I was asleep, draped over the rudder like a fisherman's wet net. Theagenes made no mention of it and allowed me to rest setting his course by some star to the south and managing to stay on it by the use of his oars. I cannot even say how long the voyage took, but after several hours, the scrape of the boat on the rocky bottom woke me. I tried to act as if I had not avoided my duties as helmsman throughout the trip, but it was of no consequence to Theagenes for we had successfully crossed the strait and thereby cut our time to the Hot Gates in half.

We knew that Xerxes was approaching from the north but could only hope that we were able to reach Lampis and his brothers-in-arms before the Spartans engaged the Medes. We raced against time. If Theagenes were to have his fight against Lampis, we would have to make the Spartan camp before the battle was joined. I am chagrined to admit that our thoughts were not on the war of nations but rather on a single fight between two men, a fight that was the farthest thing from the mind of the Spartan champion. How vain we were to think that a single boxing match was more important than the Spartan mission to halt the progress of the largest army ever assembled by men.

Theagenes dragged the vessel high on the beach and turned it to its side. That done, with hands on hips, a pose he often assumed, he surveyed the land and then, taking his aim by the heavens, pointed to the northeast. "Set your course in that direction, Simonides. You have rested like a babe as we crossed the water. I will sleep for an hour or two to regain my strength. I will follow you when Helios rises. With any luck, I will catch you by midday. Do not tarry, poet. By my reckoning, we can make the Hot Gates in two days' time, but that will be up to you. From here on, you alone set the pace of our journey. If my silent prayers be answered, there has been no encounter with the Medes and Lampis will be well rested when we arrive. If not, then we both will fight with weary arms and tired legs."

I stayed any response I might have made knowing that there would be time to talk when he overtook me later in the day. I only nodded and started to walk with a steady pace in the direction he had indicated.

As I have reluctantly told you, Hiero had given me payment for his unwritten epinicion during the banquet two nights earlier in Olympia. My purse was full but heavier with the shame I felt for having left the city with Hiero's money. I could not undo what had already been done, and in truth, I needed the money.

After several hours, the sky lightened in the east with its cool, violet color, and I chanced upon a small farm in the hills through which I marched. I stopped to draw water from the well and considered that in a short time, Theagenes would be on the path again. Although I disagreed with his chosen course of action, I respected him for what he felt compelled to do, and for that reason, I had no cause to slow him down or delay his confrontation with the Spartan. As I quenched my thirst, the farmer emerged from his house and walked toward me.

"Greetings, traveler," he said cheerfully without a hint of suspicion or fear. "It is rare, indeed, that I find such as you traveling through these hills alone. By all means, take your fill from my well."

"Thank you, kind sir. That I shall, and I will ask if you have *maza* and *opson* that I might buy from you to nourish my tired body."

He smiled, "That I have, and I will gladly share it with you for any news you might have." As Helios had yet to appear above the horizon, I concluded that I could spare a few moments with this man who was eager to talk to anyone other than his fat wife whom I glimpsed in the doorway of the house. From what I could tell, she was not large of frame, just fat for I could see the flesh falling heavily beneath her arms. I would not have expected it of a farmwoman who lived in these remote mountains. I would have thought her body to be lean and hard from daily toil.

"Agreed," I said, and he escorted me to the table that occupied the small courtyard before the doorway. I nodded toward his wife and smiled, but she did not return my greeting.

"Food, woman," he ordered his fat wife, "My new friend is hungry and will share his news of the world." The woman went back inside and retrieved a bowl of *opson* and a plate of *maza*. I greedily took a piece of the bread and covered it with the vegetables and enjoyed a large, ravenous bite. She had sweetened the vegetables with a goodly portion of honey, and I could feel my body replenish itself. The farmer shared the food with me, as this was the time he took for his early meal. Few words were exchanged as we ate, but I continued to nod my head approvingly as the farmer's wife brought fruit and even cheese to the table. The meal was simple but a feast to me after two full days on the march, particularly when I compared it to the fish stew I had wolfed down with Theagenes the previous evening. I received more satisfaction from the farmer's fare than I had at the banquet at Hiero's tent in my final evening at the games.

When we were finished he asked, "From where do you come and what news can you tell me?"

"I am Simonides of Ceos," I began. My name meant nothing to this unlearned man and his wife who had probably not ventured far from this remote farm during their simple lives. "I come from the games at Olympia and I will be joined soon by the champion who won the boxing competition. His name is Theagenes."

"Though I claim ignorance of your name, I have heard of this man Theagenes before," he commented, "The bull from Thasos."

"That is he." I recounted to my host the list of victors (at least those through the three days I was there) with some detail of each event. His wide eyes told me he was starved for news of the games. His wife, on the other hand, had no interest in athletic contests and left us alone to talk about these manly things while she went about her domestic tasks expressionless and unnoticed. It is possible that she was mute for I never heard her speak a word the entire time I was there at the farm. I gave an account of my conversations with the Spartan *ephor* and asked if he might have any news of the progress of the Persian host.

When I mentioned talk of war, his cheerful mood turned glum. "I have no quarrel with any man," he began. "Whether the land is ruled by Hellene or Persian makes no difference to me. Few men cross my path here in these hills. I live alone with my wife and I worship the gods, as all men should. They are my only masters," he said, "The gods and my wife." I nodded with a condescending smile on my face as he continued. "Once each year I leave this place and take counsel at Delphi. Once a year, I replenish what goods I cannot obtain for myself on my farm from the merchants at that holy site. No man bothers me, and I quarrel with no man. The Medes have no interest in me or in these cold and barren hills. Those things that are destined to happen will happen."

I raised my eyebrows and my surprise at his answer did not pass unnoticed. "Whether you acknowledge it or not, friend," I said, "You are a Hellene from a long heritage of brave men like Odysseus, Achilles and Jason. As such, you are a free man. To be from Hellas means to be free. If the Medes conquer our land, you will be no more than a slave to a foreign master who will be more demanding of you than the gods or your wife, and you'll not enjoy the serenity of your isolation in these hills. You will pay tribute to some satrap who demands an unjust share of your bounty to fill his already full coffers. Pray to the gods for the defense of this land because you, and all of us will pay a dear price if our armies fail."

He considered my response and shrugged his shoulders. "Each man to his own beliefs," he concluded.

"Exactly as I have said. A Hellene can have his own beliefs and express them freely; a subject of Xerxes cannot."

The first rays of the sun crested the hills and gave full light to the farm. By now, Theagenes was surely on his way. The landscape before me was verdant and beautiful, with a small open meadow surrounded by trees. To call it barren as the farmer had, was inaccurate. He had much to be thankful for but seemed not to understand that his freedom and the way of life that gave him comfort were in jeopardy.

He lowered his eyes. "Two days past a man stopped at my farm. As I have said, my wife and I have few visitors and welcomed him as we have you. He was a soldier, unarmed, with clothes dirty and torn. He was nervous, tense and very tired. I know animals," he said, "and they speak in many ways beyond the unintelligible sounds that come from their mouths. Like the hens in my coop when the fox is afoot, this man smelled of fear. It masked the stench of the filth and sweat that clung to his clothes and dried on his body. He bathed in our stream, but could not cleanse himself of that smell.

"This man had traveled all night from Locris, near the sea, where he had assembled with other men at the ancient Phocian Wall. It is there at the wall, where the pass is so narrow that a man could cross its width in fewer than 50 paces, that this man says the Spartans will make their stand. I have been there once before with my wife, many years ago, to partake of the healing waters that flow from the ground there. What he says is true."

"Was he a Spartan?" I interjected.

"No," he replied, "a Thespian. According to this man the Spartans were able to recruit several thousand men as they marched north to defend the wall at Thermopylae. There were Tegeans, Mantinians, Arcadians and others as well. In all, the soldier guessed more than 5,000 Hellene *hoplites* had answered the call of the Spartan leader and took up position in the pass near the Hot Gates. Shortly after they arrived to build their defense, the Persian host appeared far in the distance, near Trachis. The train was endless and seeped from the northern hills like rainwater that falls to the forest floor and finds many ways to rejoin itself in the stream, and the streams eventually become a mighty river. He had never seen such a number of men and animals amassed together in a single place for a single purpose. The soldier told me, he gazed at the host across the open space between the camps and then looked back on the defense the Spartans proposed to mount. Do you see that single rose amidst that mass of tangled bushes?" the farmer asked me. He directed my eyes toward the edge of the woods where ancient fence posts had been assaulted by weeds. I nodded. "The soldier pointed at that rose and said, 'We are like that lonely flower to stand against the weight of the mightiest army the world has ever seen.' Sooner or later, Simonides, that flower will wilt and die. The weeds will strangle it. Its petals will fall to the ground and rot. With that thought in mind, the Thespian left the Spartan camp and made his way here seeking safety for himself."

"A deserter?" I asked.

"Yes, a deserter. He ran away before the first arrow was every loosed."

"Was he alone or were there many more?"

"He was by himself," the farmer replied, "and I would guess there were not many cowards among the men at Thermopylae. The Thespian told me that by the direction of their march, the Medes were moving south, toward Athens. Had more soldiers deserted their positions, they would have traveled in this direction to take them out of harm's way. They would have passed through my farm. The soldier who fled and found his way here chose his path to put as many mountains between him and that massive army as he possibly could."

For many days, ever since I had encountered the *ephor* on my way to Olympia, I was unsettled and anxious. The gaiety that surrounded the celebration at the games was enough to divert the attention of the thousands who gathered there from the critical situation that imperiled us all. The rumors of war pestered me less than they should have, like a gnat instead of a harpy, but they still left me uneasy. I tried to swat them away without success. Now, in my quest with Theagenes, I approached the eye of the storm. I no longer had to speculate the whereabouts of the Medes or of the Spartans: both forces had reached Thermopylae. I was heartened to learn that Leonidas had successfully recruited soldiers from other cities to strengthen his force, but by the deserter's report their number wouldn't make much difference.

With more knowledge than what I had previously and rashly acted upon, I was now faced with a choice, but I knew I would still have to act on conjecture. Not knowing the outcome of the battle nor if it had even been joined, should I continue my journey toward Thermopylae or should I wait for my sometime traveling companion, Theagenes? I do believe the gods answered my dilemma when, just after the cock crowed, I heard the braying of a donkey, a thirsty one at that, plodding slowly from the barn not far from where we sat. It was a sign from Olympus disguised comically as a dumb animal; I felt it deep in my gut.

"You have a donkey?" I asked as if to change the subject.

"Three now. The old one foaled in the summer. Just another mouth to feed."

"That one, the old one as you call it … do you have need of it or is your barn so full of donkeys that you can spare one of the three?"

The farmer scratched his chin and answered, "No, I have no need of three donkeys."

"Then I will pay you five drachma for the animal, more than a fair price, and I will be on my way."

The farmer's eyes glistened when I placed the coins in his open palm. We struck our deal, and soon I was back on the path, headed east, but now I rode the donkey.

"You are headed in the wrong direction," the farmer yelled after me. "That path takes you toward danger. Were you not listening to me?"

You must think it my folly to set my course toward the pit of hell, but you will learn it brought me to revelation and wisdom beyond which I had never expected nor thought to attain. I awkwardly twisted my body as I teetered aboard my mount, fighting the roll of his back so as not to be dislodged and shouted, "If you see my friend, tell him I have continued east as we agreed." I turned forward with a firm grip on the leather strap to guide the animal, not daring to release it with even one hand to wave. I left the farmer scratching his head behind me.

As slow as I perceived the animal was, I knew that his pace was faster and surer than mine was as we worked our way along the rocky and uneven path. Whether or not he knew the way or the object of my journey, he responded well to my gentle tugs and nudges to keep him pointed in the direction that would lead us just to the west of Mt. Parnassus. I watched the shadows as they shrank, and when they were their shortest, I knew it was midday. By that time, I was comfortable aboard my newly acquired friend, and I began looking over my shoulder for Theagenes. My ears were alert for his footsteps. With every rise I crested, I paused briefly to search the land behind me for any sign of the Thasian. I was pleased with my progress through the afternoon and never doubted that Theagenes was gaining on me with his long, athletic strides. I patted the donkey on the side of his neck knowing that he had indeed taken me farther this day than what my legs could have. Theagenes would be surprised and pleased that I had advanced so far.

Late in the afternoon I stopped to water the beast at a stream when I heard the footsteps I waited for approach me from the west. As I suspected, it was Theagenes, for it was unlikely that any other man would be heading in the direction of the maelstrom that lay before us to the east.

"Well done, Simonides," he called as he jogged up and fell to his knees at the stream's edge. I held my donkey by his bridle while he and Theo drank from the stream. "You've made good time on the back of the ass. I have glimpsed Parnassus through the trees on the distant horizon. We'll steer west of Parnassus and straight for Kallidromos. I say with you on the animal, we'll pass the lower slopes of the larger mountain by nightfall. In two days time, we'll be in the Spartan camp." Stubble had grown in equal length on his face and on his head. He washed the dust from his body, but his face still looked dirty.

The donkey raised his head from the stream satisfied that he had consumed all of the water his body was able to hold. Like I had earlier in the day, I backed up to the animal, and in one small hop, I was atop his back and ready to travel. Theagenes grasped the leather strap that made the donkey's lead and bridle, and led us down the path.

We did not talk much as we journeyed. Whether Theagenes had determined that he would merely tolerate my presence or if he had reasons to now treat me as a trusted traveling companion I can't say, but he no longer eyed me with the wariness that was characteristic in his gaze when I first encountered him in Olympia. As he had predicted, we were passing Parnassus to its west through the foothills as darkness approached. Somewhere up there, the Pythia rested in her lair at Delphi. From here, the final leg to Thermopylae would be relatively easy compared to what we had faced since we departed Olympia three nights ago. I could see Kallidromos in the distance urging us forward, but I was glad when Theo decided to stop so that we might rest.

After we had finished our small meal and stretched our weary bodies out to sleep on pine boughs we had gathered, I said to my 'companion,' "Our relationship, if I dare refer to it as that, has been brief. Three nights ago at the temple, you left me in the trail of your dust. Now, you tolerate me. Why?" Though it had passed its fullness, the moon still shed great light, and I could see that the boxer remained awake, his eyes opened wide, staring into the starlit night sky as he lay on his back. When he did not answer, I prodded, "If silence is your only response, I will accept it."

An owl called into the night, its mellow voice softening the edge of the insects' sharp chatter. I heard movement in the nearby forest as the night creatures roamed in peace. I felt secure with Theagenes close by. I placed my hands behind my head and spotted the Big Bear.

"As a young boy on Thasos," Theagenes said in a low voice, "I studied the feats of Achilles and his comrades in the ancient war with Ilium. I read the praises of Herakles, Odysseus and others. Those men were champions. Their deeds have inspired me to strive for greatness. I want my stars in the heavens, too. I have but one goal in life and that is to be the greatest athlete the world has ever known. The Spartan stands in my path and keeps that honor from me. With Lampis fled from these games, I have been robbed of true and complete victory. As each contest began at those games, I looked upon my opponent and I saw Lampis. I did not see Euthymos in the stadium days ago, I saw the Spartan. I fight to be victorious over Lampis so that all might know that I alone am the greatest athlete, not Euthymos and not the Spartan."

I was pleased that he appeared willing to talk now, and I encouraged him to continue. "And whom, if not Lampis, do you consider the greatest athlete, not just now, but ever?"

"Herakles," he answered with no deliberation.

"But Herakles was born of Zeus, the mightiest of gods, and all know that even Achilles was protected by Hera. What man of flesh and blood, if not Lampis, is the greatest?"

We listened to the night creatures while Theagenes carefully considered his answer. "If greatness can be achieved by mortal man, then it was Milo of Kroton who was the greatest in our lifetimes. Everyone still talks of Milo. Even as a wrestler he achieved more than most men in sport. Lampis I tell you is a pretender to this thrown, and I will not honor him in any way without meeting him in a fair contest."

I smiled to myself and told him, "It is interesting to me that you would say Milo. I have seen him fight many times. It was he I saw in the first games I attended with my father as a young boy. Despite his great training by an earless man named Pythagoras, he was still boastful, like you, but unlike you, not angry. He carried himself with pleasantry that offended no one. It was after Milo's final victory nearly 30 years ago, that Pythagoras returned to the quiet of his home and walked away from sport. As a younger man, I spent many hours with Pythagoras. I wanted to know what it was that he did that enabled him to produce such an invincible champion. Pythagoras, however, did not see Milo in that light. Pythagoras considered himself a failure for Milo had not grown to be the man his trainer expected to produce."

Theagenes sat upright and said, "How can that be? He had trained the greatest athlete, perhaps ever. Yet you say the man considered himself a failure?"

"Yes he did," I replied. "He believed Milo to be a failure despite his countless victories. You see, Theagenes, Pythagoras was firm in his belief that he trained more than athletes. He trained men. As such, it was the final product of the man upon which Pythagoras judged himself and his pupil. Pythagoras trained to create not just the greatest athlete, but the perfect man, the man of superior intellect and strength, and beautiful in heart and spirit. Pythagoras observed, correctly, that Milo was victim to his own success. Even with his affable character, Milo was unable to avoid the pride that comes with victory, and hence, his character was flawed, perhaps more so than it ever would have been had he never competed in the first place."

Theagenes shook his head in disbelief. "I would say," he answered, "that this Pythagoras never tasted the pain that his champion endured to win his many *athlons*. For the agony that a man bears to achieve greatness in the arena, he has earned the right of boastful pride. Consider your own profession, Simonides. You build a fire of pride in the hearts of men like me. Your words of godly victory fan the flames of competition and inspire us to be better than other men. Yet here, alone at night, you tell me it is wrong?"

I felt trapped by his observation, for there was truth in it. Was I not like the prostitute who uses her body for no good moral value but only for the pleasure of men? Was I but a common man who worshipped these athletes and instigated the unhealthy pride that evolved in many? And only for my own reward?

When I failed to respond, Theagenes added, "I find your hypocrisy amusing, poet. And now I offer you a choice to ponder through the night. I have given much thought to you and your intentions to accompany me. I straightened your path when it would have taken you to the Isthmus. I rowed you across the strait to Naupaktos, and now I wait with you. The night will be short. At daybreak, I depart to secure my destiny with Lampis. If you agree to compose my epinicion, I will wait with you and your ungainly friend, lord donkey. If you will not agree to that, I will leave you watching my heels as I run to the Hot Gates. Consider no tricks, Simonides, for unlike what your benefactor Hiero may demand

from you for your indiscretion to him, if you run afoul of
me, you will pay with your life and by my own hand. I will
wake you when the sky lightens. Until then, ponder your
choices carefully." With those words, Theagenes rolled to
his side, away from me, and fell asleep.

Hypnos deserted me that night in the forest. Theagenes
snored loudly and perhaps frightened her away. Alecto, she
who does not rest, tormented me. Even in the lair of her
darkness, I could see her eyes weeping the blood of Uranus while Momus mocked me just beyond my vision at
the edge of the trees. I could hear his laughter like tiny
bells in the wind. My only recourse was to pray to Athena
for the wisdom that would grant me peace in the choice
I made. When darkness falls, you are trapped with your
own thoughts and the probing darts of gods and demons.
Like a child, you think that closing your eyes will protect
you, but you are wrong. And so it was that remorse washed
over me, regret for my own greed and for the part I played
in inflating this character flaw in men like Milo and now
Theagenes, a flaw that I was only now beginning to recognize and understand. I never understood until that moment
what the wise Pythagoras had told me so many years ago.
Men such as these have so much more to offer; yet their
pride confines them to the comfort of their athletic are-
nas where they know their superior skill will assure them
success with little risk of failure. Men like me encourage
them not to expand their breadth of influence, rather to
confine their abilities and the inspiration they might arouse
in others to the single act of self-gratification so that they

might reap the glorification of their fellow men based solely upon their athletic prowess. I felt hollow and empty as if I had stolen a loaf of bread from a hungry child.

Days ago, when I asked you Thasians who you considered your greatest, you agreed it was Theagenes. Now think. You answered Theagenes only because he has brought your island renown based solely upon his athletic achievement and his place of birth. Do you really believe that Theagenes has done more for your city than any another man has? What of your rulers who have insured peace and organization? What of your teachers who have helped raise your children to greater knowledge? If I asked four men of Kroton, "Who is your greatest?" I have little doubt they would answer, Milo. Do you know of Alcmaeon of Kroton? No. But I met this man once when staying with Hiero in Syracuse. Alcmaeon has studied the human body. He is a poor man, for his inquisitiveness brings him no monetary reward. But Alcmaeon says that you live through the power of your brain. Your heart beats only because your brain commands it to. Your eyes see only because they are attached to that gray mass encased by your skull. I say that Alcmaeon's studies will someday advance our ability to heal our own bodies. I ask you now, which is of more value: Milo's crowns in the games or man's ability to care for his own body? You need not answer, but we all know that a thousand Olympiads from now, men will only remember Milo. Alcmaeon's name will fade from memory like the winter snow on the mountain that melts under the spring sun. I remain convinced that Theagenes is the exile to whom the Pythia refers, but I begin to question the true value of a man's worth and how it is perceived by his fellow men.

I lay there that night deep in thought, no longer distracted by Theagenes' heavy breathing. I contemplated the foolishness of our race. There we were, all of Hellas threatened by the largest army ever assembled by humankind. Xerxes himself was prepared to violate our most sacred truce. But rather than defend ourselves, we were content to place our fate in the hands of three hundred men while the rest of us took pleasure and comfort from the games at Olympia. Are we that blind? Do we really think that the gods will intervene in our lives to protect us simply because we worship them and offer them butchered animals on an altar? What would have happened, I thought, if Theagenes and other great athletes like he had stepped away from these games much like Lampis had done? But unlike the Spartan, what would have happened if, rather than leaving silently, each had encouraged the others to take up their arms and join the army of Hellas to defend itself against the Medes. I believe that no man has more influence on his fellows than the athletes we venerate do. Once more, I knew that their influence was due in some part to men like me who raised them to godlike status with our songs of victory. Nonetheless, would it not have been better for them to turn their efforts in support of the greater good and the very defense of our land? Do the gods favor men of action or men of submission?

I made my decision in that moment: even at the risk of losing my own life at the hands of this troubled man, I would continue my journey with Theagenes in the hope that I might have the opportunity to undo what wrong I had done to him and others of his calling. I tell you now, that was ten years ago and I have written no songs since to praise the acts of one man alone on his singular quest for personal glory.

I managed to find little sleep that night, and rose early. I was atop my donkey before Theagenes stirred from his troubled dreams. He stretched like a restless beast and flexed his muscles to frighten away any tiredness that might remain. The boxer rolled to his stomach and effortlessly raised his prone body with his arms, up and then down, many times in rapid succession before he finally stood and faced the early morning sky. Clouds had gathered in the west and were moving slowly to the east to shield the power of Helios from the earth for this one day. Theagenes turned to face me. "I must be on my way. Do we travel together, or do you return in the direction from whence we came?"

"If praise is to be written, Theagenes, then it is I who will craft the words. I travel to Thermopylae with you."

"Very well," he answered, and from his simple reply I couldn't be sure if he was pleased with my choice or not. As we moved east down the path he said over his shoulder, "If you find it easier, you may call me Theo." I bowed slightly from my perch, pleased that he was ready to take me into his confidence.

Theo was more inclined to conversation that day and expressed interest in my perceptions of the Spartan champion. I told him I had heard the praises of this man who achieved great success in many contests. It was said he never lost a match. These Olympic games were to be his first where his true skill would be tested to the limit against the likes of Euthymos and Theagenes. Theo stated again, and with such conviction that I think he truly believed it, that Lampis was afraid and had used the Spartan call to arms as an excuse to leave the games, and thus keep his undefeated record intact.

"Lampis alone knows the truth of your statement," I offered. I told Theo of my encounter with Lampis and the Spartan *ephor* on my way to the games. "Lampis never once glanced in my direction," I told Theo. "His eyes were fixed on his homeland. He showed no emotion, no fear, no disappointment, and certainly not pride. I tell you this, Theo: you are a big man and no one who values his life can doubt the strength of the muscles you have developed through your training. But from what I recall from my brief encounter with the Spartan, Lampis is larger and appears no less fit. While I am certain you spared no pain in your training, I can see that from the flex of each muscle with each step and motion of his body, Lampis is a product of the *agoge*, the most intense physical training environment any man can endure. Even then, I am sure he trained beyond that to hone his boxing skills. If you consider your training, and add the brutality of the *agoge*, you will find a formidable opponent waiting for you at Thermopylae. As he passed, I noticed the mark of the lash on Lampis, yet the Spartan lash does not produce anger, only obedience and the will to perform flawlessly in the severest of conditions and without error. In the stadium, you fight for a prize and to defend your personal honor. On the battlefield, a man fights to defend his life and the integrity of his nation. With that mentality, Lampis will not easily be defeated."

"If it is as you say, Simonides," Theagenes replied, "then your journey with me to Thermopylae will be well worth the effort for you will be witness to the greatest spectacle of sport." Thinking back to my conversation with the farmer, I prayed that would be all I would see, a spectacle of sport.

My donkey was able to maintain the pace set by Theagenes. Theo held the lead in his hand and the donkey followed him willingly, perhaps glad to have escaped the drudgery of the farm where he had spent his entire life. The path was narrow and crooked and more than once I bent to the left or right to avoid a thorny branch thrust forward by an ancient tree to pester such as me who would invade its ground. Small scratches appeared on my arms when I was unable to dodge the natural barriers that appeared more frequently the farther we traveled up the slope.

The clouds continued to gather as we approached our destination and we thought we heard the rumble of thunder from a far distance. "Even Zeus prepares for the contest," Theo commented. We were soon to learn what contest Zeus truly anticipated, and it was not a boxing match between Theagenes and Lampis.

Nightfall approached, and our narrow path led us up the steep, rocky slope of Kallidromos. In short time, it became too narrow for even our faithful donkey to pass and we were forced to abandon him with silent prayers that he might find his way back home. He brayed his protest as we continued up the slope, but he soon learned he could not follow and had no other choice than to work his way back in the direction from which we had come. The path was so steep that at times I would call it a ladder, and our pace slowed considerably as we reached for purchase on the base of scruffy trees whose roots somehow clung firmly and deeply to the rocky soil. Theagenes led the way. Often times, he would have to reach back and extend his arm to me. I learned firsthand the power in his grip as he hoisted me like a child to the ledge upon which he had planted his feet. He sensed my nervousness but assured me that he would not leave me on these precipitous projections. "We are in this together, Simonides," he said, "Though I had not anticipated that this path would be so difficult, I'll admit, even for me." The journey had mellowed his tone and he began to treat me more as a companion and less as a piece of baggage. I thanked him for his kindness, and for the first time since I had met him, I saw a strange smile, an unbalanced mixture of friendliness and compassion cross his lips. At that moment, he was a handsome man, and in my heavy breath, I suggested to him that the smile was becoming to his countenance. "You are not so fearful when you smile," I commented.

"And now you know," he replied, "why I am more apt to hide it. To me, a smile shows weakness that a combatant cannot show to his foes."

As evening approached and after great labor, we rounded a bend in the path and found that it began to descend. As we turned that corner, the sea breeze struck our faces and refreshed us in a welcome way. But the scene that stretched before us was not right. It attacked our senses in a disorienting way. I feared that I would be overcome by dizziness. We paused to catch our breath and collect our strength for the descent. As we did, I studied the vista that presented itself to us. Clouds followed us through the day and covered the sky from horizon to horizon when darkness fell. Rarely did we glimpse the moon as the clouds rolled over us like an uneven mantle of torn cloth. But as I stood on that ledge with Theagenes, I saw more stars than I had ever seen in the sky at one time as if they had fallen beneath the clouds and positioned themselves unnaturally under the dim veil. They seemed to stretch endlessly to the north and they twinkled, as stars are apt to do.

Confused, Theagenes asked, "Have we reached the very end of the earth? I find it unlikely," he continued, "but the stars stretch before us in an orderly fashion, and I find myself looking down upon them, not up toward the heavens. What trick are the gods playing upon us, Simonides? Has this path taken us to the steps of Olympus?"

Have you ever tried to count the stars in the sky? It is an impossible task rarely attempted, and then, only by children and dreamers. I could not even estimate the number of flickering lights that reached north as far as our eyes could see. My mind rebelled at the thought that had entered it as I stood, dumb-founded on the slopes of Kallidromos with Theagenes, yet I had to accept the reality of that which would not vanish from my sight. No, we had not arrived at Olympus and this was no trick of the gods. What we saw was the work of men, an impossibility that spread before us in living flesh and blood. I guessed that we stood six or seven miles from the leading edge of this ocean of lights, and it flowed north from that point and disappeared over the horizon. We gazed not on the stars in an inverted sky, but at the Persian host of Xerxes, camped and assembled on the Malian plain. No city I had ever seen could match the size of the army that camped before us. Theo and I had just come from the games at Olympia where perhaps 40,000 men had gathered for celebration. What I saw at Olympia was a speck in comparison to the host that filled the plain and how far beyond the horizon, I was afraid to imagine.

"No, Theo," I finally said, "We have not reached Olympus, but more likely the house of Hades." I spoke the words that neither of us wanted to say. "There lies the Persian host, and what has been said is true. That is the largest army ever raised by mortal men." I imagined the landscape behind it upon which it had trod, barren fields and rivers reduced to puddles to quench the thirst of this giant war machine. "If it is the largest, let us pray to Zeus that it is not the greatest." I have seen men march to war. In my mind, an army was 5,000 men strong, maybe 10,000. It was said of Marathon that 10,000 Athenians faced 50,000 Medes. Even those numbers overwhelmed me, but what I saw here would dwarf the battlefield at Marathon. I could not divert my eyes from the lights that would not leave my sight. I was pulled toward them like a moth to a flame.

"Do not look upon them as a Gorgon's head," Theo finally said, "for if you do, you will truly be turned to stone and you will never leave this place. We must continue."

"What?" I asked incredulously, "Continue? Continue where? Look at the force that marches upon our country. We must return and take refuge in the Peloponnese. I fear that even Leonidas and his Spartans would have fled before this ocean of men. Surely you can see that Lampis and his comrades have far graver things to confront than a boxing match with an angry Thasian."

Theo shook his head. "No army of men will keep me from my task. I continue, Simonides, with or without you. Destiny calls to me and to Lampis."

"Pythagoras was right," I said to him, "The pride of victory has consumed you and to no good end." Theo glared at me and I saw him tightly clench his fist turning it into the weapon with which he had defeated his opponents at Olympia. I stupidly stood my ground and waited for the blow I was certain would come.

He calmed himself and opened his hand. "You have a timid heart, poet. As for me, I move on to find Lampis." He turned away from me and started to descend the rugged mountains. My emotions ran wild. I was afraid, I was disgusted, I was confused, but most of all, I was trapped on the side of a mountain with nowhere to turn. I called to him to wait and followed like a blind man would a cowbell, frightened all the while of where his steps might take us.

We walked on through the night. More than once in the darkness, I stumbled and fell. Each time, Theo would turn and raise me effortlessly by my arm even as he would a child. The sky began to lighten, and the Persian camp disappeared from our sight as we worked our way down the side of Kallidromos. We left the scrub bushes and trees behind us at the higher altitudes and approached the forest again where larger trees had sunk their taproots into deeper soil. We exchanged no words. I knew Theo's mind was set, and I think he suspected, correctly, that I believed madness had assaulted his mind. Despite the great difference of our conflicting thoughts, we kept them to ourselves and stayed together.

Without warning, Theo stopped before me and raised his hand that I should halt as well. We heard the unmistakable sound of movement amid the trees we were approaching. Theo ushered me to the side of the path where we concealed ourselves in a thicket. Thorns scraped my skin as I hunkered low behind Theagenes, thankful for his presence in this wild land. The sound was moving toward us. It was no beast of the forest or domesticated farm animal for we could identify the occasional sound of metal clanging together. Four men emerged from the woods on the path we were following. They were breathing hard, and two carried the fourth who had great difficulty finding his steps. When they had left the trees and entered the clearing, the wounded man fell to the ground and the others collapsed around him. The look of fear was unambiguous in their eyes. They were soldiers though each had discarded much of his *panoplia* to afford him the ability to move quickly and unimpeded by heavy shield or helmet. Each still carried his *xiphos*, his short sword, wielding it in a clumsy manner as they lugged their wounded comrade with them. They were not Spartans; that much I could tell for their hair, though soiled and dirty, was cropped short.

I shrank back when Theo revealed himself and boldly asked, "Who goes there breathless and weary, running away from the Persian advance?"

His voice startled the soldiers but none had the energy to stand and defend himself or his comrades. Rather, they cowered before Theo's voice and raised their hands holding swords in futile defense. "We are Phocians," one said, "and we do, indeed, flee before the Medes just as you should. Their number is such that only the gods can halt their progress. Please sirs, do not continue down that path for you will find only death and destruction, even your own end. I beg your mercy and help. Come with us to find safety in these mountains."

"Lower your weapons," Theo commanded, "for we mean you no harm." Theo and I had filled our skins with water shortly before our encounter with the Phocians, and we offered them drink, which they took greedily.

"Did the Spartans arrive as they had planned?" I asked.

"They did," one answered.

"And have they fled as well?"

"We would not know, but if they remained they are dead now or soon will be."

The exhausted and bloodied Phocians related the events of recent days. Leonidas and his 300 Spartans arrived at Thermopylae before the Medes swarmed into the Malian Plain. With Leonidas and his Spartiates was a sizeable contingent of hoplites from Thespiae and Thebes, and some others too that had joined him on the march north, but his forces numbered no more than several thousands. "He called for our help in defense of all Hellas," one said, "and we agreed for we Phocians cherish our freedom and know the Hot Gates well. Wisely, Leonidas chose our stand to be at the ancient wall that cuts the pass where a man can throw a stone across from the mountain cliffs on the west to the steep cliffs on the east that plunge to the sea.

"We were satisfied with our position and thanked the gods that we had arrived at Thermopylae well before Xerxes. We considered our force sizeable, but no man, not even Leonidas, despite the rumors that reached us from spies and fleeing countrymen of the northern lands, could have anticipated or imagined the number of enemy soldiers we would confront. When they came, they came as a flooding river that poured from the shadows of Olympus and Ossa and filled every valley until finding its place in the wide plain spread beyond the Spercheios River to our north. We could see no end to it.

"Even as we waited and fortified the wall, the Medes approached with great flourish of horns and drums. We could hear them across the gulf before we could see them, and I swear to you, their number shook the earth. When finally they emerged on the horizon, they were countless, more than the stars themselves. I and my comrades were humbled by our Spartan brothers for they showed no sign of fear, but sat calmly, preparing their weapons and combing their hair while Leonidas and other brave men strolled amongst them and us, making light of the mass of men who were intent on ending our lives. Our enemies arrived in full light of day under a blistering sun that reflected from the cloud of dust that rose in their path. I sat nearby a group of Spartans who rose quickly to their feet when one of their generals, the man they call Dienikes, strolled casually up to the warriors to make sure their spirits remained high. Standing there together and gazing toward the army amassed before us I dared to say to this great man, 'I have heard that when the Medes loose their arrows the number of shafts is so great that they block out the very light from the sun.' With no hesitation, Dienikes smiled at me and all the men who were gathered nearby and replied, 'That is good, then, for we can fight in the cool shade!' Even I laughed with the others, our spirits buoyed by the calmness, fearlessness and confidence of our leaders.

"They are so calm in battle, the Spartans," he said with reverence. "On that first night, Leonidas called us together before the wall after we had supped. 'Men of Hellas,' he said, 'I, king of my own land, heir of Herakles and leader of our common defense shall entertain you with a song composed by Sparta's own Tyrtaeus.' The men applauded. With those words, a young boy, a *helot* I am sure, stepped to the top of the wall behind the king and began to stroke his lyre. The words were so powerful that even now, in my fearful flight, I remember them. After a few notes, Leonidas the king began to sing in a deep and melodious voice:

> *'Now, since you are the seed of Herakles the in-*
> *vincible, courage!*
> *Zeus has not yet turned away from us.*
> *Do not fear the multitude of their men,*
> *Nor run away from them.*
> *Each man should bear his shield straight at the*
> *foremost ranks*
> *and make his heart a thing full of hate,*
> *And hold the black flying spirits of death*
> *As dear as he holds the flash of the sun.'*

"At that moment, my heart hardened and my spirit turned to steel. Never had I heard a man of such stature speak such words. His song dispelled our fear and transferred his own iron resolve to each and every one of us assembled before that wall. When he finished, we cheered loud and long. I am certain that Xerxes himself heard the jubilant noise from his camp across the Spercheios and wondered at our defiance. Leonidas raised his arm in thanks and walked back behind the wall. We were one man. We were one, impenetrable wall built of heavy oak shields and bronze spear points, convinced beyond reason that we would not bend before the weight of the invaders.

"The Medes camped on the plain beyond the west gate. They waited as if their presence alone would make us forsake our defense of Thermopylae. If that was Xerxes' ploy, it did not work for the mind of Leonidas and his Spartans was set like granite and would not be eroded. Their will to win was contagious and spread through our camp like a welcome wind that clears the air of smoke from a burning field. But winds never last forever; they move on.

"As I have said, we Phocians know the Hot Gates well. One of our numbers gave some concern to Leonidas when he told the king of a path that leads not far from where the Persians camped, through these mountains and to a point on the coast beyond the east gate. Learning of this path, and confident in our knowledge of the land, Leonidas dispatched our Phocian force to defend it should the Medes learn of it and attempt to encircle the defenses at the wall. As inspired as we were, I will admit that many of us were not reluctant to leave what we considered would become the killing field of Thermopylae. I am shamed to admit it, but despite the courage of the Spartans, fear slowly worked its way back into my mind and the minds of my comrades as we listened and watched the advance of the Persian horde on the northern shore of the gulf. The Spartans are different. They see a larger army and smile, for it presents them with more men to kill. Other men see a larger army and fear for their own lives.

"We were 1,000 men, all Phocians and we left the Hot Gates before the first clash of Hellenes and Persians. The two armies, one very large and one very small, faced each other for three days and neither a spear was cast nor an arrow loosed. We left them behind as we climbed hard and made our way to a plateau not more than two hours from where we now stand. We set up our position, but I fear that the unspoken relief we Phocians felt at escaping what we imagined was certain to happen at Thermopylae, deadened our senses and gave us unfounded reason to consider ourselves safe. Feeling security on the plateau with more distance now between the Persian horde and us, some in our number managed to sleep.

"A force of Persians much larger than ours struck without warning perhaps three hours ago. After an initial clash of swords and spears, the Persians retreated a short distance. When we did not leave our position and attempted to organize our phalanx, the Medes rained arrows upon us that broke our defense and sent us running into the nearby forest to escape their deadly shafts. We formed again, but the Persians continued on their trek giving us no more notice. I pray the gods forgive us for we lacked the courage to impede the enemy's progress further and they continued unopposed."

Each of the four Phocians showed blood, dried brown now, but only one was wounded so that he required the assistance of the others to move. An arrow shaft protruded from his thigh and gave him great pain, even as he lay motionless on the ground. "You failed the mission you were tasked to complete?" I asked matter-of-factly.

"We had no choice," the one answered with his eyes turned solemnly to the ground.

I looked at Theo. "And so it appears that Leonidas will be surrounded as the sun moves toward its zenith."

Another of the soldiers said, "If Leonidas chooses to remain at the Hot Gates, what you say is true: he will be trapped at the wall. But I can tell you as the Persians attacked us on this plateau, a small band of our men raced back down the path. I would say that they would report to the king what has happened giving Leonidas and his men time to retreat toward Attica. The king has great hopes that reinforcements are on their way. But as I see it, all the armies in Hellas cannot withstand the might of the Great King and his war machine."

"And the rest of your Phocians? Where are they?" Theo asked.

"Those who do not lay dead with the point of a Persian arrow buried in their chests have scattered like leaves in the wind. Many will die in their flight," he nodded toward his wounded mate.

"I am no doctor," I said kneeling to examine the wound, "But I might recommend one remedy to increase his chance of survival though the initial cure may cause him more pain than he now feels." The Phocians awaited my solution. "Break off the shaft just below the feathers and force the arrow through his leg. I can see that it has cleared all bone and will only pierce the meat. When it protrudes from the other side, take firm hold of the point and pull the shaft out of his leg. There is no other way." I stood and pointed to the south. "If you follow this path you will find a farmer's house when night falls. He and his wife will attend to your comrade as you rest and determine your next steps." I passed him a handful of drachma. "Tell the farmer, Simonides bids him care for these brave soldiers. We leave you in peace and pray that the gods still stand by us all and keep our homeland safe."

Theagenes and I departed and entered the woods. The forest was strangely devoid of the light-hearted laughter of birds, a sound that I was accustomed to hearing in such places. The silence was ominous and foreboding. The events that were being played before us had cast a pall on our, heretofore, comfortable lives. Theagenes picked up his pace as we entered the thick fir trees, and I struggled to keep up with him. Why we continued to advance, I could not be sure but Theo had set his gaze and mind once more to Thermopylae with some miraculous hope that the battle at the gates would not have been joined. I considered it unlikely but also knew that even if the fleeing Phocians had been able to warn Leonidas of the approaching force that would surround him, the Spartans would not leave. After several hours, we entered another large clearing, and I could see that the grass that grew there had been trampled and flattened by a large number of sandaled men. I suspected correctly that this was the site of the Phocians' encounter with the Persian force. From the woods on our right where the path turned east, we heard the moan of a dying man; it is a sound that no man wants to make, and no man wants to hear. Upon further investigation near the edge of the trees, we found no fewer than 100 bodies, all Phocians, most dead with more than one arrow shaft protruding from his chest or throat. Amid the death and blood, which seeped into the ground, we found the dying man whose moans had brought our attention to the eastern edge of the clearing. One arrow had taken him in the neck, just above his metal cuirass and below the cheek plate of his helmet. How the man had survived this long, I could not conceive, for the blade had grazed a major vein in his throat and he had lost much blood. Worse still, it appeared that after he had fallen, another shaft had found its mark below the bell of his cuirass and was embedded in his groin. His eyes were glazed as we approached, but I know he could see us through the mist of his struggle for they opened wider with recognition.

In a raspy, painful voice he begged, "Kill me! End my misery and my hopeless struggle with life." He tried to say more, but he could make no intelligible sound; those few, brief words allowed what blood remained in his body to pool in the back of his throat. He gagged. I turned my eyes from his suffering as bile rose in my own throat. Theagenes, however, did not hesitate to fulfill the dying man's last request. He sat next to the Phocian hoplite and cradled the man's head in his lap like a father would a sick child. I strained to keep my eyes averted and heard the bone snap at the base of the soldier's skull as Theo wrenched his neck in one swift motion that brought the man instant and permanent relief.

CHAPTER ELEVEN

Molòn Lábe

"Surely you can see that your cause is lost, Theo," I pleaded as I wiped my mouth. "We have no choice but to turn back. Death will greet us at the end of this path." Theo dropped the corpse like it was no more than an armful of cloth. His own *chiton* was smeared with fresh blood from the dead soldier. He walked back into the clearing and paced from one end to the other like the caged lion I had once seen in Athens. When he returned, he stooped to his haunches, stared at the body and scanned the other lifeless shapes that lay scattered amid the trees in the most awkward of positions.

"These men are not Spartans," he finally said. "If the Spartans are the men it is said they are, then there is hope that I will find Lampis and his companions still at the Hot Gates. If indeed I do, I will join them in their trial. When it is finished, I will turn my attention to Lampis and complete the purpose of my journey. I have come this far, and I will not flee like those soldiers we passed in the mountains. I will find Lampis, though my choice will not be to follow these Medes to the east gate." He snatched a handful of dirt and let it run through his fingers. "I will turn my step from

this path and make my own, north, directly to Thermopylae. There will I find Lampis and the Spartans." He rose
quickly and darted through the scrub at the clearing's edge,
blazing his own trail down the wooded slope that descended
through the Anopaea Mountains toward the Trachinian
Cliffs and the sea. My own reason had fled. In a moment of
panic and insanity, I called to him and followed.

His step was true as we left the dead Phocians behind
us in the umbrage of Kallidromos. In a short while, we had
no need to rely upon the unseen force that guided us north,
for soon we heard the sounds of the sea and wind as they
flew up the very channel that lies beneath us here. Then
we heard the dull roar of men. The forest thinned and we
walked through low bushes, some with thorns that grabbed
for our ankles. We were less than a *stade* from the edge of
the cliffs that loomed over Thermopylae.

Our senses sharpened and we remained alert for any
sign of men on the top of these cliffs, but there were none.
The tumult rose as we approached the edge with caution
and dropped to our stomachs, but even in the noise, my
senses were so keen that I could hear the movement of tiny
insects as they scurried within an arm's length of my face.
We crawled the final yards like two slithering snakes, low
to the ground and stealthily, beneath the sight of any man,
friend or foe who might gaze up at these heights. The dis-
sonance boomed like thunder.

"Look there," I said to Khepri and my Thasian companions, "High on those cliffs, far in the distance, just beyond
the turn in the land, that is where Theagenes and I huddled. Although you cannot quite see it from our position

here on Euboea, it is there, not far from where the water breaks against those rocks."

What I saw when I reached the edge of that cliff was unlike anything I had ever seen in my life or that I could possibly have imagined. Never had I witnessed the clash of armies, and I thank the gods that my journeys have limited me to this one abominable glimpse of hell. The sight before me captured my breath, and I tell you it stopped my heart. It was the closest to my own death as I have ever been. Only the natural convulsion of my body restored it to life and forced me to gasp for the air that had been stolen from me as I peered over the edge of the cliff. The gods had led us to this vantage point almost directly above the Phocian Wall. The Great King's army extended to the west as far as the eye could see. It was spread wide into the plain and wrapped tightly around the gulf. There was no end to it. The horde funneled into this pass at Thermopylae where it was choked in an area that thirty men standing shoulder to shoulder could block with their human wall. The Persians could advance no further, for there, directly beneath us was what remained of the Spartans, their red cloaks made even redder by the blood they had spilled and from the wounds that flowed freely from their own flesh. If, as the one soldier had told us, the Lakedaimonians had been joined by others, most of them had either fled or lay dead amid the tangled mass of bodies that was piled much higher than the top of the wall that they had their backs against. I could make out the white cloaks, dirty as they were, of a hundred or so Thespians who continued to fight madly with their allies. The carnage was deep and terrifying and bespoke of no spoils of war, only eternal death and damnation. By the looks of the butchery, this battle was not initiated this day but had commenced several days sooner. Many warriors held no weapons of their own but fought the Medes with their bare hands, savagely stripping their opponents of their own source of defense and turning it against them. Their tactics were no different than those of the wild beasts who, when cornered, resort to any means to insure their own survival. There was no mistaking the predicament that Leonidas and his army faced. These brave men no longer fought merely to protect their own lives, rather to kill as many of their enemies as they could before their last breath of life-giving air.

Theo nervously tapped my shoulder and pointed to our right, toward *Alpeni* where the narrow pass opened slightly as it approached the eastern gate. I stared in horror as I spotted the forward lines of Xerxes' Immortals who he claimed could rival the fierceness of the Spartans. These, then, were the men who had rained death on the Phocians and followed the goat path to encircle the Spartan defense. They marched with great calm and discipline toward the middle gate. The final engagement was near at hand, and though I strained with all my might to turn my eyes away, I could not, and I watched intensely. Despite the havoc, I could see Leonidas and identified him by the traverse crest on his helmet. A man I took as a Spartan helot raced over the wall to his side and directed the king's attention to the advancing troops who had now closed to within fives *stades* to the rear of the trapped warriors.

As we watched, surely by some pre-conceived plan, a flaming arrow shot from a Persian bow by the advancing troops near the east gate, ripped through the air, arced high into the sky and disappeared beneath the ledge on the opposite side of the pass. As the host on the west saw the sign, it pulled back, away from the wall and the remaining Spartans who defended it, but many men were cut down and fell into the carnage when they hastily turned their backs to escape the slashing swords and thrusting spears of the Lakedaimonians who found no reason to rest while the Persians withdrew. When the Medes on the western front had pulled back two *stades* or so, the land fell eerily quiet. It was so quiet that I could hear the huffing of the few Spartans that remained on their feet though they were doubled over, arms heavy from exertion.

"Can the gods protect them?" I heard Theagenes whisper to himself as much to me. I did not need to answer. A fly bit my shoulder and began to suck my blood, but I dared not swat it away for fear of drawing attention to our position though as I think back on it, all eyes were certainly trained on the defenders that remained in the narrow pass.

As the smoke trail from the arrow fled with the breeze, the mass of Persians parted like a field of wheat assaulted by a strong wind and the Great King took his place at the head of his army. He rode a chariot made of solid gold. It was heavy and his white horses strained to pull it forward. Hiero's image flirted with my attention but vanished quickly. Xerxes had little room to maneuver his team, but escorted by a group of 100 heavily armed men, he advanced slowly to a position not more than 100 paces from the Spartans.

With only the sound of his snorting steeds and the heavy breaths of the Hellenes on the wind, Xerxes commanded in a stern but respectful voice, "Brave Spartans, your valor in the face of certain death is unmatched by any men. There is no shame in what you have done here. Receive Xerxes' mercy and return to your wives and children. Throw down your weapons and be spared by the Great King."

I felt Theo's body tense against my own. It was as if the two of us stood with Leonidas and his men and waited for his answer. I prayed silently that Leonidas would accept Xerxes' offer of clemency. These courageous warriors had done all they could, far more than what would be expected of other men. There was no hope for a Spartan victory, but perhaps they had held off the approaching storm long enough for the rest of Hellas to better plan and prepare its defense. I prayed it was true. At that moment, the lives of the surviving warriors were in the hands of Leonidas, not Xerxes. Defeat was as certain as the setting of the sun, but I knew it was not the Spartan way to surrender. "With it or on it," the Spartan women would tell their men as they marched to war: return home carrying your shield or being carried dead upon it. I feared that neither these shields nor the men who clutched them would ever return to Sparta. Leonidas gazed from left to right, at the giant army before him, and at the valiant men around him. He took his time to answer and as he inspected his remaining troops, I'm sure his eyes locked with each and every one of his soldiers who had stood beside him through this bloodbath. His men knew what their king's answer would be, but Xerxes waited while his horses pawed the bloody ground... the

Persian host waited impatiently... Theo and I waited... The world waited for his answer. Finally, Leonidas removed his helmet, and his long locks, soaked with sweat, cascaded beyond his shoulders.

The Spartan king raised his helmet to the sky and in a loud and clear voice yelled back to the King of Persia, "Throw down our weapons? Molòn lábe, Come and take them." Leonidas rushed forward brandishing a bent sword and his men followed. Xerxes feared for his safety thinking that he was the object of the Spartan charge. With some difficulty and much assistance, he wheeled his chariot about and retreated to the protection of his huge army. But the Persian king was not the target of Leonidas's charge, for the Spartan led his remaining men to a small hill directly beneath where Theagenes and I lay prone, stunned and motionless as this dance of death proceeded to its ultimate conclusion. The hill might have been 100 feet high, and as the Spartans scrambled up it, they drew to within 200 feet of our position on the cliffs. Their dwindling numbers meant that their entire force extended seven ranks deep with a single, red-cloaked warrior, not Leonidas, capping the hill. They awaited the final Persian onslaught screaming all the while, "Come and take them, come and take them..." as each pounded whatever weapon he still held on his shield, helmet or cuirass to make an intimidating racket that I hoped might cause the earth to split and swallow the invaders. Men with no chance of escape, refusing to surrender, stood proudly and arrogantly in the face of their last moments on earth. Not a man turned aside.

A series of five long and loud trumpet blasts silenced
the Spartan warriors and signaled to the Medes who held
their position on the east side of the Phocian Wall to begin
their advance. Soon, they had reached the pile of bodies at
the wall, and they halted. A worse scenario could not have
evolved, and my gut tightened as 20 ranks of 100 archers
moved forward from the sea of men who stood silently behind the Persian king. They encircled the hill upon which
Leonidas and his men waited. The Lakedaimonians showed
no panic or fear. Those who could stand did so; those too
maimed to rise to their feet sat or lay on the ground with
whatever weapon they had and lifted it defiantly in the air.
Xerxes raised his right arm, and as he did, more than 2,000
archers pointed their bows toward the sky in the direction
of the hill and drew back their arrows.

As the Persian bows flexed, the Spartans raised what
shields they had and locked them together as best they
could. This, their only source of defense, had been greatly
depleted. No shield remained whole and without damage
and what bronze facing would have shone brilliantly in full
sun was now dull and tarnished with the blood of thousands of men who had been crushed before them. Heavy,
wooden bases were no longer intact, and some men raised
large pieces of naked oak, the bronze covering having been
knocked clean off in previous confrontation. No Spartan
screamed or cried with fear and all waited boldly now in
silence for the first wave of arrows.

Xerxes lowered his arm and another trumpet blast signaled the archers to loose their shafts of death. The sound
of thousands of arrows was terrifying as the feathered bolts

cut through the still air with the deadly hiss of a striking
snake. They arced through the sky and some even reached a
height equal to where Theo and I watched. The shadow of
these bolts moved across the ground like a creeping preda-
tor and converged on the hillock. I prayed that Zeus would
stop time and freeze the arrows in flight, but I knew it
would not happen. They came from all directions, and so
many were there that when they turned back toward the
earth to fall upon the hill, they momentarily hid the scene
before us. Theo rolled to his back and stared at the charcoal
sky. He grabbed my shoulder and I could feel the strength
of his grip.

I could not turn my eyes from the sight and watched
as 2,000 arrows fell upon a hundred men. The sound was
deafening and it sickened me. Many struck the oak shields
with the quick, short 'plunk' akin to hailstones striking the
farmer's cart in a powerful summer storm. Too many more
found flesh and blood. The wooden wall of broken shields
held above the defenders began to collapse. The first rush of
death lasted only a few racing heartbeats, but when it was
over, fewer hearts on that hill continued to beat.

When the Spartans had taken their position on the hill,
I believe that Leonidas intentionally donned his helmet,
but not for protection. He did it to draw the archer's aim
to him for his traverse crest was unmistakable. After the
initial wave of arrows, the Spartans lowered their shields
to dislodge the shafts and relieve their burden of additional weight. At first, I could not see Leonidas, but then a
lump rose in my throat as I saw his body rise in the hands
of a giant of a man midway through the remaining ranks.

The king's head lay back and his helmet fell to the ground; both arms hung limply. There was no mistaking his fate. I remembered the words the Pythia had spoken to the *ephor* Leon, "Your king or your city." Staring at Leonidas's motionless body in the arms of the Lakedaimonian giant, I took some faith that Sparta would be spared because of his personal sacrifice. It had been decreed, and therefore, it must be so.

Amid the fallen bodies that surrounded him, the giant maintained his balance and struggled to the crest of the hill where he gently placed the fallen king on the ground. He and his comrades surrounded the lion's son. I strained my eyes and was soon certain that the defiant bull that had carried his dead leader to the hilltop was none other than Lampis. He stood on the top of that hill, undefended, above the body of Leonidas, and raised his broken sword to the heavens. He repeated the words of his king, and his voice ripped through the stillness that had fallen upon the land, "Molòn làbe!" Those were the only words I ever heard the man speak.

I shook myself free from Theagenes' hand and slapped his face, impervious to any reaction he might take to cause me personal harm. "Watch now, Olympian," I rasped between my clenched teeth. "Turn your eyes back to the hill, for there is the man you dare call coward!" He followed my command like a scolded child, and saw Lampis, wounded and bloodied, but standing tall, proud and defiant.

Not fifty men remained alive. They discarded the remnants of their shields and stared stoically at the thousands of arrows raised again and pointed at them. On Xerxes' command, the flood of arrows was unleashed. As they soared through the sky and fell on the hill, not a single Spartan flinched nor raised a hand to protect himself. More than 4,000 shafts had been directed at those few, remaining men who had climbed the hillock with Leonidas. Now, there was no movement on the hill. Moments passed silently. No dying man allowed a sound to pass from his lips. During those moments, stillness fell upon the Hot Gates like a giant weight from heaven. The arrows covered the bodies of these valiant men like a field of thick and ripe wheat. I buried my head in the crook of my arm and wept.

CHAPTER TWELVE

Epiphany

I struggled hopelessly to hold back my tears as I retold the story from the heights of Euboea even though so many years had passed since the events occurred.

In the pain of my recollection, the young and foolish Xeno said, "I have been correct all along. It is Theagenes who was the coward. And so too my brother was right about that arrogant man who has been undeservedly praised by his countrymen even though he had abandoned our island for so many years."

Xeno's words fell upon me like blows from a weapon that I was too weak to deflect. I swallowed hard and gathered my emotions.

"You, Xeno, may never understand what happened at the Hot Gates," Parmenides snapped back, "For while you and your family drank wine with the Medes in Thasos, these men held the horde long enough to allow other brave Hellenes to organize the full defense of our country."

"I am pleased to know you recognize the worth of the Spartan sacrifice," I said to Parmenides, "but if I may continue, the story is even more personal for you Thasians though as yet, you do not know it." I pointed at Xeno and said, "Listen to me well, young man. What I tell you is not about cowardice, nor is it solely about valor. It is about a man, arrogant and foolish, who learned deeper values of life that I truly hope can come to you without the pain and sacrifice that Theo and I witnessed that day..." I continued my story.

Xerxes and his army stared in silence at the hill and watched for any sign of life. Like the hunter who has slain the bear, the Medes remained cautious lest the wounded animal rise in one last effort to take just vengeance on his executioner. I saw fear in the eyes of the Phocians I met in the forest that day; I felt fear tremble in Theo's hand as we watched the final act of the battle; I felt fear grab my heart as the arrows flew; and now, I heard fear in the very silence of the Persian host as it gazed upon the fallen beast that was once the pride of Sparta. Their fear overcame their royal obligation to cheer when the final Spartan fell. It reminded me oddly of Theo's hollow victory at Olympia. Our Hellene brothers may have lost this battle, but their savage resistance had certainly created doubts in the minds of the victors. The Persian archers withdrew, and Xerxes' Immortals began to cautiously climb the hill.

Not all the Spartans were dead, though not one had the strength to inflict any more damage upon his foes. For a full hour, the Persians methodically scoured that hill and mercifully ended the suffering of any man who had not fallen dead with a Persian arrow impaled in his body. Each Immortal's strike with the blade was hurried but true, and soon all life had fled the slaughtered Spartan army.

When the grisly task was completed, bearers lifted the Great King on his golden litter and carried him slowly to the top of the hill on a path the Immortals had cleared through the bodies. He dismounted his litter and covered his nose and mouth with a cloth to fend off the stench of death. As if to avenge Hector whose lifeless body Achilles dragged around the walls of Ilium tied to the back of his chariot, Xerxes ordered two men to raise the lifeless body of Leonidas to its knees. The dead king's head hung forward loosely so that his chin touched his chest. Standing before his vanquished foe, Xerxes extended his right arm and into it was placed a large, curved blade. In a horrible moment of extreme sacrilege, the king, whom I would no longer refer to as great, raised the weapon and swung it swiftly and accurately to sever the head of the man who had withstood the might of the Persian Empire not with weapons alone, but with the strength of his resolve and courage. On command, but reluctantly, an Immortal took the head and impaled it upon a Persian spear for no unbroken Spartan shaft could be found. He planted the butt spike in the ground at the top of the hill, and blood dripped freely from the ragged edges of the neck. Having erected his gruesome monument, the king and his men retreated from the hill.

As you no doubt can tell, friends, I am a man of words. Forgive me if they run long. Through my entire life, I talk, I sing, I write, but on that day, no words escaped my lips for none would enter my mind to describe the horror that I had seen. I had been reduced from a man of words to a child of tears. There we were, two men as far apart in character as the Pillars of Herakles to the Hellespont, a poet and a boxer.

We had been witnesses to a slaughter. Neither Theagenes nor I could find the strength to speak. We cried and whimpered like babies, but neither said a word. Our stomachs grumbled and our throats were parched, but we did not eat or drink. Through that day and well into the night, we sat and wept until we had no more tears to shed. The Persians had emptied our rivers, they drained our blood, and now they depleted our tears. We continued to watch in silence.

Xerxes pulled his army back to the camp that covered the Malian Plain. The Immortals who had followed the goatherd's path the previous night to surround the Spartans and bring them to their end marched solemnly by the hill and back to the bivouac to rejoin their comrades. They were somber and lacked the sense of joy that comes with victory, and though their king had erected his ghastly monument for the purpose of motivating his army, it seemed that the Medes were reluctant to look upon it fearing that even the gaze from Leonidas's dead eyes would bring an evil end to them.

As soon as the middle gate had been cleared of survivors, a large group of men, perhaps a thousand or more, and slaves by the look of them, entered the area with carts drawn by oxen. They worked persistently into the darkness separating the dead bodies and body parts that littered the field of combat into two separate groups. They irreverently dragged the Spartan bodies to the hillock. They loaded the Persian bodies and their allies' corpses into their carts and hauled them to the edge of the narrow Thermopylae plain, and dumped them like garbage over the cliffs and into the water below. Xerxes' plan was clear. He feared that his army would see the thousands of dead Medes and lose heart when they passed the small group of Hellenes who had visited such destruction upon them. Persian morale would suffer. And so Xerxes tried to hide the bodies of his own dead and publicly display the decimated Spartans, crowned by the head of Leonidas impaled at the top of the hill. The king's strategy was loathsome, but I am certain it minimized the disastrous effect on morale that would otherwise have ensued had he not taken the sickening measure.

By dawn the next morning, the pass was clear of the preceding days' butchery, save for the bloody hillside covered with dead Spartans left there to rot in full view of the Persian army as it passed by on its journey to Attica. Xerxes pitched his tent near the base of the hillock and his army marched by. All men were commanded to salute their king. They were forced to gaze upon his magnificence and upon the grisly monument that stood behind him in silence. No man turned his eyes toward the sea or down from the cliffs to see the thousands of dead Persian soldiers who floated in the rocks below. It was a clever deception from a king, no doubt perplexed at the ferocity of his opponent, who at this very moment was unable to understand how this small force of warriors could have withstood his might and power for so long without ever considering retreat an option. It was cause for concern that he would discuss with his generals, but he did not wish to share his anxiety with the common soldier.

You continue to wonder at the size of the invading force? Let me help you. It took three days for it to pass through the Hot Gates, such was the number of men, beasts and baggage to support it. For a time, I thought there would be no end in sight. For three days, Theagenes and I held our ground on the cliffs above Thermopylae. We watched as men from the farthest reaches on the earth, men the likes of which we had never seen, passed beneath us. Persians marched by the king with soft hats and tunics with many-colored sleeves covered with iron scales so that they appeared as angry armored fish that had walked from the depths of the sea to join the onslaught of our land. Each carried a wicker shield and a short spear and a large bow was hung from his back. Syrians passed with brass helmets, and they carried with them wooden clubs laced with sharp pieces of jagged metal. Scythians followed in great numbers wearing tall, pointed caps and wielding the wicked battle-axes that are their weapons of choice in the plains warfare they are expert at in the northern lands. I saw men clad in cloaks of animal skin such as I had never seen before. They carried large, curved weapons that appeared best suited for taking a man's head from his body in one swift, clean motion. Men of black skin, like Khepri's own workers shuffled through the pass and bowed to Xerxes, whether of fear or respect, I cannot say. These black men wore leopard skins and painted their bodies with white chalk giving them the appearance of skeletons most fearful to look at. No less terrifying was a large number of woolly-haired men, black also, who wore the scalps of horses on their heads as the Thracians to our north wear fox skins. The ears were erect and the horses' manes flowed like long crests down their backs. As frightful as this host appeared to my eyes, I knew that their wicker shields and shields made of animal skins were of little protection against the iron points of a well-trained phalanx. I thought with some satisfaction that it was only their number that allowed them to pass over the men who held the pass for so many days.

When the sun rose on the second day, we could still see no end to their number in sight, but those coming from the north halted unexpectedly while those moving south continued in cadence. A thousand horsemen entered the pass and filled the open space, each atop a giant breed of stallion called Nisaean by the place of their birth. Xerxes' own Immortals followed the horsemen. Each had preened himself like a pretty bird, taking elaborate care to groom himself immaculately for his king. They marched now in unison, each a perfect image of the other, spearheads pointing to the ground. The sacred chariot reserved for the gods and pulled by a team of eight pure white Nisaean horses followed the Immortals; the charioteer walked behind them with the reins in his hands. Xerxes' golden chariot came next, and amid much ballyhoo, the king left his throne before the mound of dead Spartans, boarded his coach and departed the Hot Gates with his army. Another thousand spearmen followed and then the calico patchwork of an endless train of soldiers who had followed their king from the ends of the earth.

Theo shared no thoughts with me or I with him. We were as two, dumb and mute men whose voices had been stolen by the horrifying events played before us while we watched in secrecy. We hungered and we thirsted, but neither made an effort to leave the place. We did not sleep but maintained our vigil, often dozing into a trance-like state, but never fully losing consciousness. I prayed.

Through each night, I watched the hill and the broken clouds about it, and as I did, my mind played tricks with me. As the waning moon illuminated the moving clouds, I saw a large, ethereal and delicate image of a crowned god loom above the hillock with open arms, and I swear I saw the spirit of some man, maybe even Leonidas, rise with the deity and then disappear as the clouds moved to the east. Perhaps I was disappointed when I faced the fact that it did not happen. I had another vision of these men, clad in full armor and formed in their feared phalanx on the banks of the river of death, unafraid, even defiant of the boatman as he made his way to the shore to ferry them into eternity.

Midway through the third day, the last of the Persian host was gone, and a rag tag assemblage of carts followed that moved haphazardly and without the discipline and organization of the armed men who marched before it. Three days it took for the behemoth to pass through Thermopylae, and for the first time since I drew Theo's attention to Lampis in the Spartan's final living moments on the hilltop, I spoke. I was exhausted, emotionally and physically.

"We have lingered long in this place of death," I said in a tired voice. Theo's eyes were dark and hollow when he looked at me. "The land is lost," I added.

"If not lost," he answered solemnly, "It is only because of the efforts of these valorous men who lie still and quiet before us on that hillock."

Theagenes and I struggled to our feet for our legs had not been used for many days and were stiff; our muscles begged for nourishment. We still had food in our satchels though up until now, neither of us had the stomach to eat. Theo grabbed a piece of bread and stuffed it into his mouth. He washed it down with a welcome drink of warm wine. Rain had threatened to fall since we first arrived, but only now did it come in a soft drizzle. "Where will you go, Simonides?" he asked me.

I, too, took bread from my satchel but needed more wine for my mouth was dry and parched. "If the sea is safe, I will find my way to Sicily even though Hiero will probably have my head at our next meeting. Perhaps in Sicily, we can escape the advance of the invaders, though I doubt this man's craving for power will allow him to be satisfied only with the mainland of Hellas. He will not stop until he reaches our colonies at the end of the world for I would say his army is that large."

"Wherever your path might take you, I beg that you delay it only for a few more hours. My task here is not complete and I will go now to finish it. Come with me?" he pleaded, as a child would beg his mother.

"There is nothing more that can be done here," I answered.

Theo did not reply. He raised his wineskin to his lips and took a final draft. With not another word, he strode off, and I was compelled to follow. After a difficult mile, we intercepted the path of Anopaea and descended from our perch to the east gate. For a moment, I believed that Theo's intention was to follow Xerxes, but instead, we headed in the opposite direction toward the middle gate, the object of our observation for three days and nights. The ground

was hard and bare, and our footsteps made little sound for
the land had been crushed and compacted by the weight of
Xerxes' army as it moved toward Attica. In a short while,
we could see what was once the Phocian Wall was reduced
to rubble as engineers had cleared it from the army's path.
No physical obstacle could stay the advance of Xerxes. Not
even the sea at the Hellespont could stop his march. Only
men could turn him aside, but I doubted that all of Hellas had enough. If I was right, that only men could defeat
the Persian army, I concluded that it would only be men of
exceptional courage who could save our land, for weapons
alone would be useless against the war machine I observed
for three days.

Vultures gathered beyond the wall and circled high in
the sky, the same sky that rained a torrent of arrows only
days earlier. They soared in their lazy way and several would
leave their dance of death and descend to the hillock that
rose beyond the wall. The closer we got to that wall, the
stronger the smell of death and destruction. The sweetness
of blood mingled with the stench of human feces and entrails that were spilled and scattered in that narrow pass
and now trod into the earth by a million men so that the
ground had an odd, red color that I had never seen before.

Xerxes' engineers had built a ramp with the rubble of
the wall. We walked to its apex and stopped. The hill towered silently before us, a *stade* from our position at the wall.
I was taken by the serenity of the scene. The slaves had done
a remarkable job in clearing the Persian dead from the field
of combat, and the passage of the army made a smooth and
clear path through the narrow confines of the middle gate.

The hill rose like the breast of a woman from the flatness of the pass, and the sharp and jagged cliffs where Theo and I had waited and watched loomed behind it like a giant, gray curtain built by the hands of the gods to protect the pass from further corruption.

I studied the bodies that lay still and silent on the hill. No more than a thousand corpses covered it, and Xerxes slaves were careful to follow his orders. They had collected as many of the Hellene bodies as could easily be identified and arranged the corpses in such a way that they covered the upper half of the hillock and circled it so they were in full view of the army as it passed by. On the crown of the hill, the spear with the impaled head of Leonidas rocked slightly and the fallen king's long wet locks, once dreadful in the eyes of his enemies, waved harmlessly in the sea breeze that brought the drizzle in from the gulf.

Theo and I dared to walk down the ramp from the top of the wall toward the short cliffs that rose from the water. We stood aghast when we gazed over the edge. The army had marched through the pass in an orderly fashion, men of each nation grouped together by race to create a colorful parade for their king. He relished his victory and acknowledged each group by a small wave of his hand as each tilted its spears, bows or swords in reverence to him. The seaward image below the cliffs that Xerxes tried so hard to conceal was far different. There was no sense of balance and order as dead men from all reaches of the earth floated in a jumbled mass, dark men, turned even blacker amidst men of lighter color now painted a putrid purple by the death wrought upon them. Wicker shields floated out toward the open sea with shreds of garments of all colors holding desperately to rotting men hoping that they would not be dragged to the bottom. Xerxes' plan to hide the bodies of his fallen soldiers had failed. If it was 100 feet to the rocky beach below the cliffs, the pile of Persian bodies climbed halfway to the top. The Spartan burial mound on the hill was but a speck of dust compared to the mountain of bodies that lay seaward of the cliffs. It was not and could not be concealed from the allied survivors merely by throwing the dead bodies from the cliff, there were simply too many. I was certain that the Medes saw the destruction wreaked upon their army even though the king demanded that they pay him homage at that very spot as they passed their vanquished opponents at Thermopylae on their way through the pass to Attica. Dead men rocked in the salt sea where their bodies had rolled from the mountain of corpses. Many were bloated and their flimsy armor had burst from the pressure of their swelling entrails. Sea creatures, crabs and fish feasted on the table set before them. I am not a man of numbers, but as I looked back toward the hillock I concluded that each Spartan warrior had taken a thousand foes to their deaths. It gave me pause for some hope amidst this disaster: could the full Spartan contingent of 5,000 standing like a single, angry animal before Xerxes' army finish the work that their 300 comrades had started? I began to believe that the impossible might not be and I prayed that this was the beginning, not the end.

Theagenes stooped and picked up a handful of soil and watched it flow through his fingers, and then grabbed stones and held them in both hands. He turned back toward the hill, and then looked straight into my eyes. "I have but one thing left to do in this place of death," he said grimly, "And you, Simonides, will bear witness to it." With those words, he set off to the hillock and I followed.

At the base of the mound, in the exact position where Xerxes sat proudly on his throne while his soldiers marched by, was a large stone marker, six hands tall and ten hands wide, flat and polished smooth on both sides. In our own letters it read, "Here the Great King Xerxes, master of the world, destroyed the Lakedaimonians who were no more than insects in the path of the Persian Immortals. He slaughtered them like dogs and left their bones to be picked clean by scavengers." The words were written in Hellenic script so that all Hellenes who passed this ground would know of the power of the Medes.

I have visited many holy places. I have been to Delphi, many times. I have worshipped Athena at the Acropolis, and prayed to Zeus at his altar in Olympia, but none of those places struck me with the awe and power that enveloped me on that hill. As I climbed it, I knew I was on sacred ground. I had never experienced that feeling with such clear intensity, and I would never experience it again. I can only tell you that something physically touched my inner being as I crawled up that mound. I no longer exercised my own free will. I had no choice but to climb the hill and witness the visions that awaited me at the top like living things among all this death. I saw the men gather again on the banks of the Styx. For my entire life, I imagined the ferryman approaching his passengers with devilish glee, but such was not the case in my spectral sight. I saw the

white-haired Charon poling his craft toward the shore. His
blazing eyes had softened and were filled with tears. He
would not avoid his duty, but he knew these men belonged
in Olympus, not in Hades. He reluctantly carried them
across the black water.

Theo used his stones with great accuracy to scatter the
scavengers who poked at orifices and open wounds with no
particular pattern, but only to satisfy their insatiable hunger. Some vultures flew away and perched on the nearby
cliffs above us while the more aggressive soared to the seaward cliffs to find the Persian banquet that rocked on the
waves beneath them and tempted them to challenge the
water. My own revulsion abated as I climbed the hill behind
Theo, and I looked upon the bodies with reverence, not
disgust even though the flies continued their busy work.
Theo and I made our way to the top. It was less difficult
than what you might think, for no body was placed upon
another in Xerxes' plan to make the Spartan force look as
large as he could. Though he could not stop the rumors that
would spread through his camp from those in the advance
troops, he wanted no one to know that such a small number of Spartans could hold his massive army in check for so
many days. It was an achievement that no one but a Spartan
could comprehend.

The body of Leonidas was pitched forward near the
top of the hill not far from where his head stared toward
the sea. It had been struck and wounded many times and
was, by now, completely drained of blood. I turned my face
upwards and gazed into his dry, lifeless eyes. As tarnished
as they were, they could not hide the resolve with which

he had set them upon the enemy he encountered here at the Hot Gates. His skin was not yet burned by the sun for clouds had remained in the sky as if to conceal what had happened here from the gods themselves. I could tell he was not a particularly handsome man even in life. An old scar from a distant battle ran from the bridge of his nose to the corner of his mouth, which hung open above his beard. The morning of his death, he had prepared his hair in tight curls that would strike fear in any man who encountered him at close range, but an arrow launched from an impersonal archer a full *stade* away knows no fear.

My eyes scanned the ground at the base of the spear and came to rest upon the once mighty Lampis. His hands were affixed to the shaft of one of four arrows that had pierced his cuirass, as if to extract it and hold on to life even as his spirit struggled to flee his body. Like his comrades who surrounded him, Lampis loved life but did not fear death. I pointed to Lampis with an open palm and said to Theo, "There is Lampis. This is the man who inspired your anger, the man whom you called coward." The words were painful for me to say, but I needed to say them aloud for both of us to hear. His reaction was not important to me when I spoke.

Upon seeing the body, Theagenes fell to his knees, then surged forward and rested his head on the Spartan's bloodied shoulder. I knew my words cut Theo as deeply as the Mede's arrow had pierced his opponent's heart. My words were meant only to express my personal anger at Theo's insolence and not necessarily to hurt him, but I know they cut him with the deftness of a Scythian battle-ax. He sat up and draped his powerful arms around Lampis and pulled the lifeless body close to his breast. "I am ashamed," Theo said through tears, "And I stand here humbled before you and the spirits of all these men." He stroked the tangled hair of Lampis, clotted with sweat and blood. "I came here to fight this man," he said to me, "to defeat him in sport, to take my personal vengeance on him, a man whom I now see I had no reason to loathe. I find him dead by a Persian bolt, but in his death, he has earned great victory far beyond any to be won in the gymnasium. I am not worthy to bear the crown that should be his. I fought only for myself. Lampis fought and died for me and all men of Hellas. In his final confrontation, in his holy death, he rises above me and all others who have ever vied for the olive crown, for no man I know of is his match for strength and courage in body, mind and spirit." I began to weep as I thought of the men at the games, the men whom I doted upon like a mother would spoil her child. Theo and I had witnessed what few men do and live to recount it; Theo and I peered into the pit of hell and saw this man and his companions stand and face death itself, for there was no escaping the fate that the gods had placed at their feet. Thanatos had stepped aside and the traitorous Keres took sides with the Medes. Not a man here ran or cowered before them.

Theagenes reached for his satchel and withdrew the wreath he had taken from Hera's temple so many nights ago that it seemed to me like a lifetime. The leaves were wilting and lost some of their luster. They threatened to fall from the thin vine to which they clung, but Theo took the crown with such care that it remained intact. His body convulsed as he fought back more tears. He propped Lampis's head on the helmet he placed behind it. In the most solemn moment I have ever been witness to, Theo put the crown of olive leaves upon the fallen Spartan's head. Gazing upon his handiwork, Theo said, "This man is the champion and he now lies in peace with the crown upon his head that belongs to him and no other. I am not worthy to stand in his presence." Theo turned and made his way to the bottom of the hill.

I descended slowly and took time to study each man who had fallen in defense of his king and his country. The Spartiates like Lampis were easy to identify. I saw no more than 100 scattered on the hillside and most of those, near the top, rallied around their fallen leader. Many Thespians had stood, and then fell with Leonidas and his knights. Saddened as I was, I was heartened by the number of *helots* who lay dead in service to their lords and masters. I was told more than once that these *helots*, Messenian slaves to their Spartan overlords, hated the men they had served for a hundred years and more, yet not a one lifted a hand against his master, rather took up the arms of his fallen lord and fought side by side with those that remained. Each had the opportunity to join the Medes, but it meant more to these men to die in defense of Hellas than to abet its subjugation to an alien power of strange men from a far and distant land. Perhaps they thought that victory with Leonidas would mean their own freedom. I wanted to think they were right. They died, however, not as slaves, but as brothers-in-arms and equals of the free men they had served until they met death at the bitter end of a Persian arrow. Such was their determination. Not a one died in servitude.

I collapsed at the foot of the hill next to Theagenes who sat bent over with his head between his knees lost in thoughts known only to him and the gods to whom he prayed.

Finally he said, "You are free of my service, Simonides, for there will be no epinicion to compose."

"I have never been bound to your service, Theo. I am here of my own free will," I answered solemnly and added, "As for my work, you are wrong. I cannot leave this place without comment. True, I journeyed here with you in anticipation of your fight with Lampis. Though your encounter with the Spartan was not what I had expected, I have seen it nonetheless, and your actions speak more for you than any words I might write. I was paid well by the Athenians for my ode to the men at Marathon. What I will leave here, I do with no desire for compensation. My heart and soul demand that I write words for these fallen heroes." I looked at him and tried to smile, but there was no gladness in my heart, only sorrow. I prayed that the sacrifice these men made would not be in vain. I was committed to see that it would not go unremembered.

CHAPTER THIRTEEN

The 13th Labor of Herakles

We returned to the wall to contemplate the momentous events that we had witnessed, and then, I suppose, to determine our individual courses of action. What to do? Exhausted, we sat on the ramp staring back at the hillock. Not wishing to disturb the meditation of the other, we remained silent and kept our thoughts to ourselves. I, the old poet and Theo the young athlete. I knew our minds moved in different directions. The vultures had returned but there was nothing we could do to prevent their desecration of this sacred place. They eyed us warily, and occasionally, one would land amidst the bodies and flap his large, black wings as he tore into the rotting flesh of a corpse. The light began to fade.

We raised our heads when we heard the distant clanging of a bell and in short time, a large cart drawn by a team of oxen approached us from the west gate. Physically and emotionally spent, we lacked the energy to move and conceal ourselves. We watched and waited for any man or demon that might come our way. As the cart neared our position on the wall, we could see that it was a straggling remnant of the endless supply train, the last piece to pass through the gates in support of the Persian army that rumbled south now like a hungry monster toward the heights of Attica's fair city. The cart halted at the base of the hill for a few moments. We watched as the lone driver stooped from his perch atop the cart to read the marker that his king had left behind. He did not tarry long but continued on his way and soon drew his wagon to the base of the ramp. It was only then that he spotted us atop the stones of the wall that had been pushed aside to make way for the Persian horde.

"Greetings," he called as he jumped down and dusted his tunic. "From the looks of the ground, I need not ask you in which direction my king is moving." For an instant, Theo and I wanted to leap upon this man and extract our personal revenge from him, but knowing he was but a small and inconsequential part of the train that followed Xerxes, we merely raised our hands to return his greeting. We had no quarrel with him and he, no quarrel with us.

Leaving his cart behind him, he walked up the ramp. "You are Hellenes?" he asked. We nodded with little enthusiasm. "Strange that I should find the likes of you here. I am sorry for your loss," he said and waved toward the hill. "Stories of Hellene valor have passed through our camp like a fire through dry brush. Our army covers the land like a giant city, and word of your bravery and courage reached even me, a poor peasant, the last man at the end of this wall of destruction. As the news has reached me and I look upon their final resting ground, I will admit to you and to all men: there is no dishonor in their deaths." He stretched his back to loosen it from the long hours atop his cart. "I carry supplies to support Xerxes, but I was delayed not far from here when a wheel on my cart broke, not an easy thing to repair and I received no assistance from my companions in their haste to move forward."

"Have you food and water that we might purchase from you, trader?"

"Indeed I do, and a good thing for you, too. The army has depleted the fields and rivers on the entire course of its trek, from the northern shores of the seas to this narrow pass, particularly here where your men delayed its advance for many more days than the Great King had planned. The land has been laid to waste." He shrugged his shoulders matter-of-factly and added, "The cost of your foolish resistance." I saw Theo clench his fist, a reaction I had become accustomed to seeing whenever he was upset or offended.

I placed my hand on his forearm and interceded, "We're not combatants, friend, but those words of yours are easy for you to say in this moment as you trail a million-man army." I pointed toward the hillock that was now just a dark shape in the shadows of the cliffs behind it, "Still, as you have conceded, Xerxes has never confronted men of such courage. While he may have won this single engagement, he has many more to face. A small force has cost him dearly. If you doubt that, wait until the sun rises and gaze at the bloody waters beneath those cliffs. You will be astounded at the number of men who have joined the sea creatures below. I for one think that even your king has underestimated the will of Hellas."

"The outcome is not for us to discuss nor will we determine it," the merchant said calmly. He looked toward the seaward cliffs and said, "I am not blind, but even if I was, I could not have helped but to turn my nostrils away from the stench that comes from the sea. Even in this dim light, I could not turn my eyes from the bodies that float on the water like wrecked, abandoned ships in the wake of a savage storm. Now, I have seen with my own eyes the death that such few Hellenes have brought to such a large number of Medes. The Great King boasts that your Lakedaimonians were no match for his immortals. I read the marker he left like a foolish braggart at the foot of the hill," the man laughed. "The result of this engagement was a matter of numbers, not courage. That much is plain to see. I do not fear for my own army, but if all Hellas fights with the passion and savagery that I see displayed here, the Great King has assembled too few men to contend for your land. You see, gentlemen, by my trade, I am good with numbers. From the looks of it, each Spartan that lies dead on that hill took no fewer than a thousand Medes to hell with him. The victory here belongs to the Spartans, not to the Great King. I have no desire to see what lies beyond the edge of that precipice in the full light of day, and I have to be on my way. Come, I will give you bread and water before I take my leave and hope that we can part as friends."

We followed him to his cart, which was full of grain. Heavy skins of water hung from the rail on the side. "Take what you will," he said, "for I suspect the lack of my services will go unnoticed with the army so far in front of me." We each took a loaf of bread, and I, one skin of water, Theo two. I offered to pay, but the man would have none of it.

As he secured his baggage he commented after much thought, "I am certain I love my country no less than you do yours, but I find no joy, rather embarrassment at the words Xerxes has left at the base of this hill. Word had spread through our camp of the fierce fighting that took place in this narrow pass, but upon seeing this," he turned back toward the hill and rested an elbow on the edge of his cart, "upon seeing this, I am sickened by the words left on the marker. Surely I would have expected that only an army of equal size could have challenged ours, yet I find that fewer than a thousand men have wreaked such havoc. I must ask you. Why? Why did so few men stand here to fight the greatest army in the world? Surely each man knew his fate."

"That is the way of the Lakedaimonians," I answered without hesitation, "Surrender is not a word they are taught in their schools and they do not know its meaning."

He considered my answer while gazing in the direction his army had marched. Then, the merchant took the harness on his oxen and turned his cart back toward the west gate from where he had come. "Call me coward then, my friends," he finally said with a sense of resignation. "For I have no desire to meet more Spartans. As surely as I share my provisions with you, they will find their way through our wicker shields. I will not be the last man in the line to face them! My path will take me in peace back to my homeland, though the journey is apt to take me longer than I now imagine." He climbed aboard his cart and coaxed his team awkwardly back toward the west gate. He shouted over his shoulder, "As I will pray to Ahura Mazdah for your safety, please do the same to your gods that I may find my way back to Susa." We waved and watched as he slowly made his way toward the west gate.

Within and hour, darkness had fallen. The clouds in the sky moved swiftly with the night wind, and Selene showed herself for heartbeats at a time and bathed the ravaged landscape in a pale light that continued to challenge my senses. Did that body actually move from one position to another between the shifts in illumination? I was exhausted and Hypnos took me in his slumber as I struggled to maintain my hold on reality. With a full stomach, my body welcomed him as it had never done in all my years. I feared that I would never wake as I submitted to his promise of escape. I slept soundly and dreamlessly despite the ordeal I had witnessed in these days. I resigned myself to the comfort of darkness and nothing more.

The first rays of Helios struck me directly in the face and took the chill from my body. I opened my eyes and found that I was alone on the wall. Rising, my gaze was drawn to an astonishing sight such that I could not believe what I was seeing with my own eyes. Rested, I left my perch and walked toward the hill. A wide and deep gash, one hundred paces long, marked the base of the hillock and it curved like a smooth arc. My first thought was that the gods had worked through the night to create this opening in the ground, that they had split the earth itself to mark this spot of heroes. But on further observation, I saw Theagenes, sweating and covered with dirt, sitting in the ditch gulping water from his skin. Impossible, I thought. What heavenly trickery was this?

He had not seen me, and I watched as he sealed his skin and tossed it to the edge of the ditch, which was a full head deeper than he was tall. Theo dropped to his knees and picked up a dirty sword with which he began to attack the ground at the bottom of the ditch to loosen the dirt. He worked that way for several minutes. Satisfied, he retrieved the remnant of a shield. The oak had split precisely in its middle leaving a half-moon of wood held by the bronze rim that still maintained its circular shape. I watched with incredulity as he scooped the dirt he had loosened from the bottom of the ditch and tossed it out, over his shoulder. As he began to repeat the process I called to him, "Theo, what madness is this that has taken hold of you?" He wearily dropped his implements and climbed from the trench. On closer inspection, I could see that his hands were swollen and bloodied from his labor.

"No madness has taken me, Simonides, only a vision from the gods." He wiped his hands on his filthy *chiton* and squinted from the burning pain that throbbed in his open wounds.

"Let me help you," I said. Not far from where we stood, a torn, scarlet cloak lay on the ground. I ripped pieces of cloth from it. "If you must continue, wrap your hands in these to protect them as best you can." At first he didn't move, but then extended his arms and I carefully wound the cloth around his hands and between his fingers, securing it at his wrists.

He smiled, somewhat painfully, and said, *"Himantes."* He raised his hands so that we could inspect my handiwork.

"And what vision came to you, friend, that has inspired you to complete this feat of insanity?"

"Sleep came quickly to you and with little resistance last night. While Hypnos took you in his gentle arms, he watched as his son Morpheus played within my own mind. As I tossed and turned, he steered my mind toward images of Herakles, the greatest champion of all. Perhaps Herakles alone could have changed the tide of this battle. When I was a child, I fancied myself to be Herakles. Like every child of Thasos, I was schooled in numbers but I was far more successful with my letters. I thank my teacher, Peta, for he taught us our letters through the words of the blind poet who recounted the deeds of our champions at Ilium, and those of Herakles and Jason. I remember with great clarity the Labors of Herakles that old Peta painted before us on his invisible sheet using his tongue as his brush and words as his pigments.

"Last night as I struggled with Hypnos and Morpheus, I recounted the twelve labors in my mind, thinking that as I did, Hypnos would close my eyes and allow me to find peace. As I envisioned the fifth labor, my mind became alert and I opened my eyes and gazed upon this hill, then, nothing more than a dark shape in the night. The two gods had awakened a thought and left me to it. As a boy, I was told that the stables held 3,000 of the finest cattle in the entire world, but due to the negligence of their owner, King Augeias, they wallowed in the filth that had remained in the stables untouched for thirty years. You know the story, Simonides. Herakles dug a ditch to divert the rivers to clean the stables and restore health to the beasts that lived there."

Theo placed his wrapped hands on his hips and looked upon his handiwork. "No, Simonides, I am not too bold as to think I will dig this ditch to the nearest river, but watch and you will see how I will restore this holy site and purify it with an offering that will cleanse it far more deeply than water alone." Without further explanation, Theagenes was back in his ditch. He worked for two more hours as Helios climbed in the sky and I watched with no understanding of his intention while Theo continued to dig. Finally it appeared he was satisfied with his own labor. He climbed from the ditch. Indeed, it measured a hundred paces long and fifteen paces wide; it was as deep as a long, hoplite spear. Had I not seen the construction with my own eyes I would have called any man a liar who said he could do what Theo had done in a single night.

"Although I do not understand it, I am impressed, but still utterly confused with your work. Please tell me, Theo. What is the purpose of your trench and how will it cleanse this place of death?" He answered with action, not words.

He walked halfway up the hillock behind his ditch to where the first bodies had fallen. He bowed his head as if in prayer, then gently lifted the closest body. Despite the work he had completed through the hours of the night and into the morning, he carried the man to the ditch as if the body weighed no more than a cloth draped over his arms. There being no dignified way to do it, Theagenes dropped the corpse into the ditch. He looked at me briefly as if to confirm that I understood what he was doing, then walked back up the hill to retrieve another body, which he promptly deposited with the first. I nodded supportively and returned to the rubble that was once the Phocian Wall.

As you can see, I travel with no heavy burden to slow my step. My satchel contains but few items: my lyre, sturdy but light, food for a day or two, and my writing implements: a roll of *papuro*, several reeds, two vials of soot from which I can make my ink, and a small mallet and chisel if I choose to work with stone. Theagenes continued to use every muscle in his body to complete his task. As he did, I searched my mind to find perfect words with which I could mark this tomb to commemorate what I had personally witnessed. As he went about the task he was compelled to complete, I embarked upon mine.

Truly, I knew that no words could capture what I saw and felt, and so I was resolved to use as few as I could, but enough that all men could grasp the significance of what had happened here. I would add no water to my pigment until I was satisfied with the words I would use. Only then, would I dip my brush and put the words on the *papuro*. Our tasks were different, but I considered mine to be no less demanding than Theo's. While he used his muscles, I used my mind. The undertaking of one could not be minimized by the undertaking of the other. This was not a race or a competition where only one man would stand victorious. No, it was an effort from each of us to honor this sacrifice of human flesh and blood as best our personal strengths could serve us to that end.

My life has been dedicated to the praise of athletes, yet I had been commissioned to commemorate other events. I was paid well for my words on the Athenian victory at

Marathon ten years earlier. But as I pondered this event, I realized that unlike Marathon, there were no survivors at Thermopylae. Theagenes and I were the only two Hellenes who witnessed the final stand and remained alive to tell it to others. If we failed in that obligation, the only memory men would have would be what I came to detest as the false words on the stone tablet raised by Xerxes in its prominent position at the base of the hill. Xerxes' story was twisted and ugly and would not be promulgated by warriors of true virtue. Still, if he could stoop so low as to raise his lies at the foot of this hill, he would tell the same lies, and even worse as he made his way through Hellas. That would be the most profound travesty.

Deep in thought, I feared for all of Hellas as I imagined the Persian war machine advancing toward Athens. Would the men who conquered Ilium cower before the advancing Medes? Would Xerxes' telling of the tale be the only one to exist? My mind wrestled with these thoughts even as Theo struggled to complete the labor that he had taken upon himself. Would what Theo and I do here mean nothing? Would it vanish unnoticed like the spirits of these men? Those were the questions that echoed in my mind as I sat on the remnants of the Phocian Wall and watched the young Thasian carry body after body to the grave he had dug for them.

For his part, your countryman worked tirelessly, but as the day wore on, his strength was slowly sapped by his exertion and his step slowed and became unsteady. I approached him infrequently, only to stop him for a few brief moments to give him water and to rest his heart. Though his muscles

weakened, his heart and his soul never did. He would drink
deeply, thank me with a nod of his head and stumble back
up the hill often using his arms as two more legs, like a
beast of burden he continued his grim task.

By late afternoon, he had crested the hill and only two
bodies remained: those of Leonidas and Lampis. I wondered
how his task would end, how he would bring closure to it.
As I watched with emotion swelling inside me, he raised
the body of Lampis in his arms and stared for a moment at
the head of Leonidas that looked down from its grisly perch
atop the spear. With no more aplomb, he carried the body
down the hill. His legs shook with every flex, but he was
careful not to stumble or fall with his precious burden. By
now, the ditch was nearly full which allowed Theagenes
to place the body gently in the pit as if it was still alive
and breathing so that he would do it no harm. He repo-
sitioned the olive crown such that it looked natural upon
the dead man. I could not argue with his act of giving the
olive wreath to Lampis, for what we had seen the Spartan
do far surpassed any act I have ever witnessed by any athlete. My Thasian friend was correct: Lampis was indeed
the true champion. And in recognizing that fact on that
day, Theo glimpsed truth as he recognized the impact of a
man's life on his brothers regardless of their walk and path
in life. Theo sat down by the edge of the tomb and stared
toward the summit of the hill knowing that a single body
remained.

I took a vial of soot from my satchel and added but a few
drops of water to it and mixed it with my reed. I took my
position, cross-legged, stretched the *papuro* tightly across

my lap and began to write. The words were brief and short but said everything that needed to be said about the men who fell here. It did not take me long. When I finished, I gathered my things and walked to the ditch.

I lifted Theagenes to his feet. His tortured hands were now completely raw, the flesh exposed and damp as the scarlet cloth I had covered them with had unwound and descended from his wrists.

"One more," he said gravely.

"I will help," I answered and followed him to the summit fearing more than once that I would have to catch his body as he struggled to maintain his balance. I doubted I could do it if he chanced to fall backward, but I was prepared to try. Without ceremony, he managed to dislodge the spear from the crest of the hill while I removed the red cloak, torn and sullied, from the body of Leonidas and handed it to him. The fluids had long since drained from the king's disfigured head and Theo wrapped it carefully in the cloak. I was not repulsed by the package I took from Theo, rather honored to be able to carry it down the hill, honored, as I would be to carry the ivory shoulder of Pelops if it were mine to bear. Theo followed with the body.

After placing the remains of Leonidas in the ditch, Theo drew a deep breath. His body shook violently and then he began to weep again. Giant sobs from a tired, confused and broken man. "I will rest until morning," he said and retreated to the wall. I let him go without a word. The hill was cleared of bodies. They lay in Theo's ditch, many assuming distorted, unnatural and awkward poses that did not portray the dignity with which each breathed his last

breath as a living man. It stuck me that what little armor
and few weapons the Spartans had carried with them to
the hillock were still strewn haphazardly on the face of the
mound creating an unearthly landscape that few men have
imagined and fewer still have seen. With what daylight remained, I used the last of my strength to retrieve those implements of war that spoke loudly and clearly on behalf of
the men who wielded them in a conflict they could not win.
I put them in the tomb that Theagenes had built with his
bare hands, much like you Egyptians place the possessions
of your deceased pharaohs in their impressive monuments.
The weapons covered the bodies and gave them some protection from the vultures that still waited hungrily on the
cliffs above us. We Hellenes place an obol in the mouths of
our dead so that they can pay the ferryman his due. These
men had already paid their fare in a way that no men before
them ever had. Charon would be satisfied, and if not, these
Spartans would have their weapons with them to convince
him that they had already paid for their journey across the
Styx. Swords were bent, spears shafts were broken, the
ground littered with Persian arrows that grew now like a
stiff field of wheat from the hill. One shield and one shield
only retained its original, unbroken shape. Though dented
and bruised, I could still see the symbol on its face, a symbol that struck fear into the hearts of all who opposed it,
a large, red *lambda*, Λ ... the sign of the Lakedaimonians.
It was too heavy for an old man, but I struggled to take it
with me. As I drug it down the hill, I imagined the ease
with which a trained Spartiate brandished it. His ability to
use it effectively was all that stood between him and death,

but even the most expert could not withstand the weight of a million men or the onslaught of a hail of sharpened arrows. I placed the shield on the ground before the marker Xerxes had raised days earlier in his effort to intimidate all men who passed this place.

With the hill clear now of everything save the Persian arrows that I would leave to rot in the rain, I began my final task while Theo slept like a dead man at the Phocian wall.

Xerxes' message was chiseled into a sandstone slab. He no doubt had an ample supply of such tablets to leave messages like this and others as he ravaged our land and crushed all men who tried to stand in his path. I was sure that one of the thousands of carts I had watched roll through the pass two days earlier carried a large supply of these tablets. Sandstone is not heavy, but it must be handled with some care so as not to break or fracture it. I managed to dislodge the stone and at once, with my own small mallet and chisel, turn Xerxes' script into a meaningless jumble of shapes that could not be deciphered. Then, with some effort, I turned the stone to its other side, flat and pristine. It stared at me and invited the touch of my chisel. I had no need to refer to my *papuro* for I had chosen my words carefully and remembered them well. I set to work, meticulously tapping the chisel with my mallet to fashion the words I had composed for this place. It was painstaking work, but it lacked the physicality of what my companion had accomplished through the previous day; his effort was Herculean, mine was not.

The letters fell into place, and the letters became words. It took me the full night, but when I was finished, I was satisfied with my labor, even as I hoped that Theo would be pleased with the final touches I made to the tomb he had single-handedly created. With the final letter in place, I stretched my body atop the stone, lay my head on my satchel and fell asleep even as light touched the night sky in the east.

Several hours later, the heat of the sun, now high in the sky, woke me from my sound and dreamless sleep, the second I had enjoyed in as many nights. I made my way to the wall and found Theo still asleep. For a few seconds, I feared him dead from his exertion. We had slept little in five days and nights; sleep or death left him here motionless. My shadow crossed his face and his eyes opened. He closed them and said in a cracked, dry voice, "My body aches and screams for more rest. No training I have ever performed can match the work I have forced upon myself since I left Olympia. Yet in those old days, I trained only for myself." He raised his body into a sitting position. His hands were swollen and he squinted as he flexed them open and closed, the dry skin cracking as he did. "The task I accomplished yesterday, however, was not for me. It was for Lampis and his comrades, for they are the true champions and it took the largest army in the world to defeat them." He raised his hand to his face to shield his eyes and asked, "What do you think, Simonides? Were these men really defeated, or was victory theirs in the manner of their deaths under such circumstances?"

"I cannot answer your question at this moment. I believe it will be many months before the outcome of this invasion is certain. These men have done their part and cannot be called 'defeated,' for in their death, in their resistance, I hold hope that our full forces have been mobilized after the games and are prepared to deal with the Medes in a swift and decisive manner. If it were not for these men, there would have been no time for mobilization, and all could very well be lost." I helped him to his feet. "Come with me," I said. "I hope you approve of the final work I have added to your worthy creation." We walked slowly to the tomb. "Today, together, we will cover the grave, but see here what will stand before it." I led him to the center of the pit. We raised the sandstone marker and behind it, the Spartan shield to secure the marker in place.

Theagenes stepped back and said, "Allow me, friend Simonides, to read your words by which these men will be remembered."

> *Of those who perished at the Hot Gates,*
> *all glorious is the fortune, fair the doom;*
> *Their grave is an altar, ceaseless memory is theirs*
> *instead of lamentation, and their fate*
> *Is chant of praise. Such winding sheet as this*
> *no mold nor all-consuming time shall waste.*
> *This sepulchre of valiant men has taken*
> *the fair renown of Hellas for its inmate.*
> *And witness is Leonidas, once king*
> *of Sparta, who hath left behind a crown*
> *of valor mighty and undying fame.*
>
> *Go tell the Spartans, O stranger passing by,*
> *That here we lie, obedient to their laws.*

We could not look at one another for fear that each would cry although we had both learned that manhood is not defined by dry eyes and that the free flow of tears can be an intimate part our very humanity. Tears do not betray manliness. Still, neither he nor I could bear to shed another. Our labor was finished here and we had to take some satisfaction from it. "And so it is finished for them and for us," he whispered.

After some time, Theo said, "We must leave this place, Simonides. Though I've come to call you friend, we will take separate paths," he said.

"And where will yours lead you?" I asked.

"I will retrace my steps to the Peloponnese," he answered. "I will find the army of Lakonia and fight with them to avenge the deaths of their countrymen... Of our countrymen," he corrected himself, "for surely the Spartans will spearhead the defense of all Hellas. I am not a trained soldier, but I will add my strength to them if they will have me. If not, I will take my own vengeance against these foreign invaders in my own way. I owe Lampis more than that, but it is all I have to give."

We embraced one another for the first and final time. "I leave you with these words," I told him. "I have watched the athletic contests at Olympia and the other crown games my entire life. I have seen many champions crowned with the laurel and olive wreaths. But of all such men, champions in their own right, I say to you, Theagenes, you are the true Olympian for of all those men, only you know that the games are just that, games played for the entertainment of the masses and played for the individual glory of a single man. Of all those men, only you know the true sacrifice that a man must make, not for himself, but for his fellow man. That knowledge and your willingness to pursue it make you the truest of champions, the greatest Olympian. I stand humbled before you.

"As for me, my days of writing epinicions for winners of sport are finished. My pen is now reserved for such as these who know the true value of life and freedom and who are willing to sacrifice their own lives to defend it, men who are not afraid to face death to achieve a higher meaning for their lives and the lives of their countrymen. These are the heroes of our age whose names will endure any test that time can throw against them."

Theagenes did not reply. His slightest of smiles reflected some gratitude and satisfaction. He bowed respectfully and turned and walked east toward the wall to find the path that brought us here three days earlier. I never spoke to him again.

CHAPTER FOURTEEN

The Oracle Fulfilled

"And now you know, friends," I said to Khepri and my Thasian companions, "why I say to you that the statue you have cast to the sea is the exile the Pythia tells you to welcome home. Theagenes is the greatest among you, and his place is well deserved in your *agora*. Whether your people honor his memory as the great athlete he was, or as the human being I've told you he became is of no consequence. The gods will be satisfied either way."

With my final words, sound ceased and an unnatural silence fell upon all the earth. No wind touched our faces; no bird, insect or animal dared break the eerie silence. Khepri gazed down to the water and answered our unspoken question. "The tide has changed in the strait beneath us, and it brings an unspoken sense of peace to the world. I have seen it happen only once before. As the water reverses its direction, a great calm settles over the land."

We acknowledged his explanation and returned quietly to our camp to rest for the remainder of the night. I did not know what each man felt for no one offered comment to my tale of Theagenes at the Hot Gates.

The sky was clear and the water reflected its blueness as we rounded the northern end of Euboea the next morning and made our way into the deep waters of the Aegean. We followed the coast north with Thessaly on our left so that we never lost sight of land. On the third day with Mt. Olympus dominating the western horizon, its peaks shrouded with large, white clouds, we turned directly east toward Thasos. I said a prayer to Zeus. On and off throughout the journey, we glimpsed great Athenian triremes prowling the waters like proud sea monsters to fend off the feared Macedonian pirates that we never saw but heard many a tale about. We always heard the triremes before we saw them, as the dull thud of the drummer's beat and the chant of the oarsmen to keep an even stroke drew our eyes to the horizon. As it rose above the splash of the waves on our hull, the rhythmic and distant noise was comforting in these dangerous waters that had seen many an unwary merchant fall prey to the renegade seamen from Macedonia. Once, we saw a pirate ship far in the distance, but it turned and raced to the north when a trireme appeared off our bow moving swiftly in that direction. Though vessels of destruction, they are things of grace and beauty as they slide effortlessly through the water. They are like the athletes who compete at the games. The crewmen are well trained and each movement of the boat appears natural as if the boat itself was a living-breathing thing with a mind of its own.

In truth, I was as surprised as I was hurt that what little conversation passed between us, me and the Thasians, included no words about the events I had related to them about what happened to me and Theagenes at Thermopylae.

The Thasians spent their time alone reflecting upon the story I had told them of their champion. Few words passed between us and they turned taciturn, even amongst themselves. If in some way, inexplicable to me, I had offended them, so be it; they needed to know these unknown facts about the man whose image they had cast from their homeland to the bottom of the sea. Even the garrulous Khepri said little, but at least he offered me more than one friendly pat on the shoulder and he continued to smile as we sailed north to port at Thasos.

On the fourth day of our voyage, Khepri announced that we would make Thasos by sundown and my fellow travelers' spirits were lifted by the news. Physical travel to distant shores can be a test of a man's endurance, physical and mental, but the farther away he gets, the closer to his homeland his heart becomes. If a man never travels, he has nowhere to come home to.

The wind was stronger that day than any other day we had been upon the waters. I sat by myself high on the aft deck and watched the horizon for the first glimpse of the island when Parmenides and the other Thasians climbed the steps and took seats on the hard floor with me.

Xeno spoke first. "Parmenides has wisely suggested that we convene to discuss what we will tell our people when we return to our home." It was over a week now since I had first joined their group and these were the first words I heard him speak that were not laced with anger and spoken with defiance.

Parmenides interrupted briefly to say, "And it was Xeno's idea that you should be a part of that discussion."

I tried to conceal my surprise, but my eyes widened and Parmenides passed me a wisp of a smile unnoticed by the others. Episcles and Cimon nodded their approval.

Xeno bowed to his elder and continued, "You, Simonides, have traveled long with us these many days, and you have told us much that we would have had no way of knowing if it had not been for your openness and willingness to share these stories with us in such a passionate way. For that, we thank you. I now stand before you humbled for I alone seethed with hatred at the sound of his name—Theagenes. Theagenes, the object of my brother's wrath that I have come to see as jealousy born of ignorance. Theagenes, the cause of my brother's death, a death brought about by Alcamenes' own hand, cast upon him by his own resentment and by no ill will from the Olympian himself. If only we had known..." his voice faded.

"No man can be faulted for what he does not know," I said.

"Perhaps," he answered, "but Alcamenes paid a dear price for his ignorance, and that can never change." Sea birds circled our mast, and more than one stopped to rest on our rigging. They called to one another as they fluttered about the sail. "I loved my brother, and that love blinded me from the ignorance of his actions. This man, Theagenes, was as foolish and brass, but he learned the true value of a man those days you spent with him at Thermopylae. All men should be so blessed by the gods that he can look down upon the earth and other men and see them for who they really are and not just for the person we and others have made them out to be in our own minds."

"We raised the statue to Theagenes as an Olympic hero and called him countryman. Though he had long since departed from our shores, we honored his name and took pleasure in calling him our own even though we did not really know him. We tore that statue down and tossed it into the sea because," Parmenides hesitated, "… because our lawmakers said it murdered this man's brother. The four of us now, including Xeno can only shake our heads in disbelief at our own stupidity." The four men cast their eyes to the floor. "But we have come to realize that true honor is due him and not only because of his victories in the games, but in what he has taught us through his own revelation and actions in an arena with consequences of far more import than those that occur on the stadium floor. We thank you for that knowledge. As you have told it, it is not when men stand tall for their own benefit that the gods smile, but when they bond together for a cause of greater calling for the good of all men. Those are the men to be remembered and revered, men whose deeds are selfless. Those are the actions of great men and they may be more common than what we are apt to realize."

Khepri stood silently behind us with his helmsman. When Parmenides had finished, the Egyptian stepped forward and bowed deeply, extending his arm to all of us. "I have learned much from you Hellenes," he said, "And you speak now with the wisdom that Hellas is known for; it flows from your land like fresh spring water from the desert oasis. I am honored to have traveled with you. Particularly you, friend Simonides." I blushed like a girl and he added, "No man could understand the breadth of your wisdom only through your written words. I am enlightened and will speak your praise and that of your countrymen wherever I might go."

For the first time, all of us shared a sincere smile that bespoke of our common understanding.

"And so we are agreed," Episcles said cheerfully, "The statue will be raised again."

"And I will lead the search for it with my own boat," Cimon declared. "We will not fail in our quest to retrieve our exile, and we will honor him as the Pythia has decreed." We rose and embraced each other as a sailor who had climbed the mast yelled down to us in a loud, clear voice, "Thasos!" He pointed to the east where the crests of the island's mountains had shown themselves above the smooth waters.

The Pythia is correct too often to doubt her words. The wooden wall she foretold would not fail, Themistocles and his proud Athenian fleet, indeed brought death to the seafaring sons of Persian mothers at Salamis, and sent Xerxes and what remained of his fleet back to its homeland shrouded in shame and failure. Like a coward, the once great king abandoned his army. The following spring, the combined forces of Hellas met the Medes in Boetia on the plains of Plataea and destroyed the remnants of Xerxes' million-man force and sent it back to Persia like a whipped dog who has no more desire or strength to fight. Indeed, Zeus battled the forces of Ahura Mazdah and was victorious by the hand of his mortal soldiers.

True to my word, I composed no more victory songs for the great athletes, though I continued to attend the games, but only by convenience and not by plan. Rather, I wrote the odes to the men at Salamis and Plataea, like I had at Marathon before them. My travels took me to Sparta where a tomb, guarded by a stone lion, had been raised in honor of Leonidas and his men. Pleistarchos, who took the place of the fallen king, and Leotychidas, who reigned with Leonidas, commissioned me to write the words on the tomb. This is what I wrote, and I would not accept any compensation for it:

> *I am the most valiant of beasts,*
> *and most valiant of men is he*
> *Whom I guard standing on this stone tomb.*
>
> *Leonidas, king of the open fields of Sparta,*
> *those slain with you lie famous in their graves,*
> *For they attacked absorbing the head-long as-*
> *sault of endless Persian men, arrows and swift*
> *horse.*

And for the men at Plataea:

> *These men left an altar of glory on their land,*
> *shining in all weather,*
> *When they were enveloped by the black mists of*
> *death.*
> *But though they died*
> *They are not dead, for their courage raises them*
> *in glory from the rooms of Hell.*

I take pride in my work, even more so in these words for they came from my heart to satisfy my soul, not to fill my pockets with drachma. In my travels, I often still hear my epinicions to runners and charioteers and boxers sung by traveling troupes at parties, at wayside inns, and even along the paths that lead to places of frequent pilgrimage. Yes, they bring me some pleasure, but today I find them empty and meaningless, snippets to moments in time that came and passed in a brief, glorious moment, but will not endure. The thought does not bother or concern me. The other songs I've written, the songs to the men of valor... Those are the songs that will stand through time and still be sung by men when my bones have long since turned to dust. That is what remains important to me.

Theagenes competed for several more years in the games before returning, at last, to his homeland, 16 years after he had fled Thasos after taking the beating from his father. Yes, he went back to the gymnasiums and fought for the pleasure of the spectators, but never again, since the fight with Euthymos, did he participate in the *pyx*. He turned to the *pankration* and enjoyed great success. He was never beaten, or so I've been told. It is said that his courage never failed him in the games though he approached each match without the anger that spurred him on as a youth.

As I travel to Delphi every year, so too do I make pilgrimage to Thermopylae. What I witnessed at the Hot Gates had more effect on my life, even in its waning years, than any event I had ever experienced before or since. I am certain it was the same for Theo, for every trip I have made to visit the tomb of the 300, I have found a gathering pile of withered olive leaves laying before that very stone I had inscribed many years ago. The stone still stands, propped by the beaten shield with the Spartan symbol. I knew those offerings did not fall from the sky; I find it odd that the winds never scatter them.

The Spartans tell the story of a 'wild man' at Plataea. Pleistarchos told it to me in a joking way as we dined one evening in his home after the men who had gathered there had more than their share of undiluted wine. Men who have faced death and survived are often apt to talk about their experiences with laughter. I think it hides the fear that still lingers in their hearts.

As Pleistarchos relates the story, word of Leonidas's stand came to Sparta from a large, hairy and dirty man who told of the final engagement in great detail. This man, who refused to give his name, begged the *gerousia* that he be allowed to take up arms with the Spartans, but as you know, Spartan society is closed and secretive. The Lakedaimonians would have none of it and bid the man and his fleas to leave at once. He would not go despite more than one savage beating from the *Krypteia*. The man simply refused to be chased away. He lived in the woods and rose early each day. From a distance the warriors could see him as he mimicked their training. He was filthy and did not bathe. His hair was not shorn and as it grew, he wound it in tight locks that fell to his shoulders. When beckoned, the man would not respond, but when the army set out in the spring, he followed at a distance. There were some that forebode that he was bad luck and would be the ruin of the men, but others thought the opposite and found diversion in monitoring his movements and even waved to him. He did not respond.

On a calm morning not long after the full moon of Mounychion, the combined armies of Hellas stood across the field in Plataea from what remained of Xerxes' expeditionary force. Reduced now to 60,000 men, it was still a formidable and imposing sight, but a mere shadow of what he had brought to our land the previous year.

As the phalanxes prepared to advance, the combined forces of Sparta, Athens and their unified allies were heartened when a solitary figure, upon hearing the Spartan flutes as they called the men to battle, rose from the dust in the open field as if he had burst from the dry soil like a newborn plant. With no armor, he raced toward the Persian line and threw his body amidst them, his hands and arms flailing and striking blow upon blow. Such was his deftness that no man saw him wounded, and all swear he never went down. His courage rallied the Hellenes and quickened their pace.

The victorious Spartan general Pausanias was at the table with us and described the man as wild and feral. "He had wrapped his hands in *himantes*," the general said, "and between each finger in the leather straps, the wild man wedged long, sharp thorns that did much damage to any man unfortunate enough to meet him on the field."

The fury of the battle consumed this stranger and he melted into the melee that ensued, just a single man who wanted to die a Spartan death but still fought to preserve his own, insane life. That is what Pleistarchos said. The man was never seen again, but neither was the nameless stranger forgotten.

The four Thasians called their people together when we landed at the island and bid me tell what I knew of Theagenes. I could see that most, if not all shared the initial thoughts of Parmenides: that the banishment of the statue had been idiotic and served no purpose. Each man found joy in the stories I told. It took no effort, particularly after Xeno spoke of his own stupidity in the matter, for them to convince their fellows that they needed to retrieve the statue from the water. After many days in the harbor with a fleet of a dozen small boats and at least 30 divers and men with strong ropes, Cimon found the statue of Theagenes and brought it to shore. It was cleaned and raised again in the agora amid much celebration. I was pleased and left the island with the hope that the Pythia's request had been satisfied.

It was, for as I returned to the island on this trip, the land is green and fertile. The treasuries are no longer sapped to bring food to Thasos. The children are happy, and the men and women proud. Thasos is once again a beautiful place.

The hour is late, Selene has left the sky to darkness, and soon all Thasians will awaken to this new day. Further rumination serves no purpose. Theagenes' place in history will be preserved, but only as a victorious boxer and *pankratiast* who ruled the gymnasiums during his too few years among mortal men. We flash through time like the heavenly bodies which streak through the sky, seen but briefly from the corners of our eyes — where have they been, what have they seen, what impact will they have on our world, today and in the future?

The sky has turned above me as the gods play among themselves and toy with the other creatures that inhabit the heavens. I rise to my feet and stare into the blackness. I see Herakles. I smile and wave at him, but he does not wave back. Dressed in the skin of the Nemean lion, kneeling, he wields his club and threatens Cerberus, the three-headed dog from Hell; his foot keeps Draco in check. I feel safe. Another day is behind me, and I look forward to this one with much anticipation.

EPILOGUE

Simonides died that year in 469 BC at the age of 84.

GLOSSARY

Aeschylus: (525-456 BCE) the earliest of the three great Greek tragic dramatists. "Prometheus Bound" is considered his best-known work.

Aethon: one of the horses of the sun god Helios.

Agoge: the training regimen of all Spartan citizens.

Agora: the Greek marketplace.

Ahura Mazdah ("Lord of Wisdom"): the supreme Persian god who created the heavens and the Earth. His symbol is the winged disc.

Aition: the cause of the ritual.

Alcmaeon: an early Greek medical writer and philosopher-scientist from Kroton who wrote between 500 and 450 BCE.

Alecto: one of the Furies spawned from the blood of the wounds of Uranus during the Titan rebellion.

Altis: the sacred grove of Olympia.

Alutarches: the head of police.

Archons: the officers of state.

Artemis: the Moon goddess in charge of the movement of the moon across the Sky. She was the protector of animals and small children. She saved Iphigenia when Agamemnon was about to sacrifice her. Shining and silver like the moon, Artemis drove a stag-drawn chariot and carried a silver bow and arrows. Three hunting hounds accompanied her.

Artemisium: a cape in northern Euboea that is named for a great temple of Artemis.

Aryballos: a small container of athlete's oil.

Athlon: the Olympic prize.

Augeias: a king of Elis. In his fifth labor, Herakles was tasked with cleansing the stables of Augeias in a single day. Augeias had a herd of three thousand oxen, but his stables had not been cleansed for 30 years.

Aulis: a port city of Boeotia where the Greek forces led by Agamemnon set out for Troy. It was in Aulis where Agamemnon made his fateful sacrifice to Artemis of his daughter Iphigenia.

Aulos: the chief wind instrument of ancient Greece. It is similar to a modern oboe or clarinet.

Boeotia: an area of central Greece. The main city was Thebes. Pindar, Hesiod and Plutarch were all Boeotians.

Bouleuterion: the council building at Olympia where the Hellanodikai met.

Calchas: the seer who told Agamemnon to sacrifice his daughter Iphigenia to the goddess Artemis at Aulis to gain favorable winds to take the Greek fleet to Troy.

Cerberus: the three-headed guard dog from the underworld.

Charon: the ferryman who rowed the dead across the River Styx into the Underworld. His fee was one Obol.

The Greeks always buried their dead with an Obol in their mouths to pay Charon.

Charybdis: a gigantic whirlpool wrecking ships and drowning humans. Charybdis was encountered by Odysseus who managed to escape.

Chiton: a tunic made from linen in the hot months and wool in the cold months.

Cithara: a stringed instrument similar to but more elaborate than the lyre.

Diaulos: the double-course foot race.

Drachma: an ancient currency unit. A mercenary soldier or an artisan earned about a drachma per day.

Ecclesia: the Spartiate Assembly made up of men over 18-years-old.

Ekecheiria: the Olympic truce. In Greek, ekecheiria literally means "holding of hands." The ekecheiria was announced before and during each of the Olympic festivals, to allow visitors to travel safely to Olympia. An inscription describing the truce was written on a bronze discus, which was displayed at Olympia. During the truce, wars were suspended, armies were prohibited from entering Elis or threatening the Games, and legal disputes and the carrying out of death penalties were forbidden.

Eos: the goddess of the dawn and sister of Helios and Selene. Eos was the mother of the winds: Zephyrus, the west wind, Boreas, the north wind, Notus, the south wind and Eurus, the east wind.

Ephebos: an 18-year-old young man who has reached the age of training for and ultimately entry into citizenship. His training was called ephebike and was vital to the state in the creation of a military reserve.

Ephedros: an athlete in waiting. When odd numbers drew lots, the odd man was the athlete in waiting which provided a great advantage, as he was fresh for his first match against an opponent who had already competed.

Ephors: five Spartiate "overseers" elected annually by the Ecclesia. Any Spartiate could be an ephor. They had financial, judicial, and administrative powers even over the kings. Two Ephors always went with a king on campaign to control arrogance and to protect the interests of the whole state.

Epinicion: a victory ode.

Euboea: the large island to the east of the Greek mainland.

Gemini: the Twins Castor and Pollux. They were always represented as riding splendid snow white horses.

Gerousia: the Spartan elders. Once he passed 60, a Spartan was considered beyond the age for military service. Thirty men in all were included in the Gerousia, 28 Spartiates and the two kings. The Gerontes, the Senators were elected by the Assembly of Spartiates for life.

Hades: the king of the underworld.

Hellanodikai: the judges and the organizers of the Olympic games in Elis.

Helot: one of a class of serfs in Sparta. A helot was neither a slave nor a free citizen.

Heraclitus: a philosopher of Ephesus, c.535–c.475 BCE.

Hesiod: an early Greek poet, c. 700 BCE.

Hiero: a Sicilian who succeeded his brother Gelon as tyrant of Syracuse, BCE 478. His chariots repeatedly won the prize at the Olympic Games. Pindar, Aeschylus, Simonides, Bacchylides and Epicharmus were well-received at his court.

Hoplite: a heavy infantry soldier.

Hoplitodromos: an Olympic event in which competitors ran two lengths of the stadium wearing helmets and carrying shields.

Husplex: the starting gate for races.

Hypnos: the god of sleep.

Kalos kagathos: the physical and mental state in which a youth is beautiful and balanced in body and soul.

Karneia: a Spartan festival in honor of the soldierly way of life.

Keres: the horrible, black-winged, female spirits of death and doom who also act as avenging spirits.

Khepri: an Egyptian god associated with the scarab beetle.

Klimax: a contest resolution when each man in turn stood motionless and received a blow from his opponent without making an attempt to avoid it. When a contest continued for a long time, the opponents had the option to declare klimax.

Knucklebones: a game of chance where bones are thrown from a cup. Each bone had four long sides: flat, irregular, concave and convex, which has the value of one, six, three and four. The worst throw was a dog throw.

Krypteia: a tradition involving young Spartans who have completed the agoge. After the agoge, the young men were reintegrated into society by undertaking the krypteia. The krypteia was partaken of by select individuals rather than by the entire population. During the krypteia, armed with a small knife, no shelter, clothing, or food, the youths hid during the day. In the evening they secretively patrolled the helot land plots and roamed the mountainside. Once the krypteia was complete, the individuals who survived it were given high standing in the army, and potentially became a part of the Three Hundred Knights.

Kybernetes: a trireme helmsman.

Lachesis: one of the three Fates who dispensed lots and assigned destiny.

Lakedaimonia: the proper name of Sparta.

Maza: a flat bread made most often from barley.

Melikertes: the Isthmian Games were held in his honor.

Metageitnion: July and August when both the Olympic games and the Spartan Karneia festival were held.

Moirai: the personifications of the inescapable destiny of man.

Momus: the god of mockery.

Muses: a sisterhood of nine spirits who embody the arts. Calliope was the Muse of epic poetry and eloquence; Euterpe, of music or of lyric poetry; Erato, of the poetry of love; Polyhymnia, of oratory or sacred poetry; Clio, of history; Melpomene, of tragedy;

Thalia, of comedy; Terpsichore, of choral song and dance; Urania, of astronomy.

Naupaktos: the naval shipyard of the Dorians.

Notus: the South wind.

Nymphs: the beautiful female divinities of nature.

Nyx: the goddess of the night and mother of the fates.

Obol: a currency equal to one-sixth of a drachma. A rower might make two obols per day.

Oinomaos: a king and father of the beautiful maiden Hippodamia. The king did not want his daughter to marry, so he made a contest for Hippodamia's suitors. The king excelled in chariot racing. Knowing he would win each race, he set the contest as the winner would get Hippodamia, but the loser would die. Hippodamia was sure she would be a spinster for the rest of her life, but then the hero Pelops appeared. Pelops knew of the 13 suitors Oinomaos had already killed. He persuaded the king's charioteer to loosen the pins, which held the wheels of his master's chariot to the axle. On the day of the race at the first turn the pins sprang free, letting both wheels fall from the axle. King Oinomaos was killed and Pelops married Hippodamia.

Olympiad: the chronological unit in ancient Greece. Each Olympiad was a four-year period, and each one began with the Olympic games. The first Olympiad was reckoned to have begun in 776 BCE.

Opson: an accompaniment to maza that could be fish or vegetables, but rarely meat.

Pankratiast: a participant in pankration, a brutal Olympic event that combined boxing and wrestling.

Papuro: the ancient Egyptian word, which means "royal." Papuro is papyrus, the most common writing medium in ancient times. This paper-like material was easy to use, handle, transport and make.

Pelopeion: the Tumulus, or burial ground of Pelops at Olympia.

Pelops: the son of Tantalus who married Hippodamia. Pelops was killed by his father and served to the gods at a feast. He was revived by the gods and given an ivory shoulder to replace one eaten by Demeter. Legend says that the games at Olympia were founded in his honor.

Pentecontarchos: the lowest ranked officer on a trireme who is in charge of wages and the administrative duties of running a ship of war.

Pindar: a Greek poet c.518?–c.438 BCE.

Piraeus: the port of Athens

Polyphemus: a Cyclops.

Potamoi: the sons of the Great River Okeanos that encircled the earth, and brothers of the Okeanides, goddesses of clouds.

Proreus: the lookout on a trireme in charge of the foredeck.

Pythia: the Oracle at Delphi.

Pyx: the boxing event.

Salamis: an island in the Saronic Gulf west of Athens.

Sirius: the 'Dog Star', named by the Egyptians after their god Osirus whose head in pictograms resembled that of a dog.

Spartiate: a Spartan male with full citizenship and a member of the elite warrior class.

Sponde: a libation. The sponde was poured from a cup called a spondeion.

Stade: the single-course foot race. A stade is approximately 200 meters.

Strigils: the scrapers used to remove the oil from an athlete's body.

Styx: the river of Hades that the souls of the dead had to cross on their journey from the realm of the living.

Tartarus: the lowest region of the world, as far below earth as earth is from heaven.

Thanatos: the twin of Hypnos and the personification of natural death.

Thyrsos: the stick of Dionysus entwined with vine leaves.

Tribon: a large cloak that was the distinctive mark of the Lakedaimonians.

Tyrtaeus: a Spartan poet, circa 630 BCE.

Xiphos: the hoplite short sword used for thrusting in close quarters.

Zephyrus: the West wind.

ACKNOWLEDGEMENT

Need it be said: to the writers of antiquity that include Simonides himself, Herodotus, Pindar, Hesiod, Homer and so many others who have preserved the stories upon which modern literature, even our very culture is founded.

I am grateful to my one and only wife of 34 years who, when I told her I wanted to hide in the woods and write a book said, "Okay."

Thanks to my F-106 brother-in-arms George Mehrtens who was willing to pour through the manuscript and give me his recommendations, suggestions and observations. Check six but never look back, Mert!

Immeasurable thanks to my friend and mentor, Steven Pressfield who told me many years ago, "You have to continue to re-invent yourself." I would have given up long ago without his constant support and inspiration. King Kong indeed lives.

Lastly to God who continues to tell us over and over, "Do not be afraid."

CPSIA information can be obtained at www.ICGtesting.com
Printed in the USA
LVOW101956060912

297712LV00017B/80/P